Praise for Cynthia D'Alba

"The first book in the *Texas Montgomery Mavericks* is a great way for readers to meet D'Alba […] D'Alba's passion for the world she's created comes across and will have readers waiting for the next book in the series."
—4 Stars, RT Book Reviews on *Texas Two Step*

"Cynthia D'Alba's *Texas Fandango* from Samhain lets readers enjoy the sensual fun in the sun […] This latest offering gives readers a sexy escape and a reason to seek out D'Alba's earlier titles."
—Library Journal Reviews

"*Texas Two Step* kept me on an emotional roller coaster […] *Texas Two Step* is an emotionally charged romance, with well-developed characters and an engaging secondary cast. A quarter of the way into the book I added Ms. D'Alba to my auto-buys."
—5 STARS and Recommended Read, Guilty Pleasures Book Reviews

"Cynthia D'Alba did herself proud with *Texas Bossa Nova* and gave readers everything they could hope for in a story of a much loved character."
—Guilty Pleasures Book Reviews

Look for these titles by
Cynthia D'Alba

Now Available:

Texas Montgomery Mavericks
Texas Two Step
Texas Tango
Texas Fandango
Texas Twist
Texas Bossa Nova

Texas Hustle

Cynthia D'Alba

SAMHAIN
PUBLISHING

Samhain Publishing, Ltd.
11821 Mason Montgomery Road, 4B
Cincinnati, OH 45249
www.samhainpublishing.com

Texas Hustle
Copyright © 2015 by Cynthia D'Alba
Print ISBN: 978-1-61923-238-9
Digital ISBN: 978-1-61923-129-0

Editing by Heidi Moore
Cover by Valerie Tibbs

First Samhain Publishing, Ltd. electronic publication: November 2015
First Samhain Publishing, Ltd. print publication: November 2015

Dedication

Thank you to Porchia Gilbreath for her beta readings and for lending her first name for the book's heroine. Also I have to give a shout out to Paula Farrell for reading the early chapters of this work. My gratitude knows no end for Delene Yochum, Tabitha Collins and Margaret Hughes (aka Book Partners in Crime) for their continued support and assistance with my book releases and parties. I seriously could not do it without you ladies. And no author has ever had a more responsive critique partner than Angela Campbell, who will drop everything to get me a fast turnaround when I need it. Finally, to my best friend in the world, my husband, whose idea it was to get into this writing biz and who continues to encourage me every day.

And I'm setting my editor, Heidi Moore, off into her own paragraph because she deserves special recognition. As usual, your edits were on target. You make me look better than I am. You push me to become a better writer. Thank you, Heidi.

THE MONTGOMERY FAMILY TREE

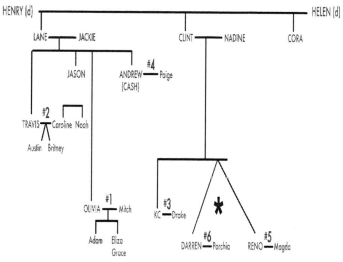

CAPITAL NAMES - denotes
MONTGOMERY Surname

* denotes twins

#1 - Texas Two Step   #4 - Texas Twist
#2 - Texas Tango   #5 - Texas Bossa Nova
#3 - Texas Fandango   #6 - Texas Hustle

Chapter One

It was still dark when Porchia Summers wheeled into the parking area behind Heavenly Delights Bakery. Her car's headlights bounced off one other vehicle, an old, rusty Jeep that looked like it should be in a junkyard instead of her bakery's parking lot. The Jeep's owner, Mallory James, adored her car and took offense at any aspersions about its paint, or rather its lack thereof.

Light filtered from windows near the ceiling. While Porchia hadn't designed the building, the construction was perfect for baking. The elevated openings were ideal to allow heat in the summer to escape. Plus, she'd gotten it at a bargain price.

She let herself in, wincing at the ear-splitting volume of the head-banging heavy-metal music blasting in the kitchen.

To her left, racks of cookies cooled. To her right, multiple ovens baked fresh muffins and pastries for the sales counter. In front of Porchia, Mallory stood with her back to the door, her hands flying as she moved fresh muffins and rolls into plastic bags for Whispering Springs's three B&Bs and restaurants.

"Mallory. How'd last night go?"

When Mallory didn't respond to Porchia's shout, she picked up the remote for the portable system and lowered the volume. Mallory whirled around, hands fisted and ready for an attack. The minute she realized it was Porchia, she loosened her fists and greeted her boss with a lift of her chin.

"Morning," Mallory muttered. "Sorry about the music. Must have lost track of time."

"Not a problem," Porchia said. "Everything go okay last night?"

Mallory shrugged. "Sure," she replied in her usual understated tone.

Mallory had served as a Marine and come back from Afghanistan unable to deal with what she'd seen and the jobs she'd had to do. Working in an environment that required her to interact with people wasn't possible. She'd approached Porchia about a job. Given that Mallory had grown up in a family that'd owned a bakery, Porchia knew she'd have been a fool to not hire her. However, Mallory's only job stipulation was that she had to work at night. At first, Porchia hadn't been sure how that would work. But it had turned out to be a win-win for both women. Mallory came in at midnight, did all the breads and most of the cookies, and left at seven when the rest of the bakery staff arrived. Before Mallory, Porchia had been at the bakery every day no later than four a.m. Since Mallory has started working for her, she'd had the luxury of sleeping until five most mornings, a serious bonus for her.

"Great," Porchia said. "I've got a couple of things to do in the office before we open."

She was headed toward her office when Mallory said, "Oh, the phone's been ringing since about four."

Porchia's brow furrowed. "Who was it?"

"Don't know. Didn't answer it. Figured nobody was ordering a cake at four in the morning."

Porchia nodded. Another one of Mallory's idiosyncrasies. She refused to answer the bakery phone, and sometimes even her own cell.

"Well, you've got a point. I guess if it's important, they'll call back or have left a message. I'll check."

Mallory didn't respond and went back to her packaging.

The bakery phone began to ring. Porchia hurried to the phone mounted on the wall to answer.

"Heavenly Delights."

"Hello, Kat. Miss me?"

Every nerve in Porchia's body ran blazing hot, then ice cold. A tremor shook her hand, banging the receiver against her ear.

"This is Heavenly Delights Bakery," Porchia said. "There's no one here by that name."

The man on the phone laughed, a deep, haunting chuckle that sent shivers skittering down her spine. "Now, Kat. Don't play games with me. Why, it's been seventeen years since I've had the pleasure of your company."

"I'm sorry," she replied, imitating her mother's dressing-down-the-staff voice. "You really have a wrong number."

It took two shaky tries to get the receiver back into its holder. Her legs wobbled like gelatin as she made her way to the office. Once there, she closed the door and leaned against it, as though that would keep her juvenile history in the past. Her lungs had seized up the minute she'd heard his voice, and they still hadn't relaxed. Her breaths came in pants and gulps as her lungs struggled to expand.

Porchia grabbed the edge of the desk and guided herself around the side until she could collapse into the chair. She rested her forehead on the desk, but that did nothing for the swirl in her brain.

Her desk phone rang. She had to answer it. Mallory wouldn't and none of the other staff had arrived yet. It could be a bakery order. She did have a business to run.

"Heavenly Delights." Her voice quivered as she spoke. She cleared her throat and said again, "Heavenly Delights Bakery. May I help you?"

"Yes, you most certainly can," the man said. "Don't hang up on me again, Kat. I don't have a wrong number either. You can call yourself Porchia or Mercedes or Range Rover, for all I care. Doesn't change who you are."

"What do you want, Slade?"

When he chuckled, Porchia felt a thousand spiders walk up her body. The worst mistake of her life had been taking a ride in the car with Slade Madden.

"So you haven't forgotten your old friend."

"Not hardly a friend. More like a bad memory."

"Well, this memory just did seventeen years in jail for you. Now it's time for you to pay your bill."

Images came racing back at her. Beer cans rolling around on the floorboard of the backseat. A flash of red as the car ran the stop sign. Bright headlights from the oncoming car. The lurch of her body as Slade jerked the steering wheel to avoid the car. A dingy white fence just before the hood of the car slammed into it. Blood as it gushed from her legs and her face.

And all the sounds. Slade's laughter. Her begging him to stop and let her out. The crunch of metal into wood. Her screams before, during and after the wreck. The gasping breaths of the old woman trapped under the car's tires.

She'd lost everything that night. Her life had never been the same.

"I don't owe you anything, Slade. You destroyed my life that night."

"Bullshit. It was an accident. You know that. You could have testified in my defense. Hell, your old man had the right contacts to get my case tossed just like he did for his little princess. For the last seventeen years, you've been free to do whatever your little heart desired."

"You're wrong. There was nothing Dad could do."

"Don't give me that. He's a judge. He knows everybody in Atlanta. He could have made some calls. Maybe I would have done a little time, like six months. Instead, my life went down the crapper. I had a full scholarship to play football and then it was on to the NFL. I could have made millions in the pros. You owe me, Kat. You and your family owe me. I figure seventeen years at, let's say a modest sixty big, and that's a cool mil. That should give me a new start on my life."

"A million dollars. That's insane. Even if I had a million bucks, and I don't, I certainly wouldn't give it to you. You are solely responsible for that night."

Using her foot, she dragged the trash can closer to her. The tangy saliva tingling the back of her tongue suggested vomiting was eminent.

"Your family has the dough, and I bet your dad will do anything for his little girl. Hell, he'd never miss a measly mil. I might have been in prison, but don't think I haven't kept up with his success. You, on the other hand, took a while to track down. Clever girl. Thought the slight name change would cover your past. But you forgot. I'm smart. So get on the phone and rattle your dad's piggy bank for my new start in life."

Porchia hesitated. She hadn't spoken to her parents since Labor Day weekend. Her relationship with them was strained at best, but she made herself see them for major holidays.

Her parents had been beyond disappointed with her actions that night. What respect they'd had for her disappeared, along with any semblance of trust. Even at fifteen, she'd known better than to get into a car with someone who'd been drinking, regardless of how popular the boy might have been. Just the first in a long line of poor decisions when it came to men, something her parents, and her conscience, never let her forget. For months afterward, they could barely look at her, speak to her. As soon as she'd been cleared of any responsibility for the accident, they'd sent her to Whispering Springs to live with her maternal grandmother, Lillian Summers, until all the talk died down.

As Porchia aged and matured and learned how the world worked, she'd come to believe they'd done what they'd thought best all those years ago, that in their minds, they were protecting her without damaging their social status. However, a scared and hurt fifteen-year-old Porchia had felt betrayed and abandoned by her parents. Two years later, when they'd asked her to come home, she'd refused, opting to remain in the loving home of her maternal grandmother and in Whispering Springs, where she'd found the joy of anonymity.

"You're working off old intel," she said. "Dear old Dad cut me off years ago."

Slade was quiet for a minute. "I know you can get the money. You owe me and I want it." His voice lost all his fake friendliness. Now it was rough and guttural and threatening.

She took a deep breath and stiffened her spine. She couldn't let him know how scared she was of him.

"Fuck you. Go back into the hole you climbed out of and leave me the hell alone." She slammed down the phone, her whole body shaking. When the phone rang again, she let it go to voice mail.

A couple of days passed with no contact from Slade. Porchia hoped he'd moved on, but in her heart, she knew she was kidding herself.

Friday morning, business was brisk, her pastries flying out of the store as though she was giving them away. She glanced at the clock. Almost noon. Someone from the fire station would be by soon to pick up all the unsold pastries from earlier this week. She'd made the firehouses a deal they couldn't refuse…all the left over pastries from the last two days at sixty percent off. The deal was a win-win for both. She got excellent public relations from it and the firefighters got some cheap treats.

The bell over the door jangled, and Porchia looked up with a smile ready to greet her next customer. But it wasn't a customer. Instead, her worst nightmare had just reentered her life. Slade Madden oozed into the shop. Her stomach roiled with the sudden influx of acid.

"Get out," she said between clenched teeth.

"Now, Kat, is that any way to greet an old friend?"

The bell over the door jangled again as a probie firefighter came in to pick up the firehouse box. He stopped short when he caught sight of Slade. Not surprising. Dressed all in black—jeans, T-shirt, boots and leather jacket—Slade looked like Lucifer himself. Adding to his threatening appearance was a skull and crossbones tattoo on his neck.

"Um, is everything okay, Porchia?" The young firefighter's eyes ricocheted from her to Slade and back.

"Everything is fine," Porchia lied. She held out the box of pastries. "Here's your box. We'll settle up later."

Chad, the rookie firefighter, took the box. "Thanks," he said with a glance at Slade. "I can hang around until you finish with this customer."

"No. That's okay. You'd better get back to the station."

As soon as the door closed behind Chad, Porchia held up a finger for Slade to not say anything. She went and closed the swinging door to the kitchen.

"I have other employees here, Slade, so make it quick and get out."

"I don't like my ladies hanging up on me." He spread his stance and fisted his hands.

"Well, that's fine since I'm not, and never have been, one of your *ladies*." She swept her hand around the small bakery. "This is all I have, so if you came here looking for money, it'll be like getting blood from a turnip. And, trust me, my dad won't give you a dime. He'll call the cops on you for some type of probation violation."

If only her internal strength matched the grit in her voice, she'd be fine. But her insides were quivering like a puppy expecting to be hit. Luckily, she only had to channel her mother talking to their cook to get her haughty tone perfect. Forcing her spine straight, she squinted her eyes in what she hoped appeared to be a glare and tightened her lips across her teeth as though she were her mother ready to give her tsk of disapproval.

When he gave her one of his greasy smiles, she noticed he'd had a gold tooth put in his mouth. "No probation worries, my dear. I served my entire sentence. I'm a free man."

"Great." Her voice dripped with sarcasm. "Now go away."

She turned to go to the kitchen, but Slade was faster. He grabbed her arm and jerked her back against the counter. The hard edge slammed into her side and back, but she wouldn't give him the satisfaction of hearing her scream as the pain shot through her.

"Not without what's due me."

"Let go of me," she said through gritted teeth.

"Hey! What's going on? Is everything okay, Porchia?"

Porchia and Slade turned toward the deep, masculine voice. Porchia's heart skipped a beat or more at the sight of Darren Montgomery standing in her kitchen door, a freshly baked apple fritter in his hand. Taller than Slade and more muscular, Darren wore a threatening scowl on his face. He pointedly moved his gaze down to where Slade's fingers were pressing into Porchia's flesh and then back up to Slade's face. He took a step toward them.

Slade released her arm. "No problem," he said, a used-car-salesman's smile on his face. "I thought I'd forgotten to pay for my coffee. I wanted to stop the lady before she got away." He glanced at Porchia. "I always pay my bills. I'm sure you do too."

Porchia rubbed her arm. "I'm fine." She gave Slade a threatening look, or least she hoped he felt threatened. "He was just leaving, isn't that right, sir? You're all paid up here."

Slade tipped an imaginary hat. "Real nice place you've got here. I'll see you around."

The minute the front door shut behind him, Porchia went on the offensive, wanting to distract Darren from any additional conversation about Slade. Her Grandmother Summers had been well loved and respected. That respect and goodwill had been extended to Porchia when she moved here. The very last thing she wanted was to darken her late grandmother's good name or her own. So the less Darren—and everyone else—knew about her past, the better.

She cocked both fists on her hips. "What are you doing coming in through my kitchen? Callie let you in the back door again?"

Darren's body relaxed and he grinned. She was positive this was the grin that got every girl in town picking out wedding dresses and checking church reservations.

"What can I say? I love Callie's apple fritters."

Her jaw tightened. Callie couldn't make an apple fritter with instructions from an "Apple Fritters for Dummies" book. Porchia had made those fritters.

"Great. That'll be two dollars."

"Two dollars? Isn't that a little steep?"

"Not when I know Callie fed you at least two more in the kitchen."

The twinkle in his eyes let her know she'd hit the bull's eye.

He tilted his chin toward the door Slade had just exited. "About that guy—" he started.

"Stop. Don't say anything. It was nothing. Just a jerk being a jerk. It's over."

"Didn't recognize him. Someone you know?"

"Nope. Never seen him before today. Probably just passing through town. Now, what are you doing here and why aren't you at the D&R?"

Darren loved the cattle ranch he and his brother Reno ran. The ranch was a good hour outside of town, so for Darren to be in Whispering Springs on a Friday morning was definitely out of the ordinary.

"Hot plans for the evening."

"Really? Do tell."

Darren pointed to the glossy brochure Porchia had on the counter. "I'm up for bids." He gave her a leer. "And, baby, let me tell you, you'll get every dime's worth."

A loud laugh bubbled up from deep inside Porchia, something she desperately needed after Slade's little visit.

"You are in the bachelor auction? You? Darren Montgomery? What is this world coming to when you have to sell your wares on the street?" She tsked. "D&R a little hard up for money this month?"

Shaggy long dark hair brushed the collar of his denim shirt. Piercing-blue eyes that could make any woman drown in them. And his voice. Oh Lord. His deep Southern drawl combined with a husky laugh made her gut tumble to her knees.

He chuckled. "What can I say? Aunt Jackie caught me in a good mood one day and I said yes. Besides, it's for a good cause. It's to raise money for an abused women and children's shelter."

"I know." She pointed toward the large plate-glass window at the front of her store. "I've had the flyer up for a couple of weeks."

"You coming tonight?"

"No. Why would I?"

He tapped on the brochure. "You have all the various information. I thought maybe you were checking out the manly goods."

She laughed again. One thing about Darren, he never failed to entertain her. If only he were her age instead of being years younger. The age thing was her problem, not his. But being thirty-two and dating a guy still in his twenties made her feel desperate, and she wasn't.

However, she didn't make the best decisions when it came to men. Slade was only one example. Somehow every loser found his way to her doorstep.

She really liked Darren and valued their friendship. If he had some fatal flaw, like every other guy in her past, she didn't want to know.

If she gave in and let herself get romantically involved with him and it didn't work, there went their friendship. And since he was the brother-in-law of one of her good friends, a failed romance could also put a damper on her girl friendships.

No, she had just too much to lose if everything went south. It was in her best interest to keep him as her friend and nothing more.

"Manly goods? It might be worth it if there were any manly goods to be seen."

He leaned over to whisper in her ear. The scent of man and sugar and cinnamon was an aphrodisiac for her. She felt a tug in her gut just behind her navel. Her breath caught, holding all that deliciousness in.

"The date I'm offering is very special. It's not just any girl that I'd want to take. Check it out."

His warm breath on her neck had her knees going weak and her head wanting to turn until her lips could meet his. In the end, she grinned and pushed him back.

"I'm sure you'll raise a lot of money tonight. Have fun."

Six hours later, Porchia locked the back door of the bakery, exhausted and ready to put her feet up. Her car was the only one in the lot, which was not unusual. However, what was different was finding a piece of paper on her windshield held down by a wiper blade.

"See you soon."

The note wasn't signed, but it didn't have to be. Slade Madden was fully aware of where she worked and what she drove. He'd probably already scoped out where she lived. That thought didn't bring any comfort.

During the drive from the bakery to her house, which was a mere five miles, Porchia watched her rearview mirror for any sign of Slade, but if he was back there, he was doing an excellent job staying hidden.

Her house phone was ringing when she walked in. She dropped her purse and tote bag on the couch and hurried to answer.

"Hello?"

"Hey, Kat. Nice house."

Her eyes shut in frustration. "Slade. There's nothing here for you. I have nothing. If you don't stop calling me, I'm going to go to the sheriff's office and file a complaint."

"No, you won't. I've asked around town about you. Everybody I've spoken to thinks you're a wonderful addition to their little community. What would they think of their nice addition if they learned about your part in killing a nice little old lady?"

Bile began rising in her throat as her nervous stomach spasmed.

"I had nothing to do with the accident. The courts found you totally liable, and that's why you went to jail and I didn't. I'm sorry it happened, but it did. Like you said. You did your time and now you're out. There's nothing I can do to help you restart your life. Nothing."

"Yeah, there is. Money. Starting over takes money, money you can provide. That's a nice little shop you have. I bet you have it insured and everything. Be a shame if something happened to it."

His threat came through loud and clear. He wasn't going away empty handed. What was arson to someone like him?

"Give me some time. There's no way I can get a million dollars, but I might be able to scrape up twenty thousand."

"Chump change."

"Twenty grand is it. Take or leave it."

"One week."

"Two, at least. I don't have that kind of money lying around."

"Two weeks, and if I don't have my money by then, I'll look for ways you might could get it."

He hung up. Porchia stood with the phone receiver in her hand, tears flowing down her cheeks. She'd been so stupid getting in that car with Slade Madden. It'd been the perfect *screw you* to her parents, who'd never approved of any boy she liked, unless he happened to be the son of close friends in the same social class. Dating someone like Slade Madden had been completely out of the question.

Where was she going to get twenty thousand dollars in two weeks?

Asking her parents wasn't an option. They didn't approve of her living in Texas or of her owning a simple bakery. So they'd never give her money unless it was to move back closer to them.

Getting into the small trust fund her paternal aunt had left her wasn't an option either. She couldn't access that until she was thirty-five or married. Right now, her father controlled it, so even if she could get into it, there'd be many questions.

She had nothing she could sell worth twenty grand.

She had to think. She'd bought herself a couple of weeks to come up with a solution to her Slade problem. What, she hadn't a clue, but the answer had to be there…somewhere.

Chapter Two

Porchia had bought herself a small window of time to figure out how to handle Slade's demands. She knew if she stayed in town, he would continue to dog her.

Frankly, she didn't know if he was dangerous or all hot air. If he was as threatening as he wanted her to believe, she could put her employees at risk if he kept coming to the bakery.

She'd not known him all that well seventeen years ago, more by reputation than personal interaction. How far he would take his threats was anyone's guess.

Prison changed a man. Sometimes for the better. She was thinking not so much in this case.

Slade Madden had been a popular senior at her high school. Captain of the football team. President of the senior class. But he'd also been known for being quite the party boy. Born into a lower middle-class family, he hadn't met the criteria her parents believed acceptable for their daughter.

They'd believed her too young to date at fifteen, other than the occasional country club dance where they could keep an eye on her.

Plus, it was their opinion that any senior—particularly Slade Madden—was simply too fast for her. As her parents had told her numerous times, she was too immature to be dating a senior.

However, Porchia believed the bottom line had been that his family simply hadn't been in the same social and economic class as hers.

One night, he'd come to a party where she was a guest. He'd been tall and handsome and smelled dreamy. When he'd asked her to take a ride with him, she'd jumped at the chance. All her friends had been so envious.

She knew he'd been drinking but had thought it was only beer. It hadn't been real booze or anything. But she hadn't realized how much he'd had to drink before she got in the car.

He drove his car like he faced life…fast and reckless. A corner taken too fast. A missed stop at a stop sign. A momentary loss of control. An elderly woman standing in her yard.

Everything had happened so fast. Lives had been irreparably changed.

Porchia pulled herself back from the memories. She had to get out of her house tonight. She needed something to distract her, and nothing could be more distracting than a bachelor auction, not that she planned to bid on anyone. But Tina and Delene were going, and she'd said she'd try to come.

At eight, she went to the Whispering Springs Country Club, purchased an admission ticket, was handed a bid paddle with a number on it and walked into a room of giggling, twitching, loud-talking women. The mix of perfumes, hair sprays and other assorted scents was almost overwhelming. The ladies of Whispering Springs and its surrounding areas had shown up in full force and dressed to grab attention.

She looked down at the simple black slacks and multi-colored sweater set she wore. She was a simple glazed doughnut on a tray with fancy petit-fours.

Whatever. She wasn't here to impress. She was here for the entertainment.

"Porchia!"

She turned toward the voice. Tina stood on a chair waving her arms. Leave it to Tina and Delene to get a front-row table.

Getting to them was a challenge. She weaved among throngs of ladies crowded around small tables littered with empty glasses. Apparently, the organizers believed the better oiled the crowd, the looser the purse strings.

"You made it," Delene said, giving Porchia a quick shoulder hug.

"I'm here. Now who do you two have your eyes on?" Porchia held up the auction date brochure. "There are some juicy ones here."

Tina and Delene exchanged glances.

"Okay, which one of you is buying Sheriff Singer?" Marc Singer had recently been voted in as county sheriff, and she knew both her friends had laid claims.

"Neither," said Tina. "We figure he'll go high and neither of us has the money. And second, Delene can kick my ass."

Delene laughed. "You know it." She looked at Porchia. "You got your eye on anyone?"

Porchia shook her head. "Just bored, so I came to watch you two."

"You sure? Darren Montgomery is on the auction block."

"I'm sure," Porchia said with a smile. "And why would you think I would be interested in a date with Darren?"

"Good evening," a tall, older woman yelled into a microphone on the stage. "I'm Reese McClure, your host for the evening. Thank you all for coming and supporting this very worthwhile cause. Each bachelor has outlined his planned date that's up for sale." She held up the glossy brochure. "If you don't have a program, please see the ladies at the ticket counter. You can't know the players without a program."

The room of ladies chuckled.

"Let's get started, shall we? First up is Michael Buchannan. Michael is a lawyer with Montgomery and Montgomery Law Offices. He's new to Whispering Springs, so let's make him feel welcome. Bid high and bid often."

An attractive blond man strutted onto the stage wearing a three-piece suit. Smiling, he waved to the crowd. And the auction got underway. Porchia leaned back in her chair and enjoyed watching the bidding frenzy as one attractive bachelor after another came on the stage. While the three ladies laughed, gossiped and critiqued the bachelors and the bidders, there were no bids offered up from their table.

"Okay, ladies," Reese McClure said. "Everybody loves a firefighter, right? Welcome Chad Jamison."

The rookie firefighter walked onto the stage wearing his turnout pants with the suspenders hanging down around his hips. The tight muscles in his chest were nicely highlighted by the spotlight operator as he'd apparently lost his shirt.

There was a ripple of female sighs through the crowd. The opening bid was fifty dollars and Porchia was a little concerned. The last bachelor had sold for over three hundred dollars.

Then Chad grinned and flexed his biceps and the bidding became fierce.

Tina stood and waved her bid paddle at the emcee. "Three twenty-five," she shouted.

A woman Porchia didn't know called, "Three seventy-five."

Tina glared at the other bidder. Porchia bit her lip to keep from laughing. Chad continued to strut the stage, pausing to flex and pose.

"Five hundred," Tina shouted.

"Are you kidding?" Porchia said. "Where are you going to come up with five hundred dollars?"

Tina waved her off. "VISA."

Delene shrugged. "A girl's gotta do what a girl's gotta do."

The other bidder blew a kiss to Chad and sat.

"I have five hundred dollars. Do I have another bid?" the emcee asked. When there were no more bids, she said, "I have five hundred going once, going twice, sold to paddle number one-forty-five. Go meet your date, Bachelor Chad."

Chad jumped from the stage and headed for their table.

"I'm dying," Tina said. "I can't believe I just did that. But O-M-G, is he cute or what?"

Chad came over and kissed Tina on the cheek. "Thank you." He took her arm and led her back to the cashier's stand. Porchia had noticed that as soon as the bachelor sold, the group running the auction got their payment. She figured each man had been instructed to take his winner to the cashier immediately.

"We are so honored to have the next bachelor tonight. Help me welcome our new sheriff to the stage. Marc Singer."

Marc walked out dressed in his sheriff uniform. His hair was tousled as though he'd been running his fingers through it. The excitement in the audience was electric. Porchia knew this was one of the organizers' big draws. She expected Delene to bid on him since Tina had bought Chad, but she was wrong. Delene stayed true to her word and let the bidding go on around her.

Five hundred came and went quickly. As did seven-fifty. As the bidding neared a thousand, the bidders began dropping out, but there were still a few diehards who apparently wanted to be patted down by their sheriff.

From a dark corner at the back of the room, a voice rang out. "Five thousand dollars."

There was a momentary stunned silence at the bid before the emcee collected herself.

"I have a five-thousand-dollar bid from paddle number two-ninety-five. Do I have any other bids? Going once. Going twice. Sold to the lady in the back for five thousand dollars."

Marc hopped from the stage and made his way to the back of the room. When he and his bidder made their way to the cashier, there was a growing murmur through the audience. His buyer was Dr. Lydia Henson, fiancée of Jason Montgomery.

"What's going on?" Porchia asked. "That's Jason Montgomery's fiancée. Why in the world did she buy Marc Singer?"

Delene shrugged. "No clue. I don't run in those circles. Here comes Tina. Maybe she'll know something."

"Did y'all see what I just saw?" Tina asked, dropping back into her chair.

"You mean Dr. Lydia Henson with Marc Singer?"

"Yeah. Crazy, huh?"

"We were just wondering what was going on?"

"Don't know. They were pretty closed mouth as she was paying."

The emcee tapped on the microphone. "Now here's an interesting date for sure. A ten-day camping trip with a cowboy. Who wouldn't want that? Help me welcome Darren Montgomery to our stage."

Darren strode from the right-side wing wearing jeans, a plaid snap shirt, highly polished cowboy boots and a black hat. He lifted the hat as he entered and bowed to the audience, which drove the ladies into a giggling mania and sent Porchia's heart racing. Just as every time she saw him, a familiar swirl of lust began to churn in her gut.

Then, before the bidding started, he blew a couple of kisses from the stage, one directly toward their table. Porchia pretended it was meant for all three women, but she would have sworn she felt his lips touch her cheek.

She settled in to watch the women claw each other to death for Darren, resigned that she and Darren were simply not meant to be more than the best of friends.

The opening bid came from Porchia's right. Five hundred dollars. That made her sit upright. An opening bid of five hundred? For a camping trip? She, and many other women in the room, twisted in their seats trying to get a look at the bidder. Sarah Jane Mackey was waving her paddle and glaring around as though daring anyone else to buy her man, not that Darren was her man. Last year, she'd tried to trap Darren into marriage by stabbing needles into his condom stash. It hadn't worked, but that hadn't slowed her obsession.

Another girl stood and raised her paddle. "Seven-fifty."

"Who's that?" Delene whispered.

"I was going to ask you guys that same question."

Tina leaned in. "New chick in town. Name's Rose or Violet or some flower. I forget. She's the new nursing director at the hospital. She was in the shop last week. Seems nice enough. Look." Tina tilted her head toward Sarah Jane. "I think Sarah Jane is trying to kill her competition with a death stare."

All three women turned and Porchia chuckled. Sarah Jane didn't stand a candle to June Randolph, Porchia's mother. Nobody had perfected a death stare like June Randolph. Porchia should know. She'd been on the receiving end more than once.

Tonight, Sarah Jane stood with her hands on her hips, her lips pulled tight across her teeth and glared at the new bidder. Then she raised her paddle again. "One thousand."

Porchia turned toward the stage to watch Darren's reaction. She knew him well enough to recognize he was not happy. A date with Sarah Jane had to rank high on his not-to-do list. A two-week vacation with the harpy would be nightmarish.

"Fifteen hundred," the nurse countered.

"Two thousand." Sarah Jane continued her threatening stance, which seemed to be working as the nurse pulled down her bidding paddle and sat.

Porchia saw Darren's lips move as he said something to the emcee, who nodded. Then he caught Porchia's gaze and gave her a wide-eyed help-me look.

"I have two thousand," the emcee said. "Are there any other bids?"

Sarah Jane looked around, a triumphant smile on her face.

Porchia simply couldn't let that haughty rich bitch win this date so cheaply, or at least cheap for Sarah Jane. The woman had too much money and wasn't afraid to flaunt it. If Darren had to spend time with Sarah Jane, Porchia wanted to make sure the cost took a chunk out of Sarah Jane's obscenely large allowance.

Porchia pushed to her feet. "Two thousand three hundred."

Before Sarah Jane could react, the emcee said, "Two thousand three hundred going once, twice, sold. Congratulations. Go collect your date, cowboy."

Porchia's mouth dropped open. What had just happened?

Tina grabbed Porchia's arm. "What are you doing?"

"Wow. That didn't work out like I'd planned." Porchia pushed to her feet and headed to the cashier before Darren could get to her. She'd explain to him later that she'd been trying to drive up the price.

She was digging for a credit card when Darren caught up with her.

"That surprised me," he said with a warm smile.

"Me too."

"Thank you."

"No problem." She pulled the credit card from her wallet.

"Wait. Before you pay, part of my offer for the date was if the winner didn't want to go or couldn't go for some reason, I would pay her bid and add a ten percent bonus. So, you're off the hook. I'll pay the bid. You don't have to go away with me."

Two thoughts occurred almost simultaneously.

First, hadn't she just told herself that she needed to get away? That she needed some time to think? Camping trips didn't require a lot of brain power. Eat, sleep and fish or whatever. A few days away could be just what she needed. Besides, she could always take her car and leave whenever she wanted.

Second, and this one really scared her, she wanted to spend ten days with Darren. She enjoyed his company. Relaxed and quick to laugh, he was easy to be with. She could just be herself. He accepted her no matter how she was dressed or what mood she was in.

Sure they flirted…a lot. But the flirty comments had been received with a laugh and then forgotten. That was the kind of friendship they had. So this was simply a friend helping a friend, no romantic entanglement.

She supposed camping could be fun, if dirt, bugs and sweat were on her list of fun things. They weren't, but she did owe him for stepping in with Slade this morning.

"Nope," she said and handed the card to the cashier. "I bought you, so you'll just have to put up with me."

His lips moved slowly up into a smile. "I don't think that'll be a problem at all. How about—"

Before he could finish, a loud roar went up from the ballroom where the auction was taking place.

"What was that?" Porchia asked.

Darren snorted. "I'm pretty sure the emcee just announced the surprise bachelor for this evening."

"Oh?" Porchia's eyebrows arched. "Anyone I know?"

"My cousin, Jason."

"Jason Montgomery? But aren't he and Dr. Henson engaged?"

"Not anymore. They had some big tussle last week. I have no idea over what, so don't ask. And at the last minute, he volunteered for the auction."

"Hmm, maybe I should have saved my money." She winked at him.

"Ha. Come on. Let's go see who's bidding on him."

The better question would have been who wasn't bidding on him. At least twenty women held bidding paddles high in the air. Porchia grabbed Darren's hand and dragged him back to her table. Chad had joined Tina, sitting in Delene's seat.

"Where's Delene?" Porchia asked. She retook her seat. Darren pulled over a chair and sat down.

"Paying."

"Really?" Porchia grinned. "Who did she buy?"

"Zack Marshall."

This time Darren's eyebrows rose. "For real? Good for her. Zack's a great guy."

"This is crazy," Tina said, gesturing toward the bidding women.

"Yeah," Chad said. "I'm kind of hurt it wasn't a madhouse for me and I flexed my muscles and everything."

Tina patted his thigh. "Their loss. My gain."

The emcee tapped on the microphone. "Ladies," she shouted. "Ladies. Quiet down a little so I can hear. The last bid I heard was three thousand five hundred. Is there another bid?"

"Five thousand," came the reply.

"Who's that?" Darren asked.

Tina and Porchia twisted around to see the bidder.

"Well, isn't that interesting," Delene said as she and Zack joined the table.

Zack and Darren greeted each other warmly with back slaps and then Darren introduced him to Chad.

The women ignored the male bonding. "What's interesting?" Porchia asked.

"The bidder."

"Who is she?" Tina asked.

"Her name is Katrina Murphy. She's the new hospital administrator. Rumor has it she's been dating Marc Singer. So maybe this is tit-for-tat? You buy my boyfriend and I buy yours?"

"Maybe. Who knows?"

"It's going to make our camping trip quite interesting," Darren said to Porchia.

"How so?"

"Jason had planned on bringing Lydia. Since they broke up, he was going by himself. But when he heard that my auction date was the family camping trip, he stole the idea. And Singer had planned to come for the first weekend. He and Cash were going to do some fishing while we were there."

"Wait," Porchia said. "Are you telling me your whole family is going camping with us?"

"Yeah. Didn't you read the date description?"

"Apparently not close enough. Tell me exactly what I've bought."

Darren put his arm around the back of her chair and leaned in. His woodsy cologne tickled her nose, which made her want to rub the tip up and down his neck. He smelled so good.

"It's the annual Montgomery family getaway. Because of Olivia and Caroline's pregnancies, we haven't gotten to go the last couple of years. But since no one in the family is currently pregnant—that we know of—everyone is going down to Whisky Creek Reserve for two weeks of camping, fishing and riding."

"You're taking horses?"

"ATVs. There are over a thousand acres of great riding. I was worried about you getting bored, but with Jason bringing Katrina and Singer bringing Lydia, well, we might have a front-row seat to more entertainment than I thought."

Oh dear. Two weeks, or rather ten days, with the entire Montgomery clan. What had she gotten herself into?

Chapter Three

Darren whistled as he drove home from the auction. Grinning, he kept beat with the radio by tapping his fingers on his steering wheel. If someone had told him that Porchia would be his date for the family camping trip, he'd not have believed it. But damn if it wasn't true.

His heart had been galloping in his chest when he'd been on stage. The light might have been bright, but he'd still been able to see into the audience. When Sarah Jane Mackey had started bidding and then running off the other bidders, he'd let the auctioneer know that if she won, he'd never do this again. But if someone else won, he'd personally add fifty percent to the bid as his donation. His message had been received and Sarah Jane had been shut out by Porchia's bid and a fast auction hammer.

He didn't know why Porchia had bid on him and he didn't care. She'd been on his radar for a while. Actually, more than that. He never missed a chance to be around her. He'd asked her out more than once, but she shot him down each and every time. She'd rebuffed anything beyond friendship, but he'd just been handed the gift of time alone with her, and he planned to do all he could to win her over.

To be away for a couple of weeks required a lot of advance planning for the ranch. Since his brother, Reno, and his girlfriend, Magda, were also going, he and Reno had devoted most of the week to lining up additional cowboys to help their friend, Zack Marshall, tend to their animals while they were gone. Granted, they could be back within a couple of hours if there were problems, but Darren wanted to make the most of his time with Porchia without worrying about the ranch.

His days started early and ran late. Any hopes he might have had to go into Whispering Springs before the vacation faded as he dragged his exhausted body home each evening. He spoke with Porchia on Sunday and again on Tuesday and Wednesday. With each phone call, she reiterated her excitement at getting away. However, when she'd suggested taking her own car, he'd nixed that idea immediately. Privately, he doubted her hunk of junk would make it all the way to Whiskey Creek. She did insist on meeting him at the D&R rather than him driving all the way into town to pick her up and then having to backtrack to head down to the camp.

Sleep was elusive Thursday night. Thoughts of Porchia circled through his mind. He made plans for how he could keep her entertained while they were gone. He imagined kissing her, touching her in ways she'd never allowed before. Oh, he'd kissed her, but it was always a quick touch of lips and then it was done. He wanted more. He wanted deep, soul-searching kisses that went on for days. He wanted her to feel as much for him as he felt for her.

At twenty-eight, he'd had girlfriends and lovers. But the pull he felt for Porchia was unlike any he'd experienced before. Any time he spent with her was too short. He never tired of her laugh, or her smile or the way she would roll her eyes at some of his jokes. He'd begun to think that a lifetime with Porchia might not be enough. Daylight hadn't begun to think about rising when Darren got up and made coffee. Around four, he was joined by Magda and Reno.

"How long you been up?" Magda asked. She poured two cups of coffee and handed one to Reno.

"Forever."

She chuckled. "Excited about the camping trip?"

"Yeah, that's it."

Reno snorted. "Come on. Let's get going on the chores we have to do before we leave so we can get out of here on time."

"I've already mucked the stalls. The horses are out in the pasture. Drove the road fence line and everything was okay."

Reno's eyebrows shot up. "You have been up a while. Hope you can stay awake for the drive."

"I don't think that'll be a problem." Darren poured his fourth cup of coffee. "I haven't had any breakfast yet though."

"Gotcha covered," Magda said, rising from her chair. "How about some waffles and bacon?"

"Perfect. I'm going to grab a quick shower, if you don't mind."

"We're not in your car," Reno said, "so if you stink, it's not a problem for us." He grinned. "But Porchia might appreciate if you didn't smell like horse manure."

At five a.m., headlights flashed through the living-room windows.

"Porchia's here," Magda said. "She's as good with morning hours as y'all." She yawned widely. "I don't think my internal clock will ever reset to make me a morning person." There was a knock at the kitchen door. "No, no. You two sit there like statues. I'll get it."

Reno laughed. "See why I love that woman? What a mouth."

Porchia came in carrying a white pastry box. "Too late, I see. I did bring some fresh doughnuts and apple fritters. Made this morning," she teased, waving the box toward the guys.

On the next wave, Darren snatched it from her hands. "Gimme. I need a fritter."

"Tell me there's a cream-filled doughnut in there," Reno whined.

Porchia tsked. "Do you think I'd come without a cream-filled doughnut for you?"

Magda shook her head. "I swear I would weigh five-hundred pounds if I ate like these two."

"Tell me about it. Luckily, being around this all day has sort of diminished my appetite for sweets. But notice I said sort of? I still love a fresh apple fritter."

Porchia pulled a fritter from the box and set it on the small plate Magda held out to her.

"Coffee?" Magda asked.

Porchia rolled her eyes. "You're kidding, right?"

Magda laughed and filled a large mug. "Black and strong."

Porchia took a sip. "Perfect."

Darren pushed a chair out with his foot. "Sit. Eat. Then we need to be on the road."

Porchia dropped into the chair. "Wow. You've done wonders for their manners."

Magda grinned. "Just imagine what they were like before I got here."

Reno pulled Magda into his lap. "I'll show you my manners." He nibbled on her neck as she squirmed and tried to stand.

"You two are disgusting," Darren said. "Sorry about them," he said to Porchia.

She shrugged. "Doesn't bother me. I think they're kind of sweet. What time are we leaving?" She took a big bite of her fritter and chewed.

"As soon as you're finished eating." Darren grinned. "All I need to do is load your stuff to my truck and we'll be ready."

"You sure I shouldn't take my own car? I mean, something could happen at the bakery and I'd have to head back."

"I'm sure. If you need to come back, I'll bring you."

Magda struggled up from Reno's lap. "I'm going to brush my teeth and grab my last bag and I'll be ready."

"I'll help," Reno said.

Magda rolled her eyes. "I doubt it."

After they left, Porchia looked at Darren. "We did good getting those two back together."

Darren tapped his cup against hers. "That we did."

Porchia finished her coffee and put her cup in the sink. "Okay then. Let's get me loaded."

Darren followed her outside to her car. She popped the trunk where she'd stored her luggage. She'd never been camping in her entire life. Well, if you didn't count Girl Scout Brownies. Brownie camp had been easy. She'd been given a list by the troop leader and that's what she'd taken. But adult camping? She had no idea exactly what to pack.

It was October, so the weather should be warm, but it was also Texas. Anything was possible. Finally, she'd packed shorts, T-shirts, a couple of bathing suits, jeans, a jacket and some long-sleeve shirts. She didn't even want to think about how many pairs of shoes she packed.

Darren lifted her bags out and groaned. "Good Lord, woman. We're only going to be gone ten days. On top of that, it's camping."

Porchia opened her eyes wide as though in shock. "Do you mean I didn't need to bring those two long cocktail dresses?"

Darren chuckled and stowed her bags in the back seat of his truck. "I'm hoping you packed high heels for those dresses."

Porchia flipped her long hair over her shoulder. "Of course. Don't be a rube."

She could have easily climbed into the truck, but Darren insisted on helping her climb up and in, not that she was complaining. It'd been a long time since she'd had a man's hands around her waist, and damn if it didn't feel great. And once again, Darren's scent had her craning her nose for a better sniff. One of these days, he was going to catch her sniffing him. She'd better have a good story ready to go.

By six, the Montgomery brothers' two trucks were pulling out of the D&R. Darren pulled the trailer that carried their two new Honda ATVs, early birthday presents from their parents.

"Love your new Hondas. Why are you hauling them and not Reno?"

"We agreed that I would tow them down. He's going to haul them back." He glanced over at her, his deep-blue eyes vivid even in the early morning light. "And I lost the coin toss."

She laughed. "What's it like having a twin? You two look so much alike, although not exactly the same. You're fraternal twins, right?"

He nodded. "Yep. But when we were younger, we looked more alike than we do now. You know, it's hard to say what it's like to be a twin since I've always been one. I don't know life any other way. I don't have anything to compare it with."

"Never thought about it that way."

"Reno is my best friend and my worst competitor." He chuckled. "We spent our childhood trying to outdo each other."

"Fights over girls?"

"Only once."

When he stopped there, her curiosity got the better of her. "Serious fight?"

"Oh, yeah. Very. We were six and in the first grade. We were both sure that Nancy was our girlfriend, so we fought over which one of us she liked best. We had a fistfight on the playground." He glanced over with a grin. "Very serious stuff. I got a cut over my eye," he said, pointing to a slight scar in his brow. "Reno got a chipped tooth and split lip. Sounds like we really went at it, huh?" He shook his head with a snort. "We both missed when we swung our fists. I fell against a swing and he hit his mouth on a rock when he landed on the ground."

Porchia giggled. "That's hysterical." She twisted in her seat toward him, drawing her knee up. "So what happened to Nancy?"

"Oh, well, Nancy liked Craig, who thought girls had cooties and wanted nothing to do with them. She chased him all over the playground for a month."

She gave a deep belly laugh. As she did, she felt the tension she'd been carrying ease out. This trip would be good for her. The break from work, early hours and threatening calls and visits would be a welcome relief.

"I had to get some stitches," he continued. "Reno didn't, but there's still a very light scar if you know where to look for it. Mom was not happy." He frowned. "No. That's not quite right. It was more like she was disappointed in us, which hurt more than if she'd spanked us. Told us we were brothers. Special brothers. That not many people got to have a special person like we did. Girls might come and go, but we would always be special brothers. You'd think that at only six years old, her talk would go over our heads, but it didn't. Sure we had fights over the years, but never over women."

"How did you avoid it? Surely at some point you both liked the same girl."

"Turns out we have totally different tastes in women. For example, I was never attracted to Magda. I mean, I like her. She's a great gal, but a romantic interest? Nope. Never."

"Speaking of Magda, how come you were so sure last year about getting them together?"

He grinned. "Reno is the worst at keeping secrets, even when he thinks he's great. Those two were sneaking around seeing each other. Thought the rest of us were clueless." He snorted. "Not hardly. But then something happened in August last year that sent Magda flying out of town like she'd seen the devil. Reno was total hell to live with after she left. I talked to Mom about it and she hired Magda to work for us. Of course, I acted like I was going to hit on Magda, get her in the sack, really make some moves on her. You should have seen Reno's face. He was grinding his teeth so hard, I'm surprised they didn't crack. Threatened me if I so much as looked at her funny, much less touched her, he would cram my teeth down my throat. It was all I could do to keep a straight face. Once she moved in, the way they looked at each other made me want to get out of the room."

"Puppy eyes, huh?"

"Let's-go-to-bed eyes. I was so pissed when I broke my leg but it was the best thing that happened for them." He laid his palm on her knee. "Thanks again for helping get them back together."

His rough hand on her flesh felt as if someone had placed a lit match. Hot and burning. Except she didn't have the pull-away response. Instead, she would be happy if he kept it there for the next fifty miles or so. When he put his hand back on the wheel, she was simultaneously relieved and disappointed.

She needed to keep reminding herself that he was too young for her and, more importantly, she just needed this break from life to think, not to start a romance. Not that being tangled up in bed sheets with Darren Montgomery wouldn't be a luscious way to spend a few hours…or a few days. But he was her good friend and she was determined to keep it that way.

Now what were they talking about? She'd been so focused on his thick fingers that she'd lost track of the discussion.

"How did you get away from the bakery?"

Thank goodness, Darren threw her a lifeline.

"The bakery? Right. Well, the couple of months that Magda worked with me made me realize that I really need more help, especially when she left. I hired a couple of women to help, and then one day, the ideal baker came in. Have you met Mallory James? She works at night, so she's probably been gone every time you've come in. Along with Callie's help, she's handling the kitchen. I've got a couple of women manning the counter. Plus, Tina promised to check in every day." She chuckled. "Of course, that cost me a few pastries. Anyway, it's not as if they can't call me if there is a problem." Her eyes widened. "We will have cell service where we're going, right?"

"Spotty service. It comes and goes depending on where you are on the property. But sounds like you've got it covered, so I wouldn't worry about it."

Easy for him to say. He didn't have Slade Madden breathing down his neck. Speaking of which...

"Listen, I have to tell you something," she said.

"Okay. Shoot."

"Besides your charming company, there's another reason I needed to get out of town."

He glanced at her with raised eyebrows. "Yeah? What's that?"

"Remember the guy from the bakery? The one who was holding on to my arm?"

"Yeah," he drew out. "What about him?"

"Well, he's a guy I knew back in high school. Not an old boyfriend or anything like that. Just someone I knew. Anyway, he's a little down on his luck and has been dogging old classmates for money."

A little twist on the truth, but close enough.

"And you gave it to him?" he asked incredulously.

"No, no," she hurriedly added. "But I am hoping he'll move on if he can't find me for a couple of weeks."

"You talk to Singer about him?"

"Why would I talk to the sheriff about this? It's no big deal. Just a pain in the ass I hope gets the message that he's not getting any money from me when he can't find me."

"If he's still bothering you when we get back, I'll have a word with him."

"You will not," she exclaimed. "I don't need you doing that. Really. But I felt like I had to explain why I don't want to take you up on your offer to buy me out of this trip. We're friends, and I'm sure we'll have a great time. I just wanted to be honest with you about why I'm going."

He frowned in her direction. "So it's not my sparkling personality and studly bod?"

She rolled her eyes and then laughed. "Yeah, it's those too."

He smiled. "Seriously, if this guy is a problem, let me or Singer have a talk with him when we get back."

"Sure."

Yeah, that wasn't going to happen. Still, it was nice that he'd offered. And now she could go into this vacation with a clear conscience.

Chapter Four

By the time Darren turned off the back road into the entrance for Whiskey Creek Preserve and stopped at the gate, his brother and Magda had long since left them behind. Pulling the trailer with the ATVs had them arriving after Reno by at least twenty minutes.

"I've got it," Porchia said, jumping from the truck. "Hey," she hollered back. "Want to share the code?"

He grinned and leaned out his window. "Yeah. That might help." He pulled a piece of paper from his truck's sun visor and leaned out again. "Five. Seven. Two. Seven. Four. Nine. Five."

Her fingers worked the buttons and the gate swung open. He pulled forward and then stopped to let her climb back in.

Behind them, Drake Gentry's Range Rover turned in and stopped. Darren waved out the window at his sister and her husband and drove forward. Drake followed closely on Darren's trailer's bumper and cleared the gate before it could close.

"I know that's your sister and her husband, but I don't know them very well."

Darren glanced over. "KC's pretty cool. Drake is okay, I guess. I'm sure by the end of this camping trip, you'll know them well, if we can keep them out of their cabin."

Porchia chuckled. "Really?"

"You have no idea. You'd think they invented sex."

She coughed, and he figured she was choking back another laugh.

"Actually," he went on, "I'm glad they're together. I've never seen KC happier. Of course, Reno and I did warn Drake that if he did anything to make her cry, we'd see to it that he'd be crying next."

Porchia rolled her eyes with a muttered, "Oh brother."

The truck bounced over the ruts in the dirt.

"You know," she said, "I don't really know any of your family well other than Reno and Magda. I've met the women but hardly any of the men. And I've never met your parents."

"You'll love them. And I'm sure they'll adore you." *As much as I do.* Not that he could say that out loud.

She smiled and touched his arm. "Thanks."

The drive from the gate to the lodge was a little over two miles. As each tenth of a mile passed, the tension in the truck cab rose. Porchia pulled her knee off the seat and put both feet on the floor. Then he noticed how straight she sat, eyes focused to the front. Her hands were folded in her lap. Her entire posture reminded him of the year KC had been a debutante. He and Reno had teased her mercilessly, but she'd gotten her revenge when both of them had served as debutante escorts a mere four years later.

The last bend in the road exposed the two-story log lodge. It'd been built in the early nineteen-fifties as a hunting camp for some rich banker who'd rarely ever used it. The preserve had changed hands a couple of times until it had been bought by some friends of the Montgomerys about twenty years ago. Six newer cabins had been added over the years, with the seventh one still under construction.

The drive circled in front of each log cabin and the lodge and around a large fire pit. There were folding camp chairs already set up near the stone pit.

Outside the ring of buildings, two camping sites were available for tents or recreational vehicles. Cash Montgomery stood in one of those sites directing a truck backing a fifth wheel into a site.

"Whose fifth wheel?" Porchia asked.

Darren grinned so wide his cheeks hurt. "Marc Singer. He and Cash are pretty tight." He chuckled. "With Lydia as his date, this could get interesting."

He stopped his truck in front of the lodge and climbed out. Two hours of driving had him stiff. He wasn't used to staying still for such long periods of time except when he was sleeping. Even then, if the sheets on his bed were to be believed, he tossed and turned a lot at night too.

Porchia hopped from the passenger side, flung her arms over her head and stretched. Then, bending from the waist, she touched her toes with a groan.

"Man, that feels good." She stood and twisted side-to-side.

Darren made it around the hood of his truck in time to get a good look at her tight ass when she bent. He lost his train of thought the minute she touched her toes.

"Stop staring at her and come hug your mother."

He jerked his gaze from Porchia's backside and up to the porch. His mother stood with her hands on her hips, a knowing smile on her lips.

"Hi, Mom." He hurried up the stairs and lifted his mother off her feet in a bear hug.

"Stop that," she said, slapping his shoulder.

He set her back on her feet. "When did you and Dad get here?"

"Yesterday. Your dad and Lane wanted to go riding before the rest of you got here."

"Uncle Lane brought horses?"

Nadine Montgomery snorted. "I wish. Those two fools bought new ATVs. When your dad test drove the ones we got y'all, he had to have one." She sighed dramatically. "I wonder which one of them will hit a tree first."

Darren laughed. "Lucky for us that Travis had the foresight to marry a doctor."

He sensed Porchia's presence before she said a word. Heat washed over him, followed by a tingling at the base of his spine. In all his life, he never remembered having this type of physical reaction to just being near any one woman. He turned to face Porchia and the heat notched up about a hundred degrees or so.

"Mom. This is Porchia Summers. Porchia, this is my mother, Nadine."

Porchia extended her hand. "Nice to meet you, Mrs. Montgomery."

Nadine shook Porchia's hand. "Please call me Nadine. If you yell Mrs.

Montgomery this weekend, there's no telling who'll answer."

Porchia's smile was extremely polite and formal. "Of course. Nadine it is then."

"Porchia's the best baker in the world," he said, draping his arm around Porchia's shoulders. Beneath his arm, she straightened and grew stiff. What had he said wrong?

"I know," Nadine said. "Jackie has told me about your wonderful treats. Maybe you could give me some tips while we're here? I seem to have missed the baking gene."

"I'd be honored."

"Great. Come on in. Jackie assigned the cabins and I can't remember where she put y'all."

When they came out, keys to cabin five in hand, his dad and Uncle Lane came roaring up on two new, very muddy four-wheelers. His dad flew past the lodge, rounded the drive by cabin one and skidded to a stop. He stepped off his machine, pulled his helmet off his hair, laughing loudly and pointing at his brother, Lane.

"I win," Clint shouted as Lane Montgomery came to an abrupt stop beside him.

Lane removed his helmet. "Enjoy your victory while you can. Tomorrow, you shall eat crow."

"God. Those two idiots are going to kill themselves," Nadine said.

"I don't know about you, Nadine, but I made sure Lane's life insurance was paid up."

Darren looked over at his aunt who'd joined them on the porch and laughed. "I swear, Aunt Jackie. I don't know if you're kidding or not."

"Not," she deadpanned.

"I'm pretty sure you know Porchia Summers, right? Porchia. My Aunt Jackie."

Jackie hugged her. "Of course I know Porchia. Why, at least ten of my pounds are totally her fault."

Porchia laughed. "Sorry about that?"

"Don't be. I enjoyed every delectable ounce."

"If y'all will excuse us, we'll get unpacked," Darren said.

The two older women waved them off and headed over to where their husbands stood comparing their all-terrain vehicles.

"I bet those two were quite the handful growing up," Porchia said. "Seems like they really enjoy each other."

Darren grinned. "They do and they were. I understand why Dad moved to Florida to set up his ranch, but I also know he's really missed Uncle Lane and living in Texas."

They climbed back into the truck.

"I'm going to drop the trailer and ATVs before we unload. That work for you? Or do you need to, um, go inside first."

This was pitiful. He was acting like a ninth grader on a first date with a senior.

"Do you mean do I need to pee?" Porchia grinned. "I'm fine. What can I do to help?"

"Not a thing. Sit tight."

He followed the drive past cabin four, turned left toward Marc Singer's fifth wheel, passed it and pulled to an open area where a couple of other trailers were parked. He whipped the truck and trailer around and backed them in.

Reno followed them down the trail and had the ramp on the trailer lowered and was on one of the new Hondas before Darren could get out of his truck. Reno revved the engine and then backed the machine off. Darren climbed onto the second one and followed Reno down the ramp. Once they had their new four-wheelers unloaded, Reno uncoupled the trailer from the truck and Darren pulled a couple of feet forward.

"Want to drive the ATV to our cabin?"

Porchia's face reflected her surprise. "Really?"

"Sure. You ever been on one?"

"Not in years. Why don't I drive the truck and you ride over?"

"If you're sure?"

"I'm sure."

Porchia slid into the driver's seat. Darren got on his ATV, as did Reno. The guys headed back toward the main lodge with Porchia following.

Cabin five was directly across from the lodge, separated by the drive and the large fire-pit area.

Darren pulled into a dirt parking area and jumped from his machine. "Home sweet home for the next ten days."

"This place is incredible." Porchia hopped down from the truck. "Listen to how quiet it is."

Wind rustled through the needles of the tall pines. Sunlight dappled on the ground. Somewhere in the distance, a bird trilled. Suddenly, the roar of an ATV broke the silence.

"Oh well. It was nice while it lasted," she said.

The cabin was definitely a step up from Porchia's expectations. When camping had first been mentioned, she'd envisioned tents, blow-up mattresses and hard ground. Then Darren had pointed out that they would have their own cabin.

Since the only camping in cabins she'd done was with her Brownie troop, she hadn't been too excited at the prospect. At Brownie camp, a cabin had uncomfortable cots and communal bathrooms, not to mention the rats that had begged for food at night. She'd gotten used to the environment and loved being with her friends, but camping had never found its way into her favorite to-do list.

Cabin five was definitely not her Brownie cabin. The first clue was the cedar swing that hung from the rafters on the porch. Brownie cabins didn't have swings, much less a nice porch.

When she opened the door, she didn't need any more clues that this wasn't Girl Scout camp. She walked into a small living room with hardwood floors covered with a large, geometrically designed area rug. A burgundy-colored leather sofa dominated the space. The sofa was angled to give a view of the flat-screen television and a large fireplace.

After walking through the living room, she took one step up into a small open kitchen equipped with a refrigerator, stovetop and microwave. The kitchen cabinets held dishes and glassware for four.

A short hall led to the single bedroom and bath. The king-sized bed swallowed most of the space in the small room. Also in the room was a tiny closet, a four-drawer dresser and fireplace. On the far wall, a door lead to a standard bathroom, if one considered multiple showerheads standard.

She dropped her bags on the bed and turned toward Darren who'd followed her journey through the cabin. She knew her mouth was hanging agape.

"You like?" he asked.

She got the impression he wasn't kidding and that her reaction was important to him.

"I'm stunned. I'll be honest. I wasn't expecting anything this nice."

A brief moment of relief shuttered across his face and then he smiled. "We have the newest cabin. I think Aunt Jackie was trying to impress you since there aren't any two bedroom cabins. I think that living room sofa is a pull-out bed."

"Impress me?" She frowned and then scoffed. "I'm nobody to impress. That's for sure. Still, her intention or not, I'm blown away." She wrapped her arms around his neck and brushed her mouth against his. "I love it."

She'd kissed Darren before, but usually on the cheek or in completely different, non-romantic circumstances. This slight touch of lips ricocheted like a lightning bolt through her. She jerked her arms from around his neck, afraid to leave them there longer. She liked the feeling a little too much.

"Well, then," she said on a long exhale. "I think I'll get unpacked."

Darren still stood where he'd been when she'd kissed him.

"You okay?" she asked.

He cleared his throat. "I'm fine. I'll put my stuff in here. I'm sure there are some extra sheets for the couch."

She cocked her hands on her hips. "Let's talk about this, okay? We're friends. Good friends. If you want to sleep on the sofa, or if you want me to sleep on it, fine. No problem."

"Of course I don't expect you to sleep on the sofa," he said, a scowl darkening his expression. "What kind of man do you think I am?"

"I think you're a wonderful man. Completely trustworthy. One who keeps his word once he gives it." She swept her hand over the bed. "And this bed is huge. Can't we share it? As friends. Neither of us should be subjected to sleeping on a sofa for two weeks. I promise to stay on my side and you on your side. Agreed?"

Her gut tugged at the thought of sharing a bed with Darren. She wasn't a virgin. Hadn't been in a long time, but on the other hand, she hadn't shared her bed with a man in years either. She'd been telling the truth when she'd said she trusted him. It was her she was worried about.

Darren's phone rang. Both of them looked at each other surprised.

"We have service," he announced and then answered. "Hello. Sure. When? Okay. Heading out now."

He click off his phone and shoved it in his pocket.

"That was my cousin, Travis. He needs help with something."

She waved him away. "Go. I'm fine. I'll finish unpacking and find something to do. We can finish discussing sleeping arrangements later."

"Great."

He stepped out of the bedroom and then came back. He caught her head between his hands and lowered his mouth to hers. She put her hands over his, loving how large and strong they felt under hers.

This wasn't the simple brushing of mouths as before. His kiss was a full-on attack of lips and tongues. Wet and deep kisses that made her insides go soft and liquid. Kisses that had the power to make her forget all her objections to a romantic getaway with him.

When he bit gently on her bottom lip, she willingly allowed him to sweep his tongue in like an invading army. She sucked on his tongue, not wanting to let it go.

When he pulled back, she flicked her tongue out to taste the moisture he'd left behind.

His eyes were dilated and filled with lust. His breaths were ragged.

"Okay then" he said, dropping his hands and stepping back. "I'll see you in a little bit."

As soon as she heard the front door slam, she dropped onto the mattress.

Holy Lord. That kiss had everything inside her melting, including every ounce of common sense. That man knew what to do with his mouth. She let out a long sigh.

And he was exactly the type of man her parents would hate. A cowboy. A man a little rough around the edges. Hard hands with calluses and bruises. A man who worked outside and sported a tan most of the year. A man who wasn't afraid of manual labor, and did it every day, in fact. A man whose hair brushed along his collar because he'd been too busy to get a trim. She knew exactly how her parents would react to him if she were ever to bring him to Atlanta. They would waste no time in telling her he was totally wrong.

Expelling another sigh, she stood, determined to ignore her parents' voices in her head about how she was wasting her life with her *little bakery* and needed to get serious about finding the right man to marry and producing the next generation.

Once she got her clothes hung up and stashed into drawers, she wandered onto the porch and took the swing. She bent her right knee and pulled her foot up onto the chair. With her left, she pushed off and set the swing in motion.

Darren had left ten minutes earlier when summoned to help Travis. She'd wondered what Travis was bringing that needed help.

Pretty soon, she didn't have to wonder any longer.

A high-powered truck chugged into the drive towing an extended horse trailer. The truck and trailer pulled around the circle, turned by cabin four and followed the road that'd led to the field where Darren had stored his hauler.

Behind the truck, a white Cadillac Escalade SUV pulled up to the lodge steps and stopped. The back door flew open and a couple of boys around eight or nine spilled out, followed by a black and white dog. Olivia Montgomery Landry exited from the driver's side.

"Adam. You and Norman get back here. Don't let Daisy near that lake. Do you hear me?"

The boys didn't return.

On the lodge porch, Olivia's mother, Jackie, laughed, the sound carrying easily across the yard.

From the passenger side, Caroline Graham Montgomery, Olivia's sister-in-law, stepped out, a broad grin also splitting her face.

Olivia threw her hands up in the air. "Fine," she called. "Don't come back. I'll let your fathers handle this."

That threat seemed to work, because both boys came running from behind the lodge, the dog still dry. They probably just hadn't had time to make it all the way to the pond.

The sound of metal clanking and a ramp hitting the ground drew Porchia's attention back to the long trailer. Darren walked a chestnut-colored horse out, followed by Travis with a black horse. A total of six horses were unloaded and released into the corral.

Once the horses were unloaded, Mitch Landry used two fingers to produce a sharp whistle. The two boys raced over and helped unload all the necessary tack.

Porchia rocked the porch swing in a gentle sway as she watched all the activity in the campground. Most of the other women were at the lodge. Isolating herself wasn't a good way to start an extended vacation with people she would be interacting with every day.

She made her way over to the lodge and walked up the steps in time to hear Caroline say, "You know Travis. My husband is going to do what he wants. But this time, I think he's right. Those horses needed some exercise, and with all the riders in this family, they'll get what they need. Besides, this is a gorgeous place. Perfect for riding." Her gaze met Porchia's as she was gesturing to the area. "Porchia. What a nice surprise. I heard you were coming with Darren."

The two women embraced. Porchia had supplied many a doughnut to Whispering Springs Medical Clinic where Caroline had a practice with Dr. Lydia Henson.

"You know everybody, right?"

"I do. Nice to see you, Olivia."

"You too."

"Porchia is going to teach me how to bake while we're here," Darren's mother bragged.

"Me too," said Olivia. "I could use some insider tips."

Porchia laughed. "Sure. Happy to play in the kitchen. I'm assuming the lodge has a kitchen big enough, because the kitchen in cabin five won't work."

"All the cabins have small kitchenettes," Jackie said. "Most of the groups who come here have communal meals, so the lodge kitchen is fairly well stocked. I suspect you'll find whatever you need there."

"So, Mom," Olivia said. "Was it your bright idea to put Jason and Katrina Murphy in cabin three?"

"I'm sure I don't know what you're talking about," Jackie said, fluffing her hair in such a way that left no doubt she was lying.

"Jason and his date back-to-back with Marc Singer and Lydia? Are you trying to start a fight?"

Porchia leaned against the porch rail, enjoying the family interaction. Her family had never been the touchy-feeling kind. No public displays of affection. No public arguments either. Emotional outbursts were frowned upon. Her mother was the perfect society wife. Never a strand of hair out of place. A wrinkle wouldn't dare form in her mother's tailored clothing.

"A fight?" Jackie leaned toward her daughter, her face aglow with interest. "Do you really think Jason would fight for Lydia?"

"This is a bad, bad idea, Mom. They broke up."

"For now," Jackie said. "We'll just have to see what the future holds."

Nadine braced her hip on the railing next to Porchia. "Don't worry," she whispered. "I never interfere with my children's lives."

Chapter Five

Darren had been relieved when he'd been called to help with the horses. That first kiss from Porchia had been only long enough to whet his lust. That had to be why he'd gone back to the bedroom and kissed her as though his life depended on it.

Then she'd licked his tongue and sucked it into her mouth. He'd been kicked by horses that'd had less punch than that kiss. If Travis and Reno hadn't been waiting for him to help, he'd have been tempted to drop Porchia straight into bed, and that probably wasn't the best idea.

Tonight did worry him, however. He feared their king-sized mattress wouldn't be wide enough to keep him on his side. He was used to having a king-sized bed to himself, and he had a tendency to use every square inch of mattress. Maybe a bundling board? He chuckled. Nope. He'd climb right over that to be with Porchia.

They'd met a couple of years ago and she'd intrigued him from day one. However, every advance on his part had been parried away. His ego smarted from all her rejections.

But then she'd spent money he suspected she didn't have to buy this time with him. Next, she drops the news that she really just wanted to get out of town away from some old acquaintance hitting her up for money. And finally, she lays a kiss on him that pretty much blew holes in his socks.

She had him confused and tied up in knots.

He was tired of hearing how he was younger than her. Big deal. Four years was nothing. She'd used their age difference as her reason for turning down dates. More than once, he'd wondered if that was really the reason, or if she just wasn't attracted to him.

Now he thought he had his answer on the attraction question. Buying him at the bachelor auction and following that by a kiss left little doubt in his mind that she was into him. His challenge was to prove to her that they were perfect together, age difference be damned.

He had every intention of using this camping trip to chip away at her walls. But she had to be the one in charge of moving them from friends to lovers. That was the only way it would work. He'd set the scene, give her plenty of opportunities, and if nothing happened…well, then he'd just rethink this plan.

Darren spent the next few hours greeting his relatives as they arrived or helping get cars and trucks unloaded. He kept an eye out for Porchia, worried that she would be smothered by his family. The Montgomerys were an unruly crew. Loud voices, louder arguments and shouts of laughter rang throughout the main camping area. Every time he caught a glimpse of his date, she was with his mother or his aunt or his sister, wine goblets in hands, big grins on their faces. The women kept disappearing back into the lodge, where echoes of female giggles would slip out the windows.

Their paths finally crossed again at lunch. Club sandwiches along with chips and pretzels were piled high on the kitchen counter waiting for each person to fill a plate. The group gathered, or rather crammed, around a long oak table in the dining room. Darren was able to secure a seat next to Porchia only by beating the other Montgomerys to the table. Porchia's smile lit up her entire face, or it could have been the wine.

"You okay?" he asked.

"Your mom is hysterical," she said. "I had no idea these women were so funny." She patted his cheek. "Love the story of you running away when you were five. If only you could have gotten out of the barnyard. Oh, the places you could have gone." Her laugh tinkled with gaiety.

He sighed. "Mom has been telling you stories about my growing up?"

"Oh, not just your childhood, but Reno and KC's too." She leaned in and said in a stage whisper, "I think she held back on KC's stories since KC kept giving her the stink eye."

"I did not," KC protested, but her protestation was weak. "Okay, maybe a little, but I have a professional reputation to maintain."

Reno rolled his eyes. "Professional reputation? Hey, Drake. Does she still put panties on her head and dance?"

KC threw a pretzel across the table, which bounced off Reno's forehead.

Drake chewed the bite of sandwich in his mouth and swallowed. "Nope. Most of the time she's wearing nothing when she's dancing."

KC picked up her sandwich and shoved it into Drake's mouth. "Eat," she demanded. "You'll need your strength for later."

Reno and Darren groaned.

"I don't need to know that," Darren said.

Porchia laughed and elbowed Darren. "See what I mean?" she said. "Funny."

His family was going to be the death of any romance with Porchia before he could get one started. His best defense would be to keep her far, far away from his siblings, cousins and parents.

Reno leaned forward and spoke around Porchia. "Want to try the ATVs after lunch? We haven't had them out and I want to mark some trails before we take the ladies for a ride."

Magda leaned past Reno until she caught Porchia's gaze. "Ladies?" she mouthed.

Porchia grinned and shrugged.

As much as Darren wanted to cut Porchia from the family herd and get her alone, Reno was right. It'd been a few years since the family had used Whiskey Creek. The landmarks might have changed. The last thing he needed was to take Porchia on a romantic ride somewhere on the property and then have to call for help to find their way home.

"Do you mind?" he asked Porchia.

"Not at all. This morning started very early. Add lack of sleep to a bottle of wine and an afternoon nap sounds delicious. Have fun."

The thought of Porchia in bed had his cock sitting up and begging to go with her instead of out on an ATV with his brother. He had to get that under control before he stood, or else the tent in his pants would embarrass him and probably everyone else in the room.

Mentally, he started naming state capitals. Nothing more boring than that. He'd only made it to Tallahassee, Florida, when Reno called, "Let's hit it, bro."

He wasn't entirely ready to parade his semi-erection through the room. "In a sec. I want to finish this sandwich." He looked down at his plate, his now empty plate. A quick glance at Porchia's plate revealed a little less than half a sandwich. He snatched it off her plate and took a bite. She gave him a quizzical look.

"Still hungry?" She gestured toward the kitchen. "There are more sandwiches besides mine."

He swallowed and whispered in her ear. "True, but only this one has the taste of your lips on it." He gave the rim of her ear a quick kiss and then stood, his jeans sufficiently loose to allow him to walk with ease.

The new four-wheelers started with a growl. The powerful ride vibrated between his legs.

"Ready?" Reno shouted.

Darren pulled the strap of his helmet tighter under his chin. Both men had had to agree to helmets before their mother would agree to hand over the keys to the two all-terrain vehicles. Plus, Magda had made Reno promise not to remove his helmet. Darren hadn't heard Magda's reward for Reno if he kept it on, but whatever it was made Reno grin and give Magda a long kiss.

Darren flashed a thumbs-up to Reno, who nodded, goosed the machine and roared out of the camp, throwing dirt and rocks toward Darren. He chuckled and took off after his brother.

Time had not improved the condition of the trails. Darren bumped and jerked over rocks and large tree roots but he refused to slow. In front of him, Reno's body bounced on the ATV's seat and his head bopped on his shoulders.

He figured he looked about the same, bouncing and jerking with each leap of the knobby tires over the bumps.

Reno veered off to the right on what looked like a relatively new trail. The path narrowed and began to climb, not too steeply but the quads' engines still got a workout. Ahead of him, Reno pulled to the side, turned off the engine and stood, removing his helmet. Darren did the same.

"Nice view," Darren said. "I don't remember this trail. Do you?"

Reno shook his head. "Nope."

Darren ventured around Reno and then out to the edge of a large flat rock that protruded off the precipice. From up here, they had a view of the valley, which included the camp site. Below, various members of the Montgomery family were walking around while the two younger boys were racing around the fire pit with the dog on their heels. The horses Travis had brought grazed lazily in the pasture.

"This is an amazing view," Darren said. "We're facing what? East?"

"Yep." Reno nodded behind them. "Sun's already in the west, so, yeah, we're facing East."

Perfect spot to watch a morning sunrise with Porchia. A little chill in the air, a warm blanket and they'd be snuggled in no time.

"What are you planning?" Reno asked.

"No idea what you're talking about."

Reno cocked up his mouth on one side. "When you think, I can see the wheels and gears turning." He tapped his head. "Don't forget that we think a lot alike. So what?"

Darren shrugged. "Maybe a sunrise surprise for Porchia."

"I can see that," Reno replied with a nod. "And what's going on there anyway?"

"No clue," he said with a long sigh.

"No chemistry?" Reno suggested. "If you say yes to that you're a liar. There's more chemistry between you two than all the experiments we had to do in high school chem classes."

"I really don't know." He scraped his hair off his brow. "She's got me confused." He looked at his brother. "Big time confused."

Reno chuckled. "I can see that. But she did pay big bucks for this date with you. Saved your ass from Sarah Jane's clutches is what I hear. And I'll note that this is the second time she's pulled your undeserving butt out of the fire when it comes to Sarah Jane Mackey."

"Don't remind me," Darren snarled.

It'd been almost a year ago that Sarah Jane had tried to trap Darren into marriage by sabotaging all his condoms with a pin.

"Sarah Jane still calls from time to time," Darren continued. "Short of being rude to the extreme, I can't seem to shake her. Either I'm not being clear or—"

"She's as dense as this mountain," Reno interjected.

"Exactly."

"So back to Porchia."

"What about her?"

Reno just hiked his eyebrows with an incredulous glare.

"Fine. I'm interested. Happy now? I've got to keep Mom from telling her all those idiotic stories about us growing up. She already has an issue with me being younger than her. I don't need Mom, or you, or Dad or KC adding to her resistance by reminding her of all my screw ups."

His brother grinned. "Like the time you got caught naked in the hayloft with a girl?"

"Give me a break. We were five. And, yes. That's exactly what I mean."

Reno pretended to turn a key on his lips. "Your naughty past is safe with me."

"We better get back. We've been gone a while."

"Let's take the long trail home. I want to check out that private swimming hole. I might need it."

Darren laughed. "Good idea. Think we'll need to post a schedule? We've never had so many women here with us."

"Hell, it's KC and Drake I dread coming across. Those two cannot keep their hands off each other."

Some time later, they rolled back into the compound, a little dirty and a lot tired but both wearing matching grins.

"That was freaking awesome," Reno said.

"And I thought you didn't like that old four-wheeler at home."

"Ha. Fooled you. Magda and I are going to take them out a little later, if that's okay with you."

"Sure. I'm not sure how comfortable Porchia is with these anyway. Why don't I leave it here at your cabin? That way you don't have to come get it."

"Appreciate it."

Darren left the machine but took his helmet. Two men arguing caught his attention, so he turned toward the fight instead of his cabin. He'd known this was coming. It hit a little sooner than he expected.

In the open area behind his cousin Jason's cabin stood Jason and Marc Singer. Jason's brother, Cash, stood off to the side watching. Darren sidled up alongside Cash.

"Any blows thrown?" Darren asked.

"Nope. War of words at this point."

"Hmm. Think there'll be a fight?"

Cash looked at him. "Hoping for one?"

Darren shrugged. "Been a while since I've seen a good one."

"About a year," Cash agreed. "When Reno beat the crap out of the guy who drugged Magda."

"Yep."

Jason whirled toward his brother. "This is your fault," he said, pointing his finger at Cash. "You're the one who invited this...this...traitor."

Cash and Darren both turned toward the traitor, Marc Singer.

"Hey. Not my fault you and Lydia broke up," Singer said.

"You didn't have to bring her here," Jason growled.

"What's the difference?" Marc said. "We live in a small town. You're going to be seeing Lydia with me or someone else. The men in this town aren't stupid. We recognize a prize when we see it."

Jason drew back his fist, but Darren wrapped his arms around him to keep the blow from hitting the sheriff.

"Not a good idea, Cuz," Darren said. "And besides, don't you have a date here too? How's that going to look to her if you're back here fighting over another woman?"

Jason's jaw tightened. He struggled out of Darren's hold. "Just stay away from me and Kat," he said and stormed away.

Cash and Marc high-fived. Darren frowned.

"What are you two up to?"

"Not a thing," Cash said.

Darren knew a lie when he heard it, but he had his own love life to handle. Getting involved in whatever those two were up to wasn't on his agenda for this weekend.

He let himself into the cabin and closed the door with a quiet snick. The place was silent and still. Porchia wasn't in the living room or the kitchen. She'd mentioned a nap. The door to the bedroom was ajar. When he looked in, his heart bottomed out.

Porchia was lying on her side, eyes shut, mouth slightly open. Her long blond hair fanned over a couple of pillows. The late afternoon sun threw shadows around the room, but not on Porchia. Golden rays of sun fell across her body like small spotlights aimed to highlight all her gorgeous features.

He watched her sleep for longer than necessary. Her beauty was stunning. But her looks were only a small part of what made her special. She was also smart, clever, funny and sarcastic. Honest as the day is long, as his grandfather used to say. People loved her for all that.

Darren loved her for all that and more.

He'd find a way into her heart.

Somehow.

Chapter Six

Porchia waited until she heard the front door close before she opened her eyes. She tucked her hand under her cheek. It was difficult, if not impossible, to walk on a hardwood floor in cowboy boots without making a sound. She'd heard Darren coming down the hall, even though it had been obvious he was trying to be quiet.

Staying motionless while he'd stood there had been hard. She wasn't even sure why she played opossum, except that the memory of how he tasted when he kissed her and how wonderful his rough palms felt as he tenderly held her face during that kiss had wrapped her mind in confusion. The memory sent her heart leaping as though it'd been replaced with a Mexican jumping bean.

She rolled to her back and beat her fists on the bed. Damn it. If she had to be attracted to a Montgomery, why couldn't it have been someone older with a professional career, like Jason Montgomery? Someone her parents couldn't object to.

And better yet, why should she care what they thought? At thirty-two, it was past time to stop trying to fit herself into the mold her parents wanted.

Of course, if Porchia had set her sights on Jason, Lydia Henson would have injected her with some deadly, untraceable poison.

And let's face it…Porchia liked Jason. Hell, she liked all the Montgomery men, but it was only Darren that made her heart race like a stoked engine.

Last December, Porchia had overheard Sarah Jane Mackey bragging about her Marry Darren project, which had included trying to get pregnant by jabbing pins into all the condoms she could find at Darren's house. The other girls at the table had given Sarah Jane high fives. Porchia had wanted to give her a kick in the ass for being so stupid. Of course, Porchia clued Darren into the scheme but apparently, that hadn't stopped Sarah Jane from trying to get back with Darren, thus her bidding at the auction.

Except Porchia was here with him, not Sarah Jane, and that thought made her chuckle. When she thought about how close Sarah Jane had come to trapping Darren, or hell, even the thought of him marrying any woman, her stomach would roll and she'd get physically ill.

She had to admit that her feelings for him went beyond friendship, a long way beyond, if she were being honest with herself. What she was going to do about that was the million-dollar question.

Okay, she couldn't lie in this bed any longer. Time to see what the rest of the campers were doing.

Her breath caught when she opened the front door. It was later in the day than she'd realized. The sun had fallen to behind the horizon. The warmth of the day had been replaced by cooler evening air. Not grab-a-jacket cold, but not shorts and sandals warm either. Wheeling around, she headed back to the bedroom.

After changing into a long-sleeve T-shirt, jeans and a pair of sneakers, she returned to the front porch to assess her clothing in comparison to the temperature. As she did, she noticed Darren and Reno at the fire ring layering on small limbs as fire starter in the pit.

Every time Darren picked up a stick and leaned over to set it down, the denim across his butt pulled tight, giving her a yummy view. Maybe she could find lots and lots of projects for him that required him bending at the waist.

She laughed to herself. Yeah, that wasn't going to happen. His ass was simply too tempting.

The two men began stacking heavier logs that would be added to the fire later, and Darren's biceps tested the boundaries of the arm band on his T-shirt with each movement. The sight of his shirt stretched taut over thick shoulders made her tingle.

She swallowed against the lust bubbling up. Damn. She didn't know of another guy in the world who rang her bell like Darren Montgomery.

She went over to where the two guys were working. "Fire tonight?" she asked.

Darren looked up and the warmth of his smile slammed into her. She shoved her sleeves up to her elbows, trying to cool off. His smile was mighty powerful and did little to stem the lust brewing in her gut.

"Hey, Sleeping Beauty," he said. "Have a nice nap?"

"Remind me not to drink with your mother again."

Both guys laughed.

"Yeah, Mom's got a few years of practice on you," Reno said.

"Need some help?" she asked. "What can I do?"

"Not a thing," Darren said, then put his arm around her shoulders.

That arm should have felt heavy and uncomfortable. She should have shrugged it off her, but did she? Of course not. It was as if she'd lost total control of her traitorous body.

"Where's Magda?" She looked around. "And everyone else."

"Some are in the lodge. Some are in their cabins sleeping off the early morning start."

"So, fire tonight?" she asked again.

"Family tradition is to let the youngest Montgomery plan dinner on the first night," Darren said. "That'd be Adam, and he chose hot dogs and s'mores."

"That sounds fun. How'd that get started?"

"It goes back to when Dad and Uncle Lane were little," Reno said. "Dad said the entire family was always so tired by the time they got here and got set up, and no matter what Grandma fixed for supper, everybody wanted something else. She got mad one year and said the kids could decide what they were having. Dinner that year rotated among the three kids and the tradition stuck."

"Three?" Porchia frowned. "I thought there were only your father and Lane."

"We have an aunt," Darren explained. "I haven't seen or talked to her since

Grandma Montgomery died."

"You're kidding. What happened?"

"Honestly? I'm not sure. There was some disagreement about my grandparents' estate. You know Lane is the oldest, right?"

She nodded.

"Then Dad and then there is Aunt Cora. She was the baby, younger than Dad by almost fifteen years. When Grandpa and Grandma died, she thought that since she was the only daughter, she should get everything."

Frowning, Porchia said, "I don't understand. Why would she think that?"

"No clue. Dad and Uncle Lane were both married and getting their ranches going. Aunt Cora was single and in college. She still had a bedroom at home in her parents' house. I guess she felt like her brothers had already moved out and she was still living there, so she was entitled to inherit the house and all the belongings."

"Interesting logic."

"Yeah. Except Uncle Lane was executor of the state. He had control over what happened to everything."

"Apparently," Reno said, picking up the story, "there was quite the feud between Aunt Cora and her brothers. She packed up and moved to Montana to finish college. She sent them each a registered letter from a lawyer instructing them to send her one-third of the estate to her in cash via the lawyer. Plus, if they needed to communicate with her, they should go through the lawyer but to never contact her directly again."

"Yikes."

"Exactly," Darren said. "Dad said he and Uncle Lane went to Montana, but she wouldn't see them or speak to them. They did meet with the lawyer, who they said was actually a pretty nice guy. He suggested they give her some time and she would cool off and things would get back to normal."

"And?" she prompted.

"I guess too much time passed," Reno said. "Years passed. Christmas cards were returned unopened. The lawyer died and Aunt Cora just seemed to fade into the past."

"I remember the year the Christmas card came back saying she'd moved and there was no forwarding address. Remember that, Reno?"

"Yeah. It's one of the few times I remember Dad crying."

"That's awful," she said. "Have you ever tried to find her? I mean, gosh, with the internet and the programs that will search for people, I'm sure you could locate her."

"I haven't. Have you, Darren?"

Darren shook his head. "Nope. She really hurt Dad and Uncle Lane, and I always felt like I'd be doing something behind Dad's back if I looked for her. Besides, if she wanted to contact them, Dad and Uncle Lane aren't hard to find. I don't even know if she still has the Montgomery last name."

The story hit Porchia hard. She'd never given much thought to how her physical and emotional distance from her parents might be affecting them. She believed herself to be the injured party.

Her entire life, she'd felt like they'd shunted her out of town to protect themselves and not her. But she'd only been fifteen. Young, scared and embarrassed, her view of life had been completely self-centered. Was it possible that her family felt like the Montgomerys toward this lost sibling? Even though she saw and spoke with her parents, were they waiting for her to bridge the gap in their relationship?

"Hey," Darren said. Putting two fingers under her chin, he turned her face toward his. "You got awfully quiet. You okay?"

"Sure. Sure. I was just thinking about your aunt and all she's missed."

Darren gave her shoulders a squeeze. "Sorry. We didn't mean to upset you. We've lived with the story our whole lives. I guess we didn't realize how it might affect others."

She gave him her best smile. "I'm not upset. Really."

"Good." He pressed a soft kiss on her lips. A million fireflies lit up inside her.

"Well," she said, pulling out from under his arm. That simple touch of his lips had scrambled her brains. Having carnal desire as her driver always seemed to land her in the ditch. She needed to put some space between them to give her brain time to recollect and take control. "I should probably head to the lodge and see what I can do to help with dinner."

Before she reached the lodge steps, Travis and Cash Montgomery came out carrying a huge metal cooler between them.

"Need some help?" she asked, hurrying forward.

"Nope," Cash grunted out. "Too heavy."

Darren and Reno met their cousins and the four men maneuvered the enormous ice chest into the fire-pit area. She heard the wham as the chest dropped heavily on the stones.

Starting back up the lodge steps, she glanced over her shoulder. The top had been opened on the chest, which she could now see was loaded down with ice and an assortment of drinks. It had to weigh a ton. She was glad they'd turned down her offer since she'd have been no help at all.

Female voices echoed from the rear of the lodge. Following them, Porchia found herself in a cavernous, stainless-steel kitchen. Envy oozed from every pore. It rivaled any professional kitchen she'd ever seen.

The stove was a ten-gas burner, two-oven monster that covered a good five feet of wall space. Her mouth salivated at the thought of owning one like that.

The stainless-steel refrigerator of her dreams dominated the far wall. With one wide refrigerator door and three doors to the freezer section, storing and retrieving items for her bakery kitchen would be so much more convenient.

All the countertops were stainless steel, and right now, were covered with foodstuffs that needed to be stored and refrigerated.

"Oh my. I've died and gone to heaven," she said, dramatically clutching her hands to her chest.

Nadine laughed. "It's been updated since we were last here. The old refrigerator used to hum and vibrate loud enough to be heard in the bedrooms upstairs. Speaking of which, come over here." Nadine took Porchia's wrist and pulled her off to the side of the room away from the other women.

Porchia frowned. "What's wrong?"

"I'm so sorry," Nadine replied in a low voice. "Jackie wasn't thinking when she assigned you and Darren cabin five. She didn't realize that you two aren't a couple. Darren explained that you're good friends and that you'd helped him out at the auction." She squeezed Porchia's fingers. "Thank you."

"Darren and I are good friends," Porchia assured her.

"Yes, well, I appreciate your keeping him out of Sarah Jane's clutches." Porchia's eyes widened in surprise.

Nadine patted Porchia's hand. "I know all about that little, er, witch." She glanced toward Jackie, and back to Porchia. "Jackie told me everything. Anyway, I'm afraid Jackie and I have put you in an untenable situation and I am so sorry. There are only four bedrooms in the lodge and they're all in use this weekend. But come Monday, if you want to move into one of the rooms here, you're more than welcome."

"Nadine. It's fine." Porchia smiled. "Really. Darren has already volunteered to sleep on the sofa, and given that it's cushy and long, it'll make a great bed." She didn't add that they hadn't settled the sleeping arrangement yet, but she didn't want to give his family any embarrassing information or have their imaginations work overtime...like hers was.

Nadine gave a sigh of relief. "Okay then. But come Monday, there'll be some empty rooms in the lodge if you want one."

"Thanks, but we'll be fine. I promise."

"Hey, Mom. If you two are over there gossiping, you have to share with the class," called KC. "And if you're over there to avoid all the work over here, you're busted."

Nadine laughed. "We're coming back."

After all the sacks were empty and the food stored, Porchia helped load up trays of hot dogs, buns and all the necessary condiments to transport to the fire pit area.

When she carried the bags of chips outside for the dinner picnic, she was surprised to see how dark it'd gotten outside in the time she'd been in the kitchen.

Someone had started the fire Darren and Reno had laid. Its orange flame shot up against a black backdrop. One of the guys had set up a net tent over the only picnic table in the area to protect the food from various flying insects. Porchia put the chips inside the tent on the table and went back out to join the others.

The night air had a sharp coolness that made her glad she'd put on long pants and sleeves. She made her way over to Darren, lowering herself into the chair he'd set up for her. Beside her, he was whittling the end of a stick into a sharp point. Each stroke of the knife made the tight muscles in his arm tense and jump up. There was something so sexy about forearm muscles. They made her want to swoon, or lick them, or maybe swoon while she was licking them.

"I love a fire," she said, leaning toward the flame and away from Darren's lickable arms. "I think I might have been a pyromaniac in another life."

He chuckled. "Fall bonfires are the best," he said, giving the stick one last stroke with his knife. "Cool enough to enjoy a fire but not so cold that you're freezing to death."

"What are you doing?" She hitched a thumb toward the pointed stick.

"Making the skewers for the hot dogs."

"We're using sticks?" Her voice was aghast with amazement.

Her mother had purchased specially designed stainless-steel roasting skewers when Porchia had come home from camp wanting to roast hot dogs every night. Their cook had allowed her to roast her wieners over the flame of the stove burner. Of course, her mother had made sure the wieners in their house were made only from the highest quality prime beef with no fillers. Those never tasted as good as the greasy ones from Brownie camp, but Porchia had made do.

"Well, yeah. You got another suggestion for roasting these dogs?"

"I don't know. Some type of clean skewer?"

He chuckled. "You're funny. Here," he said, handing her a freshly pointed stick. "This will be ours. It's the best one."

She hesitated for a second. "Um, okay, I guess."

He laughed again and nudged her with his shoulder. "You hold our spot. I'll go grab some dogs."

She twisted the stick around. It didn't look too dirty. Still, maybe she should take it inside and give it a good washing. Before she could do much more than have that thought, Darren was back with four hot dogs.

"Four? I might eat one."

"You just wait," he said. "My dogs are to die for. And notice I was mature enough not to say wieners."

This time, she laughed. "Appreciate it."

He wasn't lying. Within just a few minutes, she bit into the juiciest, most perfectly roasted hot dog. She immediately flashed back to Girl Scout camp and sighed.

"Good?"

"*So* good," she replied, embarrassed at answering him with food in her mouth. She could practically hear her mother and grandmother telling her not to talk with her mouth full. She devoured the first dog and really wished she hadn't already declined the second.

It must be the night air making her want to do things she knew she shouldn't, like eating that second hot dog or nibbling on Darren's neck instead of dinner.

"You keep looking at me like that, and I'll be chucking this stick into the fire and dragging you off to the cabin."

"What?" Porchia sat back in her chair. "I don't know what you're talking about."

Darren's head turned to face her. "Yeah, you do."

Before he could elaborate, a truck pulled into the drive and Leo Mabee climbed out.

"What's Paige's brother doing here?" she whispered. "Think something's wrong?"

Darren shrugged. "No clue. But I can't imagine he drove two hours just to talk to her. Our phones work, remember?"

Paige Ryan, Cash's fiancée, looked up. Her face broke into a bright smile when she saw Leo.

"You came," she said.

"Of course. What did you expect?"

Confused glances flashed around the fire, except for Marc Singer. He acknowledged Leo with a knowing nod and finished eating. Leo was greeted warmly by the Montgomerys, which Porchia decided was the manner they greeted everyone.

After declining offers of food and drink, Lane Montgomery asked, "So, Leo, what brings you all the way down here?"

He smiled at his sister and then looked at Lane. "Not my story, sir. I'll let Paige and Cash explain."

Heads turned toward Paige and Cash, who both stood. "We'll be right back," Cash said. He and Paige hurried off to their cabin.

"Well, that was odd," said Jackie. She looked at Travis. "Do you have any idea what these two are up to?"

He shook his head. "No clue."

Porchia kept her eye on Marc Singer. He and Cash were best buds, but for Cash to have invited Marc to come on this family outing had to mean something.

Marc had finished eating and had pulled some papers from his back pocket. He shuffled through the sheets of paper as though looking for something. Apparently, he either found what he was looking for or got them in the order he wanted.

The sound of a cabin door slamming echoed. Marc stood and faced the group.

"Cash and Paige have an announcement."

Chapter Seven

Cash and Paige stepped from their cabin, Paige wearing a ruffled skirt that hit at the top of the cowboy boots on her feet. With the skirt, she'd paired a white cotton shirt and white cowboy hat. Cash wore jeans, the denim so dark Porchia suspected they were new, a white shirt, black cowboy hat and boots.

Their hands interlaced, they walked over to the fire where their families sat.

"Everyone we love is here tonight," Paige said.

"Right," Cash said. "We thought, why drag all y'all off to somewhere else to see this? Why not do it right here, right now?"

"Honey," Jackie Montgomery said. "What exactly are you doing right here, right now?"

Cash smiled, then pulled their joined hands up to his mouth and kissed Paige's fingers.

"Gettin' married."

Marc Singer joined the couple. "I'm licensed to do weddings in Texas, so Cash asked me to come along this weekend and perform the ceremony."

Porchia grasped Darren's hand and leaned over. "Oh my. This is so romantic."

Darren squeezed her hand and, following Cash's example, lifted it for a quick touch of his lips to her knuckles. The brief caress momentarily stole her breath. She was glad she was seated, because she was sure her knees would have wobbled.

"Travis. Can you be my best man?"

Travis leapt from his chair. "Happy to." He slapped Cash on the back. "This is great. Just great."

Paige looked at Caroline. "Seeing as you played a huge role in getting Cash and me together, can you be my matron of honor?"

Caroline rushed up and hugged Paige.

The vision of the two females hugging became blurry. Porchia blinked rapidly, trying unsuccessfully to clear the rising tide of tears.

Paige's face glowed with immeasurable happiness. The look on Cash's face suggested he'd just won the lottery.

The little green monster who lived inside Porchia raised its head and shot a flame of jealousy into her gut. Oh, she didn't want Cash Montgomery. It wasn't that. But the look of pure love on his face for his bride was something every woman dreamed of.

The bride and groom, along with their attendants, turned toward Marc, who went into the wedding ceremony. Cash and Paige vowed to love and honor each other all the days of their lives.

Porchia surreptitiously wiped at her eyes. When she glanced around to make sure no one had noticed her silly crying, she saw the other women dabbing at their eyes. Leo Mabee, Paige's brother, wasn't trying to hide his feelings. Tears flowed freely down his cheeks.

A sniff drew her attention to Lydia Henson. She sat alone near the edge of the group, looking as miserable as if she were at a funeral instead of a wedding. Lydia's gaze rolled over to where her ex-fiancée sat. Jason Montgomery was looking straight ahead at his brother and the bride, his face an unreadable stone mask. After a couple of long seconds, Lydia's stare dropped down to the ground. When it did, Jason looked from the marrying couple to Lydia, seemed to study her for a minute before moving his gaze away. Porchia didn't think she'd ever seen two more miserable people.

And the entire episode reminded her why letting herself get emotionally invested in any other person was a set-up for heartbreak.

The rings were exchanged, followed by a kiss that went on so long Cash's parents chuckled. Still, when the newlywed couple turned around to face their families, their faces were radiant.

"I am so happy for them," Porchia whispered. "They both look insanely happy, don't they?"

Darren gave her a smile. "That's what love does for you. As far as Cash goes, loving Paige probably saved his life."

"So I've heard. Well, I'm happy for them, and I love how they did this. No pre-wedding hoopla. No wedding drama."

"I'll have to remember that," he said with a grin.

She bumped his shoulder with hers.

"If you'll join us at the lodge, Leo brought our wedding cake, right?" Paige said.

Leo stood and headed to his car. He hefted a very large white box from the backseat. "Got it right here."

The next couple of hours were spent eating a wedding cake and drinking toasts to the couple. Porchia stifled a yawn and then glanced at her watch. It was only nine p.m., but she felt like it should be midnight.

"I saw that," Darren said as he slipped up to her side.

"I'm sorry. I don't know what's gotten into me."

"It's the night air, the fire, all the excitement," he offered. "I bet you wake up early too."

"As soon as the newlyweds leave, I'm out of here." She turned toward him and lowered her voice. "I don't mind taking the couch and giving you the bed. I tried out the sofa today and it's really comfy. I'll have no problem fitting on it. You, on the other hand, need all the room the bed offers."

Irritation flashed in his eyes. "I am not letting you sleep on the sofa. What kind of man do you think I am that I'd put my date on a couch and me in the bed? Forget it," he added when she opened her mouth to argue. "I'll sleep on the sofa. It'll not be the worst place I've ever slept."

"You're not going to be comfortable. It's too short. Your feet will hang off."

"Whatever," he snapped at her. "I don't know what's changed since this morning. I thought we had the sleeping arrangements all worked out." He held up his hand. "It's fine." He blew out a long breath. "I think Cash and Paige are getting ready to head out." He nodded toward the couple making a circle of the room to speak to each person.

She and Darren stood not speaking as they waited to say their congratulations. Her heart pounded. Rushing blood throbbed in her head, giving her a headache. She hated Darren's tone, hated hearing the disappointment in his voice. Yes, he was right that they had discussed the sleeping arrangements, and she'd been honest when she'd said she'd have no problem sharing, but at this moment, she was feeling a lot of flimsiness in her firm resolve to stay on her side of the bed.

She couldn't tell him that.

He would think her another ditzy, irresponsible blonde.

The buzzing in Darren's head sounded like a hive of bees. He leaned against the stainless-steel counter and waited for his cousin and his new wife to reach him and his frustrating roommate...his beautiful-but-driving-him-crazy roommate.

"Congratulations," Porchia said, hugging Paige. "I love your outfit. And I love how you guys did this wedding. So perfect."

"Thanks," Paige said. "Did you recognize the cake? You made it last week."

Porchia laughed. "I did, you sneaky thing. I thought it was for a couple named Patti and Carlton."

"It was delicious," Cash said. "Mom's freezing the top layer. Something about an anniversary?" He shrugged. "I don't have a clue what she's talking about."

"Tradition, honey," Paige said, linking her arm through his. "We eat our cake on our one-year anniversary."

Cash frowned. "Now that sounds gross."

Porchia and Paige laughed, but Darren thought it sounded disgusting too. "Frozen year-old cake? Yuck."

"Don't worry, Cash. It'll taste just like tonight," Porchia said. "Trust me.

But if it doesn't, I'll make sure you have another one a year from now. How's that?"

His face looked relieved. "It's a deal."

"If you're through being all girly and talking about cakes, I'd like to congratulate you," Darren said.

The two men first shook hands, then Cash grabbed Darren in a hug. "Good Lord, man," Darren grunted out. "Get a hold of yourself."

That just made Cash grin. "Can't help it." He threw his arm over Paige's shoulders. "I just married the woman of my dreams. One day, you'll know exactly how I feel."

"Oh, baby. I love you," Paige said and kissed him.

Darren was stunned by the jolt of jealousy that rattled down his spine. He wanted what his cousin had found with Paige. What his brother had found with Magda. He glanced at Porchia talking with Paige.

And he wanted it with Porchia Summers.

The newlyweds moved on to Reno and Magda. Suddenly, Darren felt like a balloon whose air had been released. His shoulders sagged.

"You okay?" Porchia's eyebrows were drawn down with concern.

"Exhausted," he confessed. "It's not the work that wears me out. It's the constant talking."

She nodded. "I know exactly what you mean. Let's say our goodbyes and head out. What do you think?"

"I think it's the best idea I've heard in the last hour."

The walk back to their cabin was quiet. Darren was thinking about the sleeping arrangements and wondered if she was too. But how could he broach the subject without making a mess of everything?

She entered first, flipped on the living room lamp and toed off her shoes.

"*Oh*," she moaned, flexing her toes. "That feels so good." She rolled her eyes upward. "Now you know, I'd rather be barefoot than in fancy, high-dollar shoes."

"Nothing wrong with being a barefoot redneck," he joked. "In fact, some of my favorite people are barefoot rednecks, including me and my brother."

She extended her arms in his direction. "My people," she said with a laugh.

"See? I knew we were perfect for each other."

There was no reply from her, and he wondered if he'd stepped into a pile of manure with his comment, but then she chuckled. "You might have a valid point," she said. "I smell like a fire, so I want to take a shower before bed. You want to go first?"

"You go. I can wait." He removed his hat and set it brim up on the coffee table.

She ruffled his hair. "You like that dirty, rough cowboy smell, do ya?"

He'd vowed he'd smell like a dirty, rough cowboy for the rest of his life if she would just keep running her fingers through his hair.

"Nah. But I think I'll have a drink first. Sort of wind down from the day."

"Suit yourself." She stepped over her shoes and headed up to the bath.

"Save me some hot water," he called after her.

"I'll see what I can do," she said with a grin over her shoulder.

He couldn't take his eyes off her heart-shaped ass as she wiggled away. He sighed. He'd rather put his mouth on hers instead of the mouth of a bottle of bourbon, but the bottle appeared more attainable.

He cracked the top on the new bottle and tilted the bourbon to his lips. The smoky, rich amber liquid erased all traces of cake sweetness as it rolled across his tongue and down his throat.

He heard the water in the shower come on. Porchia was naked in there. Naked and slippery wet.

His jeans tightened as his penis grew at the mental image.

"Fuck," he muttered and lifted the bottle again.

Porchia climbed into the massive shower, determined to not use up all the hot water, but the multiple showerheads hitting and massaging her tired muscles from every direction had her moaning with pleasure. The only thing that could make this better was having Darren in here with her...not that she could ask him. Oh, he'd come, no pun intended, but she didn't want to hurt him, or herself, for that matter, if she screwed up their friendship.

She shampooed her hair and stood under one of the jet sprays, letting the soap trickle down her back while the pounding water stimulated the blood flow to her head at the same time.

He'd never hidden his interest in her. And she really, *really* liked him too.

She'd read somewhere that girls have a tendency to marry men like their fathers. She remembered that when she played wedding with her friends, her imaginary nameless husband had always been someone like her dad or the fathers of her friends—suit-wearing professionals who went to an office every morning, did whatever they did and came home.

A blue-collar guy with rough hands and a sunburned neck like Darren Montgomery had never shown up in her husband-slash-lover fantasies. Maybe it was time for her to rethink some of her more erotic daydreams.

She wasn't ready to get out of the shower. Far from it. The hot water beating her tired muscles into submission felt just too good, but she'd promised to leave Darren some hot water. She climbed out and wiped the moisture from her body, her mind continuing to throw thoughts at the speed of light. It was almost impossible to keep up with all of them.

But when she bent over to run the towel down her legs, one thought stuck. Maybe, just maybe, the ideal man for her didn't wear a thousand-dollar suit and work in an office. Maybe he wore dirty jeans, scuffed boots and a battered hat to work every day. And maybe he smelled more like hay and horse than Polo cologne and a pipe.

She pulled on the thin-strapped top and tap pants she slept in, then looked at herself in the mirror. Turning side-to-side, she knew she wasn't beautiful. Her mother had tried to show her how to make the most of her limited physical attributes. Her mother and grandmother had assured her that she was attractive enough, but even she could see that her nose was too pointed and her eyes too far apart.

Grabbing her stomach pudge, she wiggled it. This frustrating pouch had attached itself to her and wasn't going anywhere.

Her thighs were not smooth either. When she pinched them, she could see the cottage-cheese dimpling.

What did Darren see in her? Whatever it was, she didn't see it.

She covered herself with a long silk robe and headed back to the living room. Darren sat on the sofa, his fingers wrapped around the neck of a half-empty bottle of bourbon. Eyes shut, his head rested on the top of the sofa back, his shaggy dark hair tousled as though he'd been running his fingers through it.

For a long moment, she stood watching him, studying his face. Rugged. Tanned. Late-day whiskers dotted his chiseled cheeks. A chin that was a little sharp. A little bump on his nose that suggested it'd been broken in the past. But it was his full lips that drew her gaze every time. They looked made for the perfect kiss.

Her heart rate ratcheted up so hard, the pulse in her neck made it hard to swallow. The front of her robe popped with each hard stroke of her heart.

Yeah, she had it bad for this man.

The next time he kissed her—if there was a next time—he'd find a receptive woman on his hands.

Chapter Eight

She was standing right there. He always felt her presence when she was in the same room with him, but tonight, the scent of lavender had washed over him when she'd entered. Shampoo or soap, he assumed. Didn't matter. Lavender was now his new favorite aroma.

He waited for her to say something. He played opossum, like she'd done this afternoon. Oh, yes, he'd known she was awake when he'd found her after his four-wheeler ride. He didn't know why she pretended to sleep. In the end, it didn't matter. But he let her believe she'd fooled him.

And two could play this game. He could pretend she wasn't standing in the same room as long as he didn't open his eyes, because as soon as he did, he knew his gaze would give away everything.

The desire he felt for her. Just her. No one else.

The emotional hit he took every time he looked at her.

The boredom of days when he didn't talk to her.

Not a day went by that he didn't have something he wanted to tell her, be it a story about his horse, or a bird he saw or joke he'd heard. Any excuse that would let him hear her voice.

The bottle in his fingers moved. He opened his eyes to an angelic vision. Porchia leaning over him with her hand on the bottle. Her blond hair, still damp from the shower, hung like a curtain around her beautiful face.

"Hi," she said with a smile. "I didn't mean to wake you."

He released the bottle into her grasp. "You can wake me anytime, darling."

"Mind?" She indicated the bottle by lifting it. More than half of the bourbon was gone. Hadn't that been a fresh bottle he'd opened?

"What's mine's yours."

She was a little burry around the edges. And she seemed a little shaky. Hmm. Maybe he was more tired than he thought.

Porchia straightened, tilted the bottle opening to her lips and took a drink. That was the sexiest thing he'd ever seen. His cock must have agreed as it woke suddenly from its nap. If she noticed the tent forming in his jeans, she didn't mention it.

"Shower's all yours," she said. Then, with a lift of an eyebrow, she teased, "And there's plenty of cold water, should you need that." Her gaze fell to his lap, which only made him harder. Then she took another draw off the bottle and he groaned.

"Damn, woman. You're killing me."

She frowned with confusion.

"You smell great and you can toss back bourbon like a pro. Every man's dream." *Including his.*

He shoved off the couch to stand. He might have wobbled a little, but Porchia didn't rush over to help him and he appreciated that.

"You okay?" she asked. "I think you might have had a little too much hooch."

"I'm fine. Just tired."

"Uh-huh. The shower's slick. Be careful."

He leered at her. "Want to come hold my hand? Or better yet, wash my, um, back?"

She laughed again. "When I do, I'd rather you were sober enough to remember it. Now go. If I hear a crash, I'll check on you."

He grinned. "Yes, ma'am." He started toward the shower and said over his shoulder, "I would have remembered."

And he would have. There wasn't enough booze in the world to wipe out a memory like that.

What stood out in his memory was her comment *when I do.* Not *if,* but *when.* He smiled. He'd loosened a brick in the wall she had around her heart and he had every intention of continuing to pick at the mortar until enough bricks fell to leave an opening large enough for him.

Until then…he turned the cold tap to full and climbed in.

The cabin was quiet as he made his way down the hall to the bedroom. He wasn't sure where he should sleep. They'd agreed to share the bed and then Porchia had gone all I'll-sleep-on-the-sofa on him.

She wasn't on the sofa. He checked. That meant she was in the bed…his bed. But did that mean she wanted him in there too? Or was she expecting him to take the couch?

His brain was as mushy as fresh manure. The bourbon only contributed to that. He flipped a mental coin, decided it landed on bed and he headed that way. If he was wrong, she'd sure let him know.

The door to the bedroom was ajar. Light leaked into the hall. He pushed the door open, ready for anything but what he saw.

Porchia sat upright, her back against the headboard. A pair of reading glasses were perched on her nose, a book in her hand. His heart sputtered for a moment. For just a second, he saw his future. Porchia as his wife, in their bed, reading and waiting for him.

He blinked, the vision real enough to be confusing. His yearning for the domesticated scene so strong he sucked in his breath.

"You all right?" she said, setting her book upside down on her lap. She jerked the glasses off her face. "Oh my God. I forgot I was wearing these." An embarrassed flush pinked her cheeks and he thought again that she was the most beautiful woman he'd ever seen.

"Put them back on," he said. "You look adorable."

"I do not," she protested, and her cheeks reddened more. "I look stupid."

He sat on the edge of the bed and caught her chin between two fingers. "You could never, ever look stupid, because you're not. You're smart and bright and funny. And I love your glasses."

He leaned in to kiss her. Not sure what her reaction would be, his first kiss was a light touch of his mouth to hers. When she didn't pull away, his second kiss was gentle but longer. This time, she came toward him, leaning into the kiss. He pulled back and stared into her wide eyes.

For a moment, they just looked at each other, and then he traced the outline of her jaw with his fingers. And still she didn't say stop or pull away.

Threading his fingers into her hair, he pulled her toward him. She came willingly, meeting him halfway. Their mouths crashed together in a frantic kiss of tongues and teeth. Still holding her head in his hands, he changed the slant of his head and took the kiss deeper, slipping his tongue into her welcoming warmth.

The touch and taste of her mouth sent his heart roaring. She scooted closer until her breasts cushioned his chest. Snaking her arms around him and up his back, she pulled him tight against her.

He bit her bottom lip and then soothed it with his tongue. Wrapping her luscious lips around his tongue, she drew him back into her mouth. She tasted of his bourbon, and that made him crave her all the more.

When she released the suction on his tongue, he swept it around inside her mouth, sampling all the textures and tastes she had to offer. No one tasted this good to him. No one. He could taste the innate sweetness he saw in her. All he could think was *mine.*

He pulled back far enough to see her face, try to figure out what was happening here. Her striking jade-green eyes sparkled with pleasure. As her lips turned up into a smile, the corners of her eyes narrowed into smile creases. Man, he loved her laugh lines.

"What's going on?" he asked. "Not that I'm not enjoying the hell out of this, but…" He hiked an eyebrow questioningly.

"I like how you kiss."

"And I like how you kiss." He started to kiss her again but stopped. Porchia wasn't acting like herself. The sudden one-hundred-eighty-degree turn in her response to him left a storm of questions pounding inside his brain.

Had she had too much to drink? With the wine today with the ladies, the champagne at the reception and the bourbon nightcap, was it possible she wasn't in complete control of her actions? The last thing he would ever do is take advantage of a woman, especially one he had feelings for. Pushing tonight and going too far could destroy any future they might have. Regret on both their

82

parts would be a difficult pill to swallow in the morning.

And then there was the wedding. His mother and sister, heck, every woman he knew, got emotional at weddings. Was that true of Porchia too? Were her kisses simply an emotional reaction to Cash and Paige's wedding, a swept-up-in-the-moment reaction?

It could also be that she was trying to make up for their silly argument over who slept on the couch. But to kiss him like she had instead of just saying she was sorry didn't seem like something the Porchia he knew would do. So probably not that.

"Hey!" Porchia snapped her fingers in front of his face. "Where'd you go?"

He put his hands on her shoulders. "I haven't gone anywhere yet, but I'm going to." He stood, collected a pillow and said, "I'll see you in the morning." As he shut the door, he heard her pillow thud against it.

Nope. In this game, he was in it to win it, and that meant knowing when to advance and when to retreat. For tonight, retreat to the couch was the best advance he could make. Retreat and take the brick that he'd loosened tonight with him.

Bang! Darren's eyes flew open at the sound. It was early, if he read the sunlight right. He'd slept long past his usual five a.m. internal alarm. The aroma of coffee penetrated his fog. Bless her. Porchia had made coffee.

When he went to sit, his back muscles screamed with a combination of spasms and stiffness. Grabbing hold on the couch back, he maneuvered himself into a sitting position. He scratched his head and tried to figure out what had woken him. He listened for a moment. The only sound was the low hum from the refrigerator. Otherwise, the place was quiet.

He pulled on his jeans, zipped up far enough to keep them up, but left the button open. Yawning, he shuffled to the kitchen toward his required caffeine. The glass carafe in the drip coffee maker held about a mugful. Porchia had to be buzzing if she'd drunk all the rest of this.

Speaking of his date, where was she? Carrying his mug along, he checked the bathroom. The door was open and the room was empty. In the bedroom, the bed was made and the room tidy. Hmm. She was gone. Now that he thought about it, it had most likely been the front door closing that had woken him. Front door being slammed, actually. That didn't bode well for him.

After making another pot of coffee, he got dressed for the day. He was standing on his porch sipping his black gold when his mother, sister and Porchia came out of the lodge, got into his parents' SUV, and drove off.

"Well, hell," he muttered to no one.

Or he thought he was speaking to no one, except he got a reply. "You're sounding a tad irritated this morning."

He lowered his gaze and turned toward the voice. Drake, his brother-in-law, was sitting in a camp chair near a freshly stoked fire with his back turned to Darren.

"Man. You must have the hearing of a bat."

Drake looked over his shoulder. "When you've been a teacher as long as I was, you learn to hear the quietest whispers. Bring your coffee and join me."

"Let me get a refill and I'll be right there. You need a cup?"

Drake held up a mug. "Empty."

"Black? Or cream and sugar."

"Black."

Darren went in and came out with an insulated pitcher he'd found in the kitchen. He set the pitcher on a rock and dragged a chair over to where Drake was seated.

"Black and hot," he said, offering the coffee-filled thermos to Drake.

"'Preciate it. So," Drake said as he refilled his mug, "from the look on your face, I'm thinking you did something stupid."

"What? Why does it have to be me that did something stupid? Maybe it was Porchia."

Drake chuckled. "Well, we've established that you did something you wish you hadn't."

Darren scratched his morning beard that he hadn't bothered to shave. "Maybe I did, but I'm not admitting to anything."

Drake shook his head. "I've probably got ten or more years on you, so

I've had more time to screw up something with a woman. Trust me when I say, whether you did it or she did it, you'll need to be the one to fix it."

"Shit."

"Exactly," Drake agreed.

"Like what?"

Drake shrugged. "Do something nice. No flowers or anything like that. Women see that as an easy cop-out for a guy. As your sister told me once, it's easy to throw money at a problem. It's harder when you actually have to take action."

"I do not want to know what actions you take with my sister."

Drake laughed loudly. "Yeah, well, I don't believe I'll be sharing those tips with you."

"Thank God for small favors."

"Anyway, I'd suggest some gesture on your part."

"But I didn't do anything wrong," Darren protested.

"Again, doesn't matter."

Darren blew out a long, frustrated breath. "Got it. Thanks."

"No problem, man. We're family, and family helps family, especially when it's guys versus girls."

The two men tapped their coffee mugs in a salute.

Drake had been married to KC for almost a year, but Darren hadn't spent a lot of one-on-one time with him until today. Drake made KC happier than she'd ever been in her life, and for that alone, Darren would have tolerated him. But he'd always liked Drake, and more so after this talk. He figured Drake was right about taking some romantic action, and he knew exactly what he wanted to do.

Darren stood and tossed his coffee dregs into the bushes.

"You leaving?" Drake asked.

"Yeah. You gave me an idea, and as the saying goes, I've gotta talk to a man about a horse. You want to get together later and ride the four-wheelers?"

Drake's face broke into a wide smile. "Damn straight."

Chapter Nine

Porchia dropped two dozen packages of fresh yeast in the grocery cart and bent over to get a box of powdered milk off the bottom shelf.

"So what's going on with you and my brother?"

Porchia stood and placed the extra-large box of instant milk in her basket, her secret ingredient for the rolls, all the while composing her facial expression before looking at Darren's sister.

Glancing toward KC, she said, "We're friends. You know that."

She pushed the cart down the aisle and stopped at the shortening.

KC followed closely on her heels. "It's more for him," she said. "He wants more than to be friends."

Porchia added three cans of shortening to their baking supplies. "I don't think so," she lied.

Whatever happened between her and Darren was between them. She didn't need his sister poking around.

She pushed the cart a few feet and stopped for sugar and flour. "We're just very good friends."

KC helped her load twenty pounds of flour and twenty pounds of sugar. Since all the Montgomery women—except Paige, who no one expected to see for a few days—wanted to learn how to make yeast rolls, Porchia grabbed a couple of extra baking pans.

KC held on to the cart and prevented Porchia from moving. "Either you're clueless or you're lying. There's something between you two more than friendship."

Porchia didn't look at her, sure her eyes would give something away. "I like him." She shrugged and then blurted out, "But I'm older than him," as though that would explain everything, even though the words sounded ridiculous to her own ears.

"So what? Drake's older than me by six years. Nobody cares about stuff like that."

Porchia walked on down to the spices and tossed in a large container of cinnamon.

How could she put in to words that she didn't want people to call her a cougar or tease Darren about being with an older woman as a mother replacement? And even though her rational mind knew these thoughts were asinine, it was hard to let go of years of societal indoctrination that programmed the male being the older in a relationship.

KC jerked the cart to a stop again. "I love my brother. Yes, he can be a pain in my ass sometimes and, yes, he still plays too many practical jokes on me, but he's my brother. I don't want him hurt."

Porchia looked at KC. "I know. I don't want him hurt either."

"So what are you going to do?"

"There you two are," Nadine said, the effort to push a heavy cart up the aisle evident in her posture.

"We'll finish talking later," KC said under her breath.

That was exactly what Porchia was afraid of.

"You have everything you need?" Nadine asked.

"For the yeast rolls and cinnamon bread, yes. I think we should get extra eggs and some apples. I know I'll be doing fritters sometime this week. Do we need anything else for the kitchen?"

"Not that I can think of," Nadine said.

Porchia and KC studied the load of foodstuffs in Nadine's cart. She had two prime ribs, a full ham and more steaks than Porchia had seen in one place, other than the meat department at a store.

"Good Lord," Porchia said. "We aren't cooking for an army battalion."

"You weren't raised with my brothers, so you have no idea. Then add in three male cousins, my dad and uncle, and you've pretty much got the appetite of that battalion."

Porchia laughed. "I see."

"Prime rib, Mom?" KC said. "Really?"

"We had a wedding last night. We need a nice wedding dinner to celebrate, don't you think?" Nadine said in the way of explanation. "And I've got some vegetables in here too." She glanced into her meat-laden basket and back to her daughter. "Well, I've got some somewhere under all this."

"How long will this all feed this group?" Porchia asked.

The corner of Nadine's mouth tweaked up. "Maybe three days. We'll be back at the beginning of the week and do it all again."

"Yikes," Porchia said. "Count me in to help cook."

"Don't worry, dear. You have been."

The camp was fairly empty when they got back. Jackie and Olivia were sitting on the lodge porch in rocking chairs, mugs of coffee in their hands.

"Where's everybody?" Nadine asked as she climbed from her SUV.

"Drake, Darren, Clint and Lane have taken the four-wheelers out," Jackie said. "Adam and Norman are with Mitch and Jason down with the horses. Reno and Magda took off on her motorcycle. We haven't seen Cash and Paige."

"Not that we expected to," Olivia said with a laugh.

"Leo still around?" Porchia asked. She lifted a heavy bag from the car. "We could use a hand with the heavy lifting."

Jackie and Olivia set their mugs on the railing and stood.

"Leo headed out at the crack of dawn. Hold on. We're coming to help."

It took multiple trips and twenty minutes before everything was in and stored.

"Quick break and then start on the baking?" Nadine suggested. "I'd like to wash my hands."

"Sure." Porchia looked at the clock. "Let's meet back here about ten. That work?"

There were voices of agreement as the women headed off to their separate rooms. Porchia washed her hands and began assembling what they would need to make the breads today.

"I know you think you're off the hook talking to me," KC whispered into Porchia's ear. "I'm a lawyer. I don't give up easily."

"Honestly, KC. There's nothing more to say."

"Will you at least give him a chance? I've seen how he looks at you."

"How?" Porchia asked, sure she knew the answer but wanting validation from someone else.

"Like you're the hot fudge on his ice cream sundae."

Porchia turned away from KC so she wouldn't see her pleased grin. Another brick fell from the wall around Porchia's heart.

It was closer to ten-thirty by the time all the women were gathered in the kitchen. Porchia counted heads. Nine. No Magda, but then she was an excellent baker and Porchia doubted there was much left to teach her.

Her mouth gaped a little when she saw Paige tying an apron around her waist. "Paige?"

"What? You think I'm going to miss a baking lesson for sex with Cash? I only have you for a few days. Him, I have the rest of my life. Plus, he and Marc went hunting."

The other women rolled their eyes in sympathy.

Katrina and Lydia exchanged hostile stares. Porchia was a little surprised to find both of those gals here for the baking lesson as they'd done an excellent job so far of avoiding one another. She mentally crossed her fingers that there wouldn't be any warfare on her watch.

"Well, I'm a little overwhelmed and flattered you all want to learn some of my baking secrets," Porchia said. "Today we're going to make my Grandma's yeast rolls and cinnamon rolls. We'll use the same dough for both, but this way, we'll end up with two yummy treats instead of one. Okay?"

There were nods of agreement.

"We'll all start together and then divide into two groups when it comes time to decide between dinner rolls and cinnamon rolls. I set out enough large bowls and heavy spoons so each of you will get your own. We'll be manually mixing today. No electric mixer required. So grab a bowl and spread out.

"Oh," she added as the ladies began to move, "you'll also need a bowl for the hot water and yeast, so grab one of those too. And find your spot to work. You should spread out a little."

The kitchen had an island in the middle that was large enough to provide space for five. The other four moved to counters along the wall. She noticed the Katrina and Lydia went to opposite sides of the room. Probably safer.

Measuring cups had to be shared, or stolen as the case was more often than not. Same with the spoons. Shouts of, "Wait a minute. I wasn't finished," and, "Give that back," were heard over and over, usually followed by a threat and a giggle. Porchia was pretty sure she saw Olivia toss flour at her mother when Jackie swiped the measuring spoons, but who knew? Puffs of flour covered all the stainless-steel countertops, so it could have been an accident. But when Jackie snickered, Porchia decided she'd had it right the first time...flour blasting.

The first hour of measuring ingredients and mixing went much better than Porchia feared. Everyone seemed to be having a good time, if the chatter and bouts of laughter were any indication.

She walked around the kitchen and checked each woman's work.

"These look great. Now grease the top of the dough and set it somewhere out of any cool drafts. We want it to double in size."

"Yeah," Caroline said. "If I didn't kill the yeast with the water being too hot."

"I think you're okay," Porchia assured her. "It was on the upper end of acceptable temperatures, but I bet yours will do just fine."

Porchia tossed clean dishcloths over each bowl for added protection from drafts.

"We have some time while these rise. Kitchen clean up time."

"God. You're a slave driver," KC whined, and then followed that with a grin.

Caroline, bless her heart, had taken Katrina—who insisted on being called Kat—under her wing, making sure the woman felt like a part of the group. As an outsider with this family herself, Porchia appreciated Caroline's gesture and made a mental note to tell her later.

"Kat and I are done," Caroline announced. "We're heading down to the barn to check on our guys."

Every time someone said Kat, Porchia's heart leapt and her internal security alert went off. Once, she even turned around when someone asked Kat a question. Hearing Slade call her Kat after all these years had thrown her back in time. From first grade on, all her friends had known her as Kat. But no one in Whispering Springs knew her as anything other than Porchia. She hadn't disliked the name Kat until it'd oozed out of Slade's mouth. Now, she didn't ever want to be known as Kat again.

As though reading her mind, her phone gonged, signaling an incoming text message.

"I'll check back with you ladies in a little bit. Got to run to my cabin for a minute."

As soon as she was alone, she pulled her cell from her pocket to read the text. She'd hoped it was Darren. Instead, it was the last person in the world she wanted to hear from.

Where the hell are you? Your time is running out. Hiding won't help.

A cold sweat broke out on her forehead and on her neck. A shudder ran through her as a wave of nausea overtook her.

Without answering his message, she slipped the phone back into her pocket and headed to her cabin. She liked Darren's family, but having all of the women together at one time was mentally exhausting.

Slade was still on her mind as she shut her cabin door. Nervous because of his continued threat, she called and checked on the bakery. She got an everything's-great report.

She thought about calling her parents, especially her dad, to tell them that

Slade was out. In the end, she didn't. She had lots of reasons, or excuses really, why she didn't call. All of them just as valid and invalid as the next. She didn't know how they would react to the information. Her mother still got upset if the events from that night were mentioned. But the reality was she wasn't ready to have this conversation with them yet.

After thirty minutes of decompression, she felt ready to take on the Montgomery women again. She was walking from her cabin across the fire pit area when her phone's text gong brought her to a stop. She debated whether to just ignore that damn thing, but she couldn't, not with her staff doing all the work at her bakery. Even though she'd just checked with them, anything and everything can blow up in a bakery without notice.

She braced herself for either a work problem or another threatening note from Slade. Instead, her heart leapt when she realized the text was from Darren.

Riding with the guys is fun, but none of them look or smell as great as you do. Be back soon for lunch.

She was still a little put out for him sleeping on the sofa, but it was impossible to stay irritated when he seemed to know exactly what to say to her.

"Message from Darren?"

Porchia's head jerked up and toward the voice. KC was standing on the lodge porch, a mug in her hand.

"Yes. How did you know?"

KC tapped the side of her head. "Psychic. Plus, you're grinning like a crazy clown."

Porchia tried to dampen her wide grin but failed miserably. "Don't be a know-it-all," she said to KC, who simply laughed. She climbed the stairs to join KC.

"And Drake sent me a note that they were headed back for lunch."

"Okay, tell me the men in this family do not expect the women to do all the cooking and have lunch waiting on the table for them. Because Darren might be in for a surprise."

"So would Drake," KC assured her. "I helped Jackie and Mom put out stuff in the dining room so they could make their own sandwiches."

The loud rumble of four ATVs announced the arrival of the four men long before they actually roared into camp.

"And here they are now," KC added.

Porchia rubbed under her eyes to remove any eyeliner that might have smeared this morning. Then she tucked a loose piece of hair behind her ear.

"I saw that," KC said.

Porchia felt the rush of blood to her cheeks.

KC grabbed Porchia's shoulders and turned her until they were facing. "If the only reason you won't give my brother a chance is because you are four years older than him, then you're a fool."

The four men rolled in and brought the four-wheelers to a stop. It was hard to tell who was who. Identical pairs of dirty jeans. Dust-covered boots. Helmets, goggles and faces coated with grime. And four wide, bright smiles.

"God," KC said. "They all look like they got their teeth whitened at the flea market."

A laugh bubbled up and burst out of Porchia. Everyone knew about the flea market that was about sixty miles from Whispering Springs. Folks got their teeth whitened there for about half the cost of the dentist. Thanks, but no thanks for Porchia. She'd just let Dr. Key continue to do his dentistry on her.

KC bounded down the stairs and leapt into Drake's arms, wrapping her legs around his waist.

"My eyes," cried Darren. "You two are blinding me. Stop it."

KC looked over and grinned. "You're just jealous." And then she looked up at Porchia and arched an eyebrow.

"I need a shower in the worst way," Drake said. "And now that I've gotten you all dirty, you do too." He carried KC still wrapped around him to their cabin.

Porchia leaned over the railing. "You're looking pretty dirty there, cowboy."

Darren looked up with a smile. "Seems to me, I remember you liking a dirty, dirty cowboy. C'mon over here."

She leaned out farther. Her upper body hung lower, level with Darren's face. He caught her face between his hands—which were surprisingly clean due to his gloves—and kissed her. He pulled back a millimeter, changed the angle of his head and pressed his luscious lips to hers. When his tongue traced the seam between her lips, she opened her mouth and he charged in like an invading army, pillaging every drop of moisture and capturing her mouth as a prisoner of war, not that she was putting up much of a battle.

He pulled away and she licked her lips.

A groan from deep in his chest hit her like a blowtorch. "Damn. You're killing me, woman."

"You taste a little like…" She licked her lips again.

"Dirt?" he suggested.

"Maybe a little."

"I think I'll go take a shower and then I'll taste cleaner." He turned to leave but said over his shoulder, "Everywhere."

She braced herself on her forearms on the rail and stretched her legs out behind, her feet resting on her tiptoes to watch him walk away. Years of riding horses had given him a firm, mouthwatering ass that just begged to be bitten. And just maybe she was the woman to do that biting.

When their cabin door shut, she sighed.

"He's gone. You can wipe the drool from your chin."

Porchia's head snapped toward the female voice, an embarrassed heat climbing up her neck.

"Oh, Lydia. I didn't hear you come up."

Lydia held up her sock-covered feet. "Had mud on my boots so I left them by the door." She pointed to a pair of muddy hikers. "Want to join me?"

"Sure." Porchia sat in the swing next to Lydia. "How was the hike?"

Lydia shrugged. "Okay, I guess. Ready to go home though."

"Yeah, I guess it's hard to see Jason here with someone else."

Lydia pushed with her foot and set the swing in motion. "You have no idea."

"What are you going to do?"

"I don't know. I'm only in Whispering Springs because of him, and now?" She looked at Porchia. "I just don't know if I can stay. Everywhere I turn around there's a Montgomery."

"I can see that. Where's home?"

"Everywhere. My parents were military, so we pretty much lived in a million places. They've retired to Florida. My sister and her family live in Wichita, Kansas, but I've never lived in either of those places. So I guess that leaves my moving options wide open." She smiled and Porchia thought it was the saddest smile she'd ever seen.

"How'd you meet Jason?"

"I was a resident. He was on a double date with another couple. They were hit by a drunk driver. All four of them were brought to Emergency to be seen. His date was some prissy little thing who kept yelling, 'Do you know who I am?' Her daddy was a state senator from a small community, and I guess she was used to being top dog. After she yelled that the fourth time, I looked into her room and said, 'Yes, I know who you are, but if you don't, I can get Neuro and Psych down here for a consult.' That shut her up."

Porchia laughed. "Then what?"

"Her parents arrived at Emergency and acted almost as bad as she did. They demanded a plastic surgeon to sew up the small cut over her eye. No one but a plastic surgeon would do since they wanted to make sure she didn't have a scar." Lydia rolled her eyes. "She wouldn't have had one anyway, but we got a plastics resident to come in and sew her up. She left with her parents. Jason needed a few stitches in his chin and over his eye. When I was done with him, he asked me out. I told him I still had six hours left on my shift." She glanced over. "I figured that would be the last time I saw him, but six hours later when I got off, there he was in the waiting room. The desk clerk told me he'd been there the whole time waiting for me. How could I not go have breakfast with him?"

"Wow. That's determination. Is it really over between you guys? I can't believe that it is."

Tears glistened in Lydia's eyes. "I think so. This is what he wants so…" She shrugged. "If you'll excuse me." Her voice was clogged with tears, and it broke Porchia's heart to hear how much she was suffering from the break-up. Lydia stood and hurried over to her boots. After shoving in her feet, she ran from the porch.

If she and Darren got together and it didn't work…well, a Lydia-style heartache was exactly what Porchia wanted to avoid.

"Hey, darlin'. Ready to eat?"

Porchia turned toward Darren, who was walking toward the lodge. Should she risk her heart with him? Was he serious about her or had all her refusals just made her forbidden fruit? After all, when she did open up last night, hadn't he run to the living room to sleep?

"Starved," she replied, relationship questions still bouncing around in her head.

Chapter Ten

Darren knew something was still on Porchia's mind. It wasn't the words she used, or the tone of her voice, or even how she stood or sat. But still, he knew something was there. Since he'd decided she was the one he wanted, he wouldn't push her, not yet. A skittish woman was like a skittish colt. Both had trust issues.

"I was thinking after lunch, we could take a couple of horses out for some exercise," Darren said to Porchia as they ate.

"I don't know if I'll have time. I'll have to check with your mom and Jackie. We've still got a couple of hours of work with the rolls. They're planning some fancy dinner to celebrate Paige and Cash's wedding, and I might need to help with that." She wrinkled her nose. "Sorry."

Putting his arm on the back of her chair, he leaned in and kissed the tip of her pert nose. The scent of fresh lavender tickled his olfactory nerve and he liked it. He drew in another breath. The aroma was wreaking havoc on his senses, not that he minded one iota. "No problem. This is only the second day of our vacation. We have a whole week to ride or hike or do anything we want."

"Thanks. If I don't have to help with dinner, I should be done in a couple of hours."

"Hey, Mom," Darren called to Nadine. "Can I get Porchia off dinner duty tonight?"

"Darren!" Porchia elbowed him. "Stop it."

Nadine turned toward her son with a knowing smile. "Your father and Lane will be cooking the prime rib on the grill. Caroline and Lydia have volunteered to help Jackie and me tonight, so she's all yours."

If only.

"Thanks, Mom." He turned his smile back to Porchia. "You heard her. You're all mine this afternoon."

She swallowed and arched her brows. "I guess so."

After lunch, Darren left Porchia in the big kitchen with the other women to do something called punching down the dough. He had no idea what that meant, and he didn't really want to.

Reno and Magda roared back into camp on her bike about an hour later.

"Where you two been?" he asked his brother as Reno climbed off the bike.

"Took a long drive to see the leaves."

Darren frowned. "You've been gone for hours."

"Yeah, we stopped at a couple of stores, had some lunch, and you know how it is. Time just got away from us. Anything going on here?"

"I'll let you two catch up," Magda said. "I'm going to look for Porchia."

"She's at the lodge making rolls or something," Darren told her.

"Great. Thanks." She planted a long kiss on Reno. "Catch you later, hunky man." After giving Reno's ass a couple of pats, she headed off for the lodge.

"Man, she's the best," Reno said, a broad grin stretched across his face.

"Yeah, I'm glad you two worked it out. I'm headed to find Travis about taking a couple of horses out this afternoon. Want to come along?"

"You go ahead. I'm headed to my cabin for a nap."

"A nap? You sick?"

Reno yawned. "Let's just say that I didn't get a lot of sleep last night."

"Got it. Catch you later."

Travis was more than happy to loan Darren a couple of horses.

"These guys need some exercise," he explained. "I'm not worried about you, but how much riding has Porchia done?"

Darren cocked up the corner of his mouth as he thought about it. "I don't know," he finally confessed. "We've haven't talked about it. She seems comfortable around horses when I've seen her near them, but I don't know that she's had any riding experience at all. But we're not going far and I'll keep the pace at a walk."

"Fine. Why don't you ride Trailblazer? He's new to my stable and I'd love to know what you think about him. I haven't gelded him yet. He's young. Maybe good breeding stock for my cutting horses."

Darren looked at the chestnut-colored stallion Travis was indicating with his thumb. He was a beauty. A silky black mane and black socks on all four legs set off his brown coloring.

"Love to. He's definitely got the cocky look of most of your cutting horses," Darren said.

Travis laughed. "My horses have a cocky look?"

"Oh, hell yeah. Like they all think their shit don't stink."

Travis continued to laugh. "Yeah, well, I can assure you, all their shit stinks."

That made Darren grin. "Which one for Porchia?"

"Hmm. I think maybe Oreo." Travis pointed to a black and white horse standing apart from the other horses. "She's sweet but a little timid. I'm not sure what I'm going to do with her. Caroline rescued her from a horse sale we were attending. The owners were elderly and I think she might have been mistreated or ignored. But I'd love to know what you think about her too."

"Great. We'll take them this afternoon for a short ride. If Porchia does okay with the horse, I think I'll want them in the morning. Early in the morning," he clarified. "A daybreak ride."

"Sure."

Travis showed Darren where all the tack was and the guys spent almost an hour talking horses. It was close to three by the time Darren wandered back up to his cabin. Porchia sat in the swing, one foot tucked under her while using the other to rock.

"You done with the rolls?"

She nodded. "Yes. They are going through their second rise. All they'll need is to be baked and I'm not needed for that."

Darren climbed the stairs. "Scoot over." Sitting down, he ran his arm along the top board of the swing back. "You check on Heavenly Delights today? Nothing blow up?"

She didn't laugh or even chuckle at his joke. Instead, a look of concern flashed and then was gone.

"I did. Tina says everything's fine. Sales are off a little, but I think that's because you're here and not in Whispering Springs buying all my goodies."

His mouth twitched. "Well, now, I thought I was buying fritters all this time. You mean you had goodies for sale too?"

She elbowed his gut. "Goose," she said with a laugh. "Everything is fine. Seems odd though."

"What?"

"Not going to work." She set the swing in motion. "I've been getting up early with the bakery for years. Sleeping until the sun's up seems like such a luxury."

"So you're having fun then?" He held his breath for her answer. He knew she'd say yes because she was the kind of person who wouldn't want to hurt his feelings. But he wanted to hear her say it.

"I am. I'll admit that all those Montgomery women exhaust me. Where do they get all that energy?"

"Years of putting up with the men, I'd guess. Want to get away for a little while? Travis has a couple of horses he'd like us to exercise."

"Um, I guess so."

"Now, don't worry," he said, his hand on her knee. "We'll go slow. I'll show you everything you need to know about riding. I'm a great teacher."

She looked at him, her lips twitching like they wanted to break into a smile.

"What?" he asked. "I am."

"Oh, I bet," she said and hiked her eyebrows. "I'm thinking you've taught quite a few girls how to ride. And I don't necessarily mean horses."

"Jealous?" He pulled his arm off the swing back and around her shoulders. "Should I be?"

"Never. None of them ever held a candle to you."

Pink tinged her creeks. "That's a sweet thing to say."

"Come on." He stood and pulled her to her feet. "Put on some jeans and boots and let's go."

They walked down to the stable where the tack was stored. Darren had set some out earlier, knowing he'd need it for this afternoon ride.

"You want some help with the saddles?" she asked.

A new rider could take forever to get a saddle on tight enough. He knew that the woman he would spend his life with would have to be able to saddle and ride her own horse, but today, he didn't have the patience to teach her. He was in a hurry to get her alone. Maybe impress her a little with some of his riding style.

There might be some time next week when he could spend more time teaching her.

"That's nice of you, but it'll be quicker if I do it the first time. But I'll explain what I'm doing as I go."

She chuckled. "Sure thing, boss."

Darren explained each step of the saddling process as he did it. He loved how she watched closely, following each step with fascination. She didn't ask questions but nodded when he asked if she understood what he was explaining.

"This is Oreo. She's new to Travis's barn, but she seems gentle enough. You want to stroke her neck. She'd like that."

Porchia climbed down from the fence railing where she'd been sitting watching him.

"Hello, Oreo. You're a pretty lady," she cooed to the horse. "Tell me about your horse."

"That would be Trailblazer."

Porchia walked over to his chestnut stallion. "Well, aren't you a handsome guy."

"Careful, honey. Stallions can be unpredictable and hard to handle."

"So I can't ride him? But he's so gorgeous."

"No, you can't. You're riding Oreo."

"Can I at least sit on him? He's so tall. How many hands?"

Darren looked at her. "You know how horse height is measured?"

She shrugged. "I might have heard a cowboy or two mention it. Something about hands."

He nodded. "Right. He's seventeen hands."

"Wow. That's big, huh?"

"Yep. Now, you ready to get on Oreo?"

"You sure I can't ride Trailblazer? He seems to like me."

"Damn sure."

She blew out a long sigh. "Fine." She walked back to Oreo. "Not to worry. I was just pulling his chain. You're a fine gal."

Darren shook his head. Women. He would never understand how their brains worked if he lived to be a hundred.

"Okay then," he said. "Put your foot in this stirrup. Step up and lift your right leg across her back. Here. Wait. I'll help you."

"I think I can do it, Darren."

"Still, I think you might want a little help this first time." Wrapping his hands around her waist, he waited until he felt her begin to lift herself. Then he gave her a little boost.

She swung her leg over Oreo's back and settled into the saddle.

"Great job," Darren praised. "Let me adjust your stirrup to the right height."

Her stirrups were just fine, but adjusting them gave Darren the chance to run his hand up her well-developed, muscular calf. Her tight jeans showcased her legs to such a degree that most of his blood began rushing below his belt. Time to stop touching her, or else his ride would be more than uncomfortable.

He stepped back. "Your stirrups are fine."

She looked at him with a knowing smile. "If you're finished feeling up my legs, let's go."

He swung up onto Trailblazer and the stallion danced a little to the side.

"Whoa, boy," he coaxed the horse.

When the horse settled, he squeezed his calves and moved Trailblazer out of the yard at a walk. Porchia followed and then caught up behind him.

"You doing okay?" he asked.

"I am. Can we go a little faster?"

He chuckled. "Why don't you get used to riding and then we can."

"Which way?"

He pointed to the left. "Down this lane about half a mile and then there's a trail we can follow."

"Great. So tell me about growing up in Florida."

They rode along talking about Florida and how the family ranch in Florida differed from Texas ranches. When they came to the trail that led off the road and into a pasture, Darren noticed Porchia had no trouble getting Oreo to go where she wanted. In fact, the more he watched her, the more impressed he was with her innate horsemanship.

"How did you end up in Whispering Springs?" he asked. "I don't think you've ever mentioned your parents."

The look she gave him was full of mischief. It reminded him of times he'd seen something similar on his brother's face just before they did something questionable.

And then she was gone. Oreo was flying across the field in a full-out gallop. Porchia's posture was low and settled into the saddle as she moved in concert with the horse.

Darren sat stunned momentarily, then he nudged the dancing stallion and raced after her, sure Porchia was going to be furious at him for putting her on such a dangerous horse. His heart pounded painfully against his chest in rhythm to Trailblazer's hoof beats. If something happened to Porchia, he'd never forgive himself. It'd be all his fault.

But as he and Trailblazer closed the gap, he could hear Porchia's laughter.

Oreo came to an abrupt stop and, with an obviously experienced touch, Porchia whirled the mare around in a graceful arc. Her face glowed with happiness. Her laughter was high and loud.

"Gotcha," she said.

Darren reined in the stallion, both his and the horse's breaths sounding harsh. "You know how to ride." There was no question in his comment. He was positive of the findings.

"I do."

"Why didn't you tell me?"

She arched one brow in a saucy and sexy manner. "You never asked. You just assumed I was a townie, didn't you?"

He shook his head, embarrassed that he had made assumptions about her without bothering to ask. But still, he had to chuckle. It was exactly like something he'd have done. "I ought to turn you over my knee and spank you. You scared at least ten years off my life."

"I'd like to see you try."

He laughed. "Travis wanted these two exercised. Want to give them a little workout? Maybe something less than a full-out run?"

"Sure."

Setting off at a canter, they moved through the field, Darren comfortable that she didn't need to be helped or monitored.

"I suppose you know how to saddle up also?" he asked, remembering how he'd tried to impress her with all his knowledge about saddling a horse.

"Yep, I do." She tossed him a cheeky grin. "But I'm not as fast as you are."

"Well, at least that's something. There's a creek up ahead. Want to stop and let the horses get a drink?"

"Sure."

After securing the horses, Darren tossed a blanket on the ground near the creek. Porchia grinned. "Not your first rodeo." She sat and stretched her legs out in front of her.

"No, ma'am," he said as he lowered himself down beside her.

The sun was low in the sky. The warmth of the day was fading with the dropping sun.

Darren sighed. "A beer would be great right now."

"Or a bottle of wine."

"Or a bottle of wine," he agreed.

"You know, Mr. Montgomery, you're doing a really lousy job of seducing me." Porchia leaned back and braced herself on her forearms. The position pushed her breasts up and out, each breath moving them slowly.

Each of her breaths pushed more blood toward his groin. Darren bent one leg and rested his forearms on his knee. The action gave him time to process her comment as well as loosen the denim over his cock, which needed the extra space.

"Am I trying to seduce you?"

Her smile was sly and knowing. "Aren't you?"

He shifted his position, moving his hands to the ground on either side of her waist, effectively trapping her between his arms. Her gaze fell first to his right hand and then to his left. When she raised her head, her eyes met his.

"Better. Much better, Mr. Montgomery."

Chapter Eleven

Porchia didn't recognize the alien who'd taken over her body and voice. She'd never teased a man like this, but if the excited whirl in her gut was any indication, she liked it. Once Darren had her trapped between his arms, it was all she could do to not nibble on one of his bulging biceps. She swallowed as she studied them. They were like handing a fresh box of chocolates to a dieting woman…impossible to pass up.

Seduction was not a game Porchia understood or played well. Should she lean up to kiss him? Lean back and hope he followed her down to the blanket? Would he think her crazy if she took just a little bite of his muscles that bulged with each movement? Did her voice sound sexy or like she'd been fighting a cold for a week?

In the end, she only had to remain in place, because Darren leaned toward her. His mouth touched hers and released a string of firecrackers in her heart. And then she just stopped thinking so hard. She caught his lower lip between her teeth, bit it and then soothed the bite with the tip of her tongue.

A deep groan rumbled out of Darren. His heavy hands landed on her shoulders and pushed slightly. Porchia unbraced her arms so she could wrap them around his neck. As she lowered to the ground, Darren followed, their mouths never losing contact.

Her shoulder, heated from his touch, cooled in the late afternoon air when he slid his hand down until his fingertips brushed the top of her breast. Breath catching, she waited for him to caress her flesh. When his palm finally covered her breast, she pushed up, pressing herself firmly into his hand.

He moved his mouth off hers, leaving a trail of hot kisses along her chin and up her cheek until he reached her ear. His breath was warm and damp on her neck, sending a galaxy of shivers down her spine.

"I want you, Porchia. Let me love you like you've never been loved before."

She didn't have time to answer or even give a thought to what she should say. A loud bell gonged from her pocket.

"Ignore it," he said and began nibbling on the large tendon in her neck.

"I can't. What if it's the bakery? I promised I'd be available."

"Damn it." He rested his forehead on her shoulder.

Her phone gonged again before she had time to even pull it out. Maybe she could ignore it. It'd be hard to do anything from the middle of nowhere.

As she began to dig in her pocket for the phone, Darren's cell rang. She laughed and he rolled his head side-to-side across her clavicle bone.

"The universe hates me," he said and sat. He pulled out his phone and answered.

Porchia clicked her text messages, saw who they were from and stood. She walked closer to the stream to give both of them privacy to answer the respective summons.

The first text message was from Slade.

ARE YOU TRYING TO PISS ME OFF? HOW HARD DO YOU THINK IT WAS TO FIND OUT WHERE YOU ARE? GOSSIPY LITTLE TOWN YOU LIVE IN. EVERYBODY GOT THEIR NOSES IN EVERYBODY ELSE'S BUSINESS. THEY ALL HAVE THE NICEST THINGSS TO SAY ABOUT YOU AND YOUR GRANDMOTHER. WHAT WILL THEY THINK WHEN THEY FIND OUT ABOUT YOUR PAST? SO YOU HAVE FUN AT THAT LITTLE CAMPING TRIP. I'VE WAITED SEVENTEEN YEARS FOR WHAT'S DUE ME. I'LL STILL BE HERE WHEN YOU GET BACK WITH MY MONEY!

The second text was from him also.

AND YOU WILL HAVE MY MONEY, WON'T YOU? TICK-TOCK.

A gun fired in close proximity to their location. Bark splintered from the tree to their left. Darren threw her to the ground and placed himself on top of her, shielding her from whatever was going on.

Another shot fired. This time, a small limb dropped from above, landing on Darren's legs. It wasn't large enough to do damage but was enough to convey the message that the shooter could hit wherever he pointed his gun.

The third bullet scattered the leaves in the tree above them, but this time only twigs fell on them.

No more shots came. They lay there for a minute, their breaths coming in anxious gasps.

"You okay?" Darren asked.

"Fine. You can let me up." When he didn't move fast enough, she added, "I'm really okay."

Darren rolled to the side but pulled her up next to him.

"I'm going to kill Cash and Singer."

She frowned. "Why? You think they were firing at us? Why in the world would your cousin and the sheriff be shooting guns in our direction? Besides, didn't they make it clear what area they would be hunting in so the rest of us wouldn't be in the way?"

"Yes, but still. This is private property and no one else is hunting but those two."

"We probably should head back and…"

The cell phone in her pocket gonged for a third time.

"What the hell is going on? Did the bakery run out of flour and sugar or something?"

Frowning, she nodded. "I'm sure the bakery is fine. Those texts were from that old school friend I told you about. Sorry he has my number now." Surely it wasn't Slade shooting at them. He wanted money, not to kill her, right? Dead would get him nothing.

The roar of ATVs broke into their conversation and within minutes, four machines tore into their area.

Reno climbed off the first one. "Are y'all okay?"

"Yeah, but which one of you idiots shot a gun our direction?"

Marc Singer shook his head. "Cash and I came back about an hour ago. As far as we are aware, no one from our party is out here."

The acid in Porchia's stomach tore at the lining. She wrapped her arms around her waist and bent over.

"Hey," Marc said. "You okay?"

From her position, Porchia watched five pairs of cowboy boots hurry toward her. She raised her hand to stop them. "I'm fine...I think. Just a little nauseated."

She recognized Darren's scuffed brown boots seconds before she felt his warm, comforting hands rubbing her back.

"You're okay," he said in a deep whisper. "I'm going to kill the sick SOB if we find out who did this."

She slowly rose back to upright and blew out a long breath. "Sorry," she said. She gulped in some air.

Darren put his arm around her. "We'll head back." He looked at Singer. "If it wasn't you or Cash, then someone is hunting here illegally."

The sheriff nodded. "I agree. Come on, Cash. Let's take a ride and look around." To Darren and Porchia he asked, "Which direction did the shots come from?"

Both of them pointed south. Sheriff Singer nodded. "Got it."

He and Cash got back on the ATVs and headed off in that direction. That left Travis and Mitch with the other four-wheelers.

"Why are you guys out here?" Darren asked.

"Travis and I wanted to try out the new four-wheelers. We just happened to be close when we heard the shots."

"The horses?" Porchia asked. "Are they okay?"

Travis nodded. "Yep. Both are still secured."

Porchia let out a breath of relief. If something had happened to those horses, she would have felt horrible. Slade was crazy if he thought shooting at her was a good way to scare her into giving him money.

"We better head back," Darren said. "Give Cash and Singer time to check out what's going on."

Porchia nodded.

When her phone gonged again, Darren said, "You want to check that before we leave? It might be important."

"Okay." But she doubted Slade had anything to say that she wanted to hear.

Quick note to let you know we closed the bakery early. Tour bus in town. Sold out of everything! Have date with Chad tonight. Woot! Hope you're having fun—Tina

She laughed, mostly in relief that the note wasn't from Slade. Mentally, she crossed her fingers that the sheriff and Cash found evidence of poachers and not of an ex-con.

"What?" Darren asked.

"It's Tina. Just giving me an update. Everything's fine." She pushed the phone back into her pocket. "Okay. I'm ready."

"You guys want us to ride back with you?" Travis asked.

"No need," Darren assured him.

Mitch gave them a salute and he and Travis headed out in the direction Cash and Singer had taken.

"Nothing like a few gunshots to interrupt my carefully constructed seduction," Darren said.

Porchia rolled her eyes and added a snort for good measure. "And you were doing so well."

If her upbringing had taught her nothing else, she knew how to put on a good front when necessary. But that didn't mean she wasn't pissed at the thought that Slade could be out in the bushes somewhere right now, maybe even watching them.

"I'm assuming helping you onto Oreo is unnecessary?" Darren asked, busting into her musing.

"Unnecessary maybe, but it was definitely enjoyable."

Once they got the horses loose from their ties, Darren put his hands on her waist and helped her into the saddle, not that he had any real work to do.

When he started to walk to Trailblazer, she called, "Don't you need to check my stirrups again?"

The grin he gave her was wickedly suggestive. She settled her feet securely. "Never mind. I've got it," she said and turned Oreo toward the trail.

Darren and Trailblazer were at her side within moments.

Light puffs of dust rose behind them as they started down the trail toward the main campground. Guilt nibbled at Porchia. She really should tell Darren more about Slade. If Slade was the shooter, and he was still in the area, the man was dangerous. There was no telling what he could do.

Plus, she should probably talk to Singer. The sheriff needed to know what he was getting into.

"Darren, about that gunshot—" She broke off as Reno came galloping toward them.

"Hey. Slow down," Darren said. "What's up?"

"Headed out to where the rest of the guys are. I think they've got the shooters."

"Shooters?" Porchia asked, grabbing on to the word like a lifeline. If there was more than one, it couldn't have been Slade, or at least that's what she hoped.

"Yeah," Reno answered. "Some teenagers. Shooting at God knows what, but definitely not *at* you. Apparently, when they realized y'all were in the area, they freaked out and ran." He looked at Darren. "Want to come along? I'm sure I can get the rest of the guys to look the other way while you kick some asses for scaring you and your lady."

"Do you mind?" Darren asked Porchia. "You're not afraid to go back alone, are you? I can ride back with you and then meet the guys."

"Of course not," she said. "I'll take care of Oreo when I get back." She smiled. "Unless you want me to wait until you can give me step-by-step instructions while I watch."

He barked out a laugh. "I'm not falling for that again."

The men rode back the way Porchia and Darren had just come, and

Porchia continued on the short distance to the camp site, not really scared but definitely urging Oreo on at a healthy clip.

It'd been a while since she'd unsaddled and brushed a horse, but the muscle memory remained. She worked through the process without having to think about what she was doing. Her hands knew what to do and just did it.

As she dragged the brush down Oreo's back, she let go a long sigh. A calm washed over her, something she'd not experienced in years. She'd missed riding, missed giving the care to her horse post-exercise. She hugged Oreo's neck. She'd owned a horse like Oreo once. Her parents had given her Patches when she was eight, along with the equestrian training her mother felt every well-bred young lady should have. But her parents had sold him when Porchia had been sent to live with her grandmother. Not being able to stop her parents from selling him was one of the biggest loses in her life.

When her maternal grandmother died, she'd left Porchia a small inheritance, enough to start her bakery, but that was about it. From day one, Porchia had put away a little money each month, trying to get the down payment for a small farm or ranch and another Patches. She was determined to make it on her own. If only she had access to her trust fund.

However, the harsh reality was that she'd be ninety before she'd have enough money amassed for a down payment for a place like she wanted. Land around Whispering Springs was priced as though rock was gold nuggets and water was oil.

So she'd changed her plan to save enough to buy a horse. Of course, she'd need somewhere to stable it. She could afford to rent a stall, just not buy the whole barn.

After putting Oreo back into the pasture with the rest of the horses, she headed to the lodge to check the baking progress of the rolls. A mouth-watering aroma of cooking beef met her as she neared the fire pit. Grey smoke oozed from under a cover. Patriarchs Lane and Clint sat nearby, bottles of opened beer near their elbows. Clint sprang from his chair as soon as he saw Porchia.

"Are you all right?" He hurried over to her and put his arm around her shoulders. "That must have been terrifying."

"I'm okay. Well, I could be doing better." When concern flashed on both men's faces, she hurried to add, "If you've got another one of those beers."

Relief flooded Clint's face. "You bet. Here. You take my seat. I'll drag over another chair."

Lane cracked the cap on a bottle of beer and handed it to her. "Any woman who gets shot at under my watch gets all the beer she wants."

Porchia took the beer and sat. "I'd love to tell you how brave I was, but frankly, I was scared to death." She looked at Clint. "Darren was wonderful. He made sure I was safe before he worried about himself. You've raised quite a man, Clint."

Clint's face lit up with pride. "I'm sorry you went through such a horrible experience, but thank you for saying that about my son. His mother and I are mighty proud of what he and Reno have done with their ranch, starting from scratch and not taking anything from us. They've done it all on their own when it would have been easy to look to me and their mom from time to time to bail them out. Of course, we're proud of all our children," he hastened to add.

"Thanks, Dad. I wondered if I was going to get a mention."

Clint chuckled.

Porchia looked over her shoulder. KC stood with her hands on her hips and wearing a wide grin. She winked at Porchia.

KC hauled over another chair and joined the group. "Glad you're okay," she said. "The good news is Drake called. They caught the shooters. A trio of would-be teen desperadoes. They're waiting for the local sheriff's department to come pick them up."

Relief flooded through Porchia. Tension she didn't realize she'd been holding released and she sagged against the back of the chair. "Reno told us he thought it was teens." She thought about the tragic mistake of her past and added, "I'm sure they didn't mean any harm. Probably didn't even know we were here. I hope the sheriff doesn't come down on them too hard."

KC accepted a beer from her uncle. "You're nicer than I'd be."

Porchia shrugged. "I did some stupid stuff when I was growing up. I wouldn't want to wreck their lives over something where they didn't mean harm."

KC leaned forward, her elbows on her knees. "Really? Porchia has a past. Who'd have thought it? Tell us more."

"Not on a bet," Porchia said.

"Leave her alone," Clint said. "She's been through enough without being interrogated by you."

KC rolled her eyes. "I was just teasing, Dad. We'll talk later, Porchia." She sneered at her father. "When we're alone."

Porchia arched an eyebrow, took a draw off her beer and then snapped her fingers. "Darn. I was headed to the house to check on the rolls and see if they needed any help."

KC gestured for her to remain seated. "Just came from the lodge. They've got it under control, so we aren't needed right now."

Porchia sat back and enjoyed listening to Lane and Clint talk about growing up, along with some hysterical commentary from KC. The aroma from the prime ribs on the grill had her mouth watering and her stomach growling.

When Darren hadn't returned after an hour, she excused herself and headed for her cabin to get dressed for dinner. The combination of grill smoke and horse smell would do nothing for anyone's appetite at the table.

She'd finished her shower and was drying her hair when the cabin front door slammed.

"Darren?" she called. "That you?"

She fastened the towel around her more securely.

"With you looking like that, it'd better be me," he said and leaned in the doorway with his shoulder pressed against the door jam. "Damn," he said and then whistled. "If I'd known you were naked, I'd have headed back sooner."

"I'm not naked. I'm wearing a towel."

Their gazes caught in the mirror. His look was pure lust, his pupils dilated and dark with desire.

She licked her lips, which seemed terribly dry. Probably because every drop of liquid inside her had rushed to her sex.

He groaned. "The way I see it, we have two options. In one, we'll be late to dinner. The other is I leave and sit on the porch until you tell me it's safe."

"My choice?" Her voice cracked.

His Adam's apple visibly moved up and down with his swallow. His breathing was audible with a choppy rasp. His nostrils flared. Then he stood and whirled around.

"I'll be on the porch," he said in a strangled voice.

Chapter Twelve

It was somewhat amazing that a man with a dick as hard as his could even walk to the porch, much less sit down, but somehow Darren was able to do both. When he'd found Porchia wrapped only in a towel, every cell in his body had demanded he take her, right there, right then. Lust had roared through him, every inch of muscle and flesh hardening at the sight of Porchia's soft skin still dewy from the shower.

The chains holding the swing creaked when he sat and continued to give squeaking protests each time he pushed off with his foot. Around him, the sounds of nature blended with the voices of his family. He decided this vacation, the one where he finally got Porchia all to himself, would most likely be one of his favorite memories.

The front door cracked open.

"Can I join you? I come bearing beer."

Darren glanced up and smiled. Dressed in black slacks and a black sleeveless knit top, Porchia stood holding two bottles of beer. The dark clothing only served to magnify the ivory tones of her flesh. A soft pink tinged her cheeks. Her blond hair fell loosely down her back. Florescent-orange toenails peeked from under the hem of her pants.

In short, she was the most beautiful woman he'd ever seen. And nothing she did or said could ever make him want her any less.

"I think one of those bullets must have hit me," he said, "because there's an angel serving me beer. This is heaven, right?"

She chuckled and handed him a beer. "Idiot. Don't even joke about what happened today."

He patted the swing. "Sit. I'll tell you the whole story."

She sat. "I'm ready. What happened?"

"Four kids. About fourteen, I'd guess. They were shooting cans. There wasn't anyone staying here last week, and they found a gap in the fence where they could come onto the property. So they came back this week to do target practice. They had no idea we were here. By the time Reno and I caught up to the group, Marc and Cash had the boys under control, sitting on the ground waiting for the sheriff to come." He chuckled. "Seems one of the boys is the sheriff's son and to add to the trouble they're in, they'd borrowed one of the sheriff's guns from his lockbox. There won't be any charges, but it did sound like extended grounding with numerous hours of community service are on the docket for these four."

"I'm glad you found them. Their punishment sounds about right. Heaven knows, we all did some stupid stuff growing up."

"Really?" He draped an arm on the back of the swing behind her and leaned in to take in her scent. He drew in a deep breath and whispered in her ear, "Tell me more about your wicked, wicked past."

"Well," she said with a long drawl. Her face lost all playfulness as her mouth quirked up on one side and she tilted her head. "I guess I should tell you about the time I eloped."

She'd been married? The information was a sharp spear in his gut.

"You're married?"

She shrugged. "No. Not now."

"Divorced? Widowed? Did he die?"

"I'll tell you if you'll stop asking questions."

Reflexively, he drew back. "Okay."

"I was so in love. I knew he was the one and only for me. Know what I mean? His name was William Hunter, but everybody called him Bill or Billy. He was a little older than me. When he kissed me, I almost died. We decided that we'd be together the rest of our lives." She let out a long sigh. "But it didn't work out."

"What happened?"

"His dad got transferred to California and his mother made him move with them."

He studied her face and caught the twitch at the corner of her mouth.

"I see," he said. "Sounds quite tragic. Exactly how long ago was this?"

"Well, let's see. Hmm. Must be twenty-seven years ago or so."

He laughed. "You were five years old? Six?"

She grinned. "Age doesn't matter when you're in love." Then she produced a dramatic, fake sniff.

"Oh, babe." He hugged her. "I can hear the loss in your voice."

Elbowing him in the ribs, she laughed. "Well, it was tragic at the time. It took me almost a full week to replace him with Jimmy Webb."

"Ouch." He rubbed his jabbed spot and chuckled. He snapped his fingers. "You were starting to tell me something this afternoon when we came upon Reno."

"Was I? Hmm. I don't remember what it was. Must not have been important." She leaned in and nibbled on his ear. "Not as important as telling you about my first husband."

He hiked an eyebrow. "So you're on the rebound? Great. That always works out well for guys."

She giggled. "You wish." Lifting her wrist, she checked the time. "You need to get ready for dinner. We're supposed to be at the lodge in about an hour."

"Are you saying I need a shower?" he joked.

"As long as you don't sit by me at dinner, I'm fine with how you smell."

He stood. "I'll make sure I smell irresistible."

The entire group crowded around one very long table. Shoulders touched shoulders. Thighs touched thighs. But Darren wasn't complaining about having Porchia pressed snugly against him.

His mouth watered from the delicious aromas rising from the copious dishes covering the table. The bowls and meat platters moved from person to person, allowing everyone to take as much or little as wanted.

Forks clinked on plates and the conversation was loud and rowdy as dinner progressed. Before dessert was brought out, Lane stood and tapped his water glass for attention.

"Looking down this table at our family brings more joy to me than I can express, especially since we all know cowboys are too tough to cry."

That brought chuckles from the women and a loud, "Amen," from all the men.

"However," he continued, "tonight's dinner is for my son, Cash, and his beautiful wife. Paige, Jackie and I couldn't be happier to welcome you into our family. We wish you both a lifetime of happiness."

"And a bunch of kids," Jackie added. Everyone laughed, but Darren suspected his aunt wasn't kidding.

Lane lifted his wine glass. "Here's to Cash and Paige. Congratulations."

Glasses were hefted into the air as the people around the table gave their well wishes to the couple.

Cash stood. "Thank you, Dad. And Mom. Don't know about the kids yet. Can we be married a week before we decide?"

"Fair enough," Jackie replied. "I'll check with you next weekend."

Laughing, Paige stood. "We'll work on that."

"I have some more news," Cash said. He took Paige's hand. "I know I originally planned to go into the cattle business with Mitch, but sometimes life throws a curve ball and you have to adjust. Marc has offered me a deputy position in the sheriff's department and I have accepted. Thank you, Marc, for dating my wife…while she was still single," he added in haste.

Another round of shouted congratulations rang out in the dining room.

Lane stood and shook Cash's hand. "That's wonderful, son." He looked at the group. "Any more good news that needs to be shared tonight?"

Heads turned as individuals looked around to see who would stand next.

"Do you want to tell them about your prior marriage?" he whispered to

Porchia, which sent her into a fit of shaking giggles.

"Ah hum."

The room quieted and KC and Drake stood.

"We're pregnant," KC yelled.

"Oh, darling," her mother cried. "My first grandchild." Nadine shoved back her chair and hurried around the table. She grabbed KC and Drake in a hug. Clint joined them, slapping Drake on the back and then hugging his daughter.

Olivia began to clap. "Way to go, Drake. I know what a great father you'll be."

Drake and Olivia had been married when Olivia had been pregnant with Adam. Even though Adam hadn't been Drake's biological child, Darren had heard that Drake had loved the boy as his own. When Olivia and Drake had divorced and Olivia had finally married Adam's father, Mitch Landry, the relationship between Olivia and Drake had remained close. It'd been Olivia who'd encouraged the relationship between KC and Drake.

"You do realize that means your sister is having sex, right?" Porchia joked in a whisper.

"La-la-la," Darren whispered back. "I can't hear anything you're saying." As far as he was concerned, he'd just as soon not think about his sister and sex in the same sentence.

As the group settled back down into their chairs, Lane said, "I guess that's all the good news tonight."

"Not so fast, big brother," Clint said. "Nadine and I have a little news."

"Oh, God. If you're pregnant, I'll kill myself," Reno shouted, which brought grins and chuckles.

"Your mother and I are long out of the baby business. We're looking to you three for the next round of babies," Clint said. "No, ours is more of a business announcement, I guess you could say, right, honey?"

Nadine stood, nodding. "Right." She looked at Darren, then Reno and then KC. "Your dad and I decided we were just too far away from you and all those grandkids you'll all be giving us…we hope," she added with a smile. "So…" She looked toward Clint.

"We sold the Florida ranch and we're moving to Whispering Springs," Clint said.

"Oh my God," Darren said, the news hitting him with a solid blow. He'd been raised on the Florida ranch. He'd never given a minute's thought that his parents would sell the place. He stood. "Surely y'all are kidding?" His heart hammered, with excitement or confusion, he wasn't sure.

"Not kidding. And don't call me Shirley," his dad joked, quoting the line from the old Airplane movie.

Reno rolled his eyes at their father's joke. "I'm shocked. Totally waylaid."

"Me too," KC said, "but I am so happy." She hurried around the table to hug her mom. "I am so glad you guys are going to be closer. Drake and I have been talking about how we wished you were closer to us. I am so excited."

"We are too, right, Reno?" Darren said. He leaned across the table to shake his dad's hand.

"Thrilled," Reno said. "Um, you're not moving in with us, right?"

His dad laughed. "I think your mother and I can afford our own place now."

"Excuse me," Porchia said and rose. "I'll be right back."

She and Magda headed for the kitchen. In a minute, they were back with an elaborately decorated cake. Congratulations had been written in icing.

"We didn't realize there would be so many things to celebrate this evening," Porchia said.

"Really," Magda agreed. "But Porchia and I thought no good celebration dinner should end without cake."

Porchia held Darren's hand later as they walked from the lodge back to their cabin. She'd always thought she had big hands until now. Wrapped in Darren's thick, long fingers, hers felt positively tiny. She had a very nice buzz going from the wine at dinner.

"So you happy about your parents?" she asked.

After his parents' announcement, she'd asked herself if she would be happy about her parents moving to Texas. The surprising answer was, she didn't know. It'd been a long time since she'd lived with them, and while they spoke from time to time, the warmth she'd experienced among the various Montgomery family members was missing from her own family. Was that because of her? Had her actions caused the facture of her family?

"Yep. I'm glad Mom will be here for KC's baby." He glanced over at her. "And it'll help keep her off mine and Reno's backs."

"So no kids for you?" The minute the question was out of her mouth, she wanted to suck it back in. It wasn't any of her business one way or the other.

"Sure, I want kids. With the right woman." He squeezed her hand.

"Hmm."

The night air was markedly cooler than the day. The light sweater she'd thrown over her sleeveless shell was doing little to keep her warm.

"Get a move on," she said. "I'm cold."

"I've got something we could do about that."

"Me too. Let's start a fire in the fireplace. I love those."

"Fireplaces?" he asked with a frown, but the twinkle in his eye gave away his joke.

She bumped her shoulder against his. "Goose. Come on."

She picked up her pace and he followed suit. Within minutes, they were climbing the stairs to their cabin.

"Why don't I bring in some wood and we'll have a fire before bed?"

"I'll grab some too," Porchia said.

"No. You'll ruin your sweater. The wood will pull it. Go on in. I'll be there in a minute."

He hurried back down the stairs and she let herself into the cabin. It wasn't cold in there, but the air was cool. And really? Was there anything better than a nice fire on a cool night? Not if you asked her.

Porchia was in the bedroom changing into a pair of lounging pants and shirt when she heard the front door kicked shut and then the thud of logs being dropped on the hearth. She hurried to the living room to give Darren a hand with the wood and skidded to a stop at the door.

Darren was bent over the hearth, placing logs on a grate in the fireplace. She might have gasped a little at the delectable vision, because he looked over his shoulder and gave her a smile.

"There you are. Almost done. With a gas starter, there's no challenge here." He straightened. "You want to do the honors or shall I?" He held up a box of long matches.

"Go ahead. I'll just grab a seat on the couch and watch the show."

If his growing smile was any indication, he liked her answer.

As he moved around the fireplace making sure the flue was open and the logs positioned just so, muscles shifted and bulged under the T-shirt he now sported. His flannel shirt from dinner was tossed over the back of the living room chair. She settled on the couch to enjoy the display of delicious male playing out in front of her.

He flipped open the gas valve and held a lit match to the gas bar running along the floor of the fireplace. Quickly, blue flames appeared and spread down the starter bar like a chain of dominoes falling.

"There." He turned and looked at her as though waiting for her to indicate if he should join her on the couch or take the chair.

She patted the cushion next to her. "Better view from here."

He took an end seat, putting the armrest on his left and Porchia on his right. As soon as he was settled, he draped an arm along the back of the sofa behind her.

"Dinner was nice," she said as she wedged herself closer, fitting her shoulder into his arm pit.

In response, he dropped his arm from the furniture to her. "It was."

She let out a relaxing sigh. "Montgomery dinners are...loud."

He laughed. "Always have been. Usually there's at least a couple of siblings or a couple of cousins fussing about something. I remember that when I was growing up, coming to Texas and staying with Uncle Lane and Aunt Jackie was always the highlight of any vacation."

She shifted so she could look up at him. "Did you come here a lot?"

"At least a couple of times a year." He pulled her closer, which pumped her heart rate up. "That's another reason I'm so happy my parents are moving here. I know Dad missed his brother, and Mom and Jackie get along like sisters." A little chuckle shook his chest. "Those four are going to be hard to manage." He shook his head. "Look out, Whispering Springs. The original Montgomery boys are back together."

"You really love your family. I see that blush on your face. It's okay that you do. No, it's fantastic that you do. Too many families are getting farther apart these days. I love that yours is getting closer and closer." She shifted again, this time rolling onto her hip so she could arch up and kiss him. His lips were warm and full. "Thank you for bringing me. I know I bought the date and used it as an excuse to avoid someone from high school, but it's been more than I expected."

His face grew serious and he stroked his fingers along her cheek. "Thank you for buying the date and coming. There's no one else I'd want here with me."

"Even Sarah Jane?" she joked.

"Especially her."

She pushed up again and kissed him, this time running the tip of her tongue along the seam of his mouth. He spread his lips and she thrust her tongue inside. He tasted too good to slow her exploration. Teeth. Gums. The inside of his cheek. She touched and savored the flavors she found.

He welcomed her intrusion into his mouth, a deep-chested groan rattling against her. At first, he stroked her tongue with his, and finally he closed his mouth on her, sucked on her tongue, sent shock waves of desire arcing between her thighs.

Both of his arms were wrapped around her. She was pulled so tight against him that she could feel his heart thudding.

Abruptly, the kiss stopped and he pulled back. "What's going on, Porchia? You've held me at arm's length for months, and now this sudden reversal?"

She slumped and allowed her weight to be supported in his arms. "It's your sister's fault."

He arched an eyebrow and then drew both eyebrows down into a frown. "Her pregnancy?"

She chuckled. "Lord, no. Something she said yesterday made me think."

"And what did she say?"

"I can't give up all my secrets," she said with a shake of her head. "It's against the women's code of gossip."

"Fair enough. I won't break the bro code either," he said with a grin. "But this…" He gestured to her in his lap. "What is this?"

She paused, trying to find the right words. "We've been friends for a while now. Good friends." She stopped, again searching for the words. "You have to have known how attracted to you I am."

"Well, no. I didn't. You've shut me down so much I'd pretty much given up. But…" The smile that curved his full lips set her heart racing. "I'm glad to hear it. So you're attracted to me. You like me. We're friends. So why the arm's-length treatment, and why the change?"

She closed her eyes in embarrassment. "I'm older than you." She waited for him to laugh or agree or just say something. When nothing happened, she opened her eyes. A quizzical expression covered his facial features.

"Didn't you hear what I said? I'm older than you."

"I know." He shrugged, his brows still furrowed. "So?"

She sighed. "I didn't want others teasing us. You know. You dating an older woman. Me being a cougar, or jokes about robbing the cradle."

"That's ridiculous. The only thing that worries me is that you'll get bored with me, or some other guy will recognize what a prize you are and steal you away. Age…well, hell, Porchia. Age is a number. It's not a personality trait or really much of a defining factor when it comes to people."

She rested her forehead on his chest. "I know. I'm even embarrassed that I feel this way. I don't want it to be but the age thing is there, and I'm worried that it might be one of the ideas that crawls in my brain and eats me up."

Two of his callused fingers under her chin lifted her head until their gazes met. "All I can say is that I want you so bad my teeth ache. I'm more than a *little* attracted to you."

"I want to give us a try. That's what I promised myself. We're here, sorta alone."

He chuckled. "Sorta is about right. But we have our own place. There are hundreds of acres around us. There's nothing stopping us from being alone."

"But here's the downside. If we don't work as a couple, we'll probably not be friends at the end, and I hate the idea of totally losing you out of my life."

"It's a risk, but hell, life's a risk. You can't live in a glass bubble protected from anything and everything. Aren't we worth the chance?"

"Yes and that's why…" she indicated their position, her lying on her side facing him, wrapped in his arms, their mouths only inches apart, "…this."

He nodded. "So we give this…us…a chance? That's what you want?"

"That's what I want."

Chapter Thirteen

The only sound was the crackle coming from the fireplace logs. Porchia flexed and re-flexed her abdominal muscles in nervous tension as she waited for Darren to say something.

He didn't. Instead, he pushed her shoulder away until he could stand. Then he picked her up off the couch and cradled her in his arms. Through her thin lounging pants, his thick forearms pressed into the sides of her thighs as he held her snugly against his well-developed chest. He turned and started walking toward their bedroom.

"Wait. I'm too heavy. You're going to hurt yourself."

"Hush, woman. You've agreed to give us a chance. Now we're going to do this my way."

His voice was rough and harsh. The guttural tone excited her, sent a sexual hunger through her like she'd never experienced. The man carrying her wasn't the good-old boy she'd been friends with. This was a highly sensual man who was going to get what he wanted. The realization made her vagina throb and her panties much, *much* damper.

When they got to the bedside, he slowly lowered her legs to the floor, allowing her to slide down his brick-hard body until she was standing.

He stepped away and flipped on the lights. "I've waited to see you naked for a long time. I plan to enjoy every second of my viewing pleasure."

The raw desire on his face jolted her heart and her lungs. She'd never been shy or bashful with previous lovers, but it'd been a while since she'd been naked in front of a man, or make that naked in the presence of a man. Anxious tension made her arms and legs quake. What if his idea of how she looked and the reality were far enough apart to make him regret this?

He sat on the edge of the bed. "Take off your shirt."

With shaking fingers, she caught the hem of her T-shirt and pulled it slowly up her body and over her head. She had to fight the impulse to cover herself with the now loose material.

"Throw it over there." He indicated the dresser with a tilt of his head.

When she hesitated, he lifted an eyebrow questioningly, as though asking if she was really sure this was what she wanted. She had no reservations about the sex. Only about him seeing her naked, exposed.

With a deep breath of resolution, she tossed the yellow shirt to the dresser, which left her standing in her bra and lounging pants. She swallowed, but it was damn hard to push down the lump her throat.

"Now the pants," he said, leaning forward to rest his forearms on his thighs as though studying a prize.

She straightened. Fine. If he wanted to play seduction games, she'd play too.

She caught the end of the tie string with her fingers and slowly, as slowly as she could manage, pulled the material to untie the bow holding up her pants. His gaze fell to her fingers and stayed there. Even though he wasn't physically touching her, his stare was a hot wash over her. As though being stroked, her nipples hardened and poked at the thin silk of her bra.

As the bow became a string, the waist loosened and she released her hold, letting the soft material glide down her legs and pool about her feet.

Darren's nostrils flared as he drew in a deep breath.

She lifted one foot out of the mound of material and then used the other one to kick the discarded pants off and over closer to the dresser. Now dressed only in a pair of bikini panties and a barely there bra, Porchia stilled, letting Darren study her.

His sapphire-blue eyes darkened with desire as his gaze rode up and down her exposed skin. She shivered under the intense stare, and at the same time felt pieces of her melt into her core.

"More?" Her voice was thick with lust.

"More," he growled. "The bra."

She unclasped the bra and let the straps fall down her arms. For a minute, she continued holding the loose cups over her breasts. She'd never stripped for a guy. As nerve-racking as it was, it was also highly erotic and extremely arousing for her too. She was strung as tight as a bow string. Would she simply explode the first time he touched her?

Gathering up her courage, she tossed the bra across the room to join her T-shirt.

He held out his hands. She laid her fingers on his and he gently pulled her toward him.

"You are the most beautiful woman I've ever seen." The gravel in his voice drove a chill down her spine.

His gaze glided slowly from her face to her breasts, which swelled and grew heavy under his intense look. Her nipples tightened and her areola puckered. His study of her body slowed at her abdomen, where she sucked in her gut as much as she could, before he again stilled on her mons covered by her thin, peach-colored silk panties. Leaning over, he put his mouth on her mons and gave her an open-mouth kiss. With a groan, he drew in a deep breath.

"I love how you smell, how aroused you are right now."

He was right. She was so turned on, and yet he'd barely touched her. He held her hands as though holding her in place, as if she could walk away from this...from him. Impossible. Her legs were trembling. Her knees were weak. How long could she remain standing before she melted to the floor in a heap?

"Spread your legs."

The command sent a gush of arousal fluid to her panties. He knew what he was doing to her and he was loving it. But then so was she.

As he'd ordered, she separated her legs. Her knees shook just a little. Her heart pounded so violently against her chest she was sure he could see it.

Placing her hands on his shoulders, he said, "Leave them there." He looked at her, his eyes so filled with desire she felt an old-fashion swoon coming over her. "I am so crazy about you, Porchia. I want nothing more than to show you, make you believe in me, in us."

And then, just when she thought she couldn't be any more turned-on, he put his hands on the insides of her thighs, pushed her stance as wide as she would go, and put his mouth on the crotch of her panties. He sucked, pulled the silk with all her fluids into his mouth. She looked down and was so overwhelmed with the vision she had to shut her eyes. Darren between her legs, sucking on her as though she possessed the only life-sustaining fluid, had to be the most erotic view she'd ever had in her life. She moaned and arched her hips forward to give him better access.

He must have liked that, if his low growl was an indication. His reaction only spurred her on. Using his shoulders for stability, she moved her hips, grinding her aching groin into his mouth. He tongued her, shoving the silk and his tongue inside her. She swayed, her legs shaking.

Then he bit her, just a nibble through the silk, but hard enough to catch her vulva lips in his teeth.

She hissed in a breath. "Payback will be a bitch, cowboy."

He laughed against her sex, blowing hot air on her. "Oh, honey. We've just begun to play." He gave one long lick along the crotch of her panties. "Let's get these off you."

Pulling her legs together enough to release the tension, Porchia reached for the elastic holding the bikini panties up. He knocked her hands away and grabbed the material to jerk it down her legs. Once she'd stepped free of the material, Darren pitched them in the corner.

His gaze dropped to her feet and crept up her body, slowing when it reached her sex and again at her breasts. A thick blanket of warmth rode up her body along with his gaze. Trickles of fluid ran down her inner thighs.

"Damn, Porchia. Just damn."

His gaze moved on up to meet hers.

"Get on the bed, on your knees. Face the headboard. In fact, hold on to the headboard."

She climbed onto the mattress and rested on her knees. As he'd instructed, she grasped the headboard.

His broad, hot hands wrapped around her ankles. She caught her breath, waiting to see what he was going to do. At first, he made no movement, but she knew he was studying her ass, could probably see the glisten from her arousal as liquid continued to dribble down her thighs.

He traced his thick fingers along her calves to her knees, followed by the palms of his hands up her inner thighs.

"You're so wet, so turned on." He tongued the watery secretions from her thighs. "Honey. You taste like the sweetest honey imaginable."

He pressed on her thighs. "Open wider for me."

She did, moving her knees to spread her legs.

"What a beautiful sight. You're so pink and so swollen. That I get to taste you is my best fantasy ever."

The tip of his tongue dug between her vulva lips, separating them, licking a long path between the sides.

As suddenly as his tongue was there, it was gone. The bed shifted with Darren's weight, and for a minute Porchia feared he'd stopped. But then something tickled her thigh. She glanced down and almost collapsed from the sheer eroticism of seeing his face sliding between her parted knees. He'd turned to lie on his back and position himself under her, his mouth below her sex.

Using the flat of his tongue, he stroked it down her center.

"Spread your knees for me, babe. Bring yourself to my mouth."

She did. He stabbed his tongue into her vagina, as deep as it would go, moving it in circles and taking it out long enough to lick her clitoris. He moved his hands to her ass, holding each cheek in the palms. He used his hold to move her, angle her in different ways, hold her still so he could torture her again and again.

Her legs began to quiver. It was impossible for her to move her gaze from where he was licking and nibbling on her like she were ice on the sidewalk on a hot day, which was a fitting thought given she was sure everything inside her had melted and was now flowing down to her center.

He put his lips on her clit and sucked on it. She groaned and, if as of their own mind, her hips began to move and grind on his mouth. With his teeth, he bit her labial lips, licked the bite and did it again. Over and over, he would lick, stab into her canal and suck various pieces of flesh between his lips.

For her part, she couldn't remain still. She humped, grinded and gyrated against his mouth. She was dying from all the tension inside her. Her muscles were tightened to the point of near cramping. At the headboard, her fingers were white from the pressure of her grip. The bed banged on the wall as she pulled on it for leverage.

"I can't stand this much longer," she said in a strained voice. "I'm going to come, Darren. And soon."

He didn't reply, only tongued her clit with circular swipes. He walked his fingers down her ass until both hands were between her legs, then he pulled his hands around her legs. He massaged the underside of her thighs while using his thumbs to spread her labia wide.

"What a view," he muttered. "So pink. So swollen. So wet. Gorgeous. So mine." He pushed one thick thumb inside her while his mouth worked her nub.

That was all she could take. Every muscle tensed and he pushed her over the edge. Her climax shook her, sent her muscles into spasms. She cried out, arching her back, banging the headboard on the wall.

As the orgasmic force began to ebb, he jerked her opening down to his mouth, drawing violently on her, sucking her flesh into his mouth.

She cried out as another, even more forceful explosive wave rolled through her. Her entire body shook from the power of her release.

She screamed his name.

Her legs weren't going to hold her up much longer. They were weak, shaking.

"Stay right there," Darren ordered. "Don't move." He shimmied out on his back and disappeared from her view. She heard his zipper followed by the ripping of foil. And then he was back.

She adjusted her hold on the headboard, praying it would support her for whatever else the man had in mind.

"Sorry, but this is going to be fast and hard," he warned. "I'm so fucking hard I could hit a ball for a homerun. Instead..." he grabbed her waist, "...I'm going to fuck you like I've wanted to do for months."

He thrust into her from behind, shoving himself to the hilt. Her breath rushed from her lungs in a gasp. Her vaginal walls stretched to an almost painful level to accommodate him. He was so much bigger than any of her past lovers. Longer. Thicker. Meatier.

Shoving her hips forward, he withdrew and slammed in again, pounding himself inside her. She arched her back. He angled her hips higher and rammed her again, this time hitting a spot she'd never believed existed. She gasped and cried out as he continued to beat against her G-spot.

Her orgasm stuck her with a solid punch and rolled from her head to her toes within an intensity that produced tears. Liquid ran from her eyes and from her vagina.

With her climax crescendo, Darren thrust a couple more times and then ground against her as his cock jerked his release inside her.

"Holy shit," he said and laid his head on her back. His breathing was labored and hot on her flesh as he panted. He kissed her back and then her shoulder. "Holy shit," he repeated.

He pulled from her and Porchia's legs gave out. She collapsed to the mattress and rolled to her back. Darren, fully dressed with only his zipper open, his cock exposed, lay on his back, his forearm over his brow.

"What the fuck was that?" he gasped out.

She rolled to her side and caught his gaze. "The best goddamn sex I've ever had."

Chapter Fourteen

"Hey, sleepyhead. Wake up."

Porchia groaned. "Go away. It's too early."

Darren chuckled and sat on the edge of the bed. "Wake up. I've got a surprise."

"If it's the same surprise you had for me at midnight and again at two, it's not that much of a surprise." Porchia pushed her hair out of her eyes and looked at him. She frowned. "You're dressed. Don't I remember getting those jeans off you last night?"

"Don't dawdle. We'll miss it."

She covered her mouth as she yawned. "You're serious?"

"Yup." He slapped her playfully on the ass. "Get a move on. Jeans, long-sleeve shirt and your boots. Hurry."

He gave her a quick kiss before standing and leaving.

In the kitchen, he poured fresh coffee into a large thermos and set it on the counter next to the knapsack that held their breakfast.

In under five minutes, Porchia strode into the living room, dressed as he'd requested, her hair freshly brushed.

"I'm here," she said. "What am I supposed to see? It's still dark outside. What time is it any way?" She squinted toward the kitchen clock. "Does that clock say four, as in four in the morning?"

"It does."

"But I'm on vacation. That means sleeping later than normal."

"You'll have time to nap later. I promise." He pulled her to him for a kiss that tasted of mint toothpaste. For some reason, he found that endearing, but then again, he found everything she did endearing. "Here." He handed her the thermos of coffee and grabbed the knapsack for him to carry. "Let's move."

She yawned again but followed him outside.

She looked at him. "You saddled horses?"

"The only way to travel," he said with a grin. God, she was so cute in the morning. "And, for this trip, the only way to travel. Need help getting on?"

She stuck out her tongue at him. "Funny man. Good morning, Oreo." She stroked the mare's neck a couple of times before she swung into the saddle like the pro she was. "Lead on."

Darren turned Bandit, another of Travis's geldings, toward the road and the sunrise spot he'd found. He hoped she would enjoy seeing the day start in his arms.

"So, want to let me in on what we're doing?" she asked, riding alongside him.

"Nope. It's a surprise."

"As long as the surprise involves the coffee you made me carry, I'm sure I'll be happy. Plus..." she reached over and pulled his horse to a stop, "...if it involves you, I'm sure I'll be elated." She leaned over the distance separating their horses and kissed him.

His tongue sought and found her mouth. He stroked inside, loving both how she tasted like toothpaste and how she let out a low groan.

He broke the kiss and pulled back. "If you start that, we'll never make it in time." Pressing his calves against the horse's sides, he set off in a trot with Porchia close behind.

"In time for what?"

"Patience, honey. You'll see."

"And you now know I have no patience," she reminded him.

He glanced over at her. "I seem to have a few demanding memories from last night. Something like, now, now, now and more and harder."

There wasn't enough light to see a blush, but he knew her well enough to know there was one on her face.

"You are a bad man," she said, followed by a deep chuckle.

Her chuckle sent an arrow straight to his heart. He was in deep. He knew it. What he didn't know was if he was in this by himself or if she felt the same depth of emotions.

And shouldn't he be more freaked out about what he was feeling?

"That's not what you said last night."

She laughed again. "So how far are we riding this morning?"

"A change of subject. Have I embarrassed you? I'm sorry if I did."

"You didn't," she assured him, but he still wondered if it was the teasing that'd bothered her or how very much they'd done last night.

"We've got about a twenty-minute ride. The last part is up the side of a hill, but I think you can handle it."

"Do you?" she teased. "I'd offer to race if I had any idea of direction."

They rode along in a companionable silence, broken only by the sounds of their horses' hooves and the occasional hoot from a night owl. The cool early morning air held a pine and sage scent from the vegetation around them. Light clouds of dust rose from the trail as they moved.

"Turn here," Darren said, guiding Bandit onto the narrow path that lead to the rock overhang.

It hadn't rained in a while. Heavier dust rose as their horses stomped toward the top. When he'd originally thought about doing this, he'd been under the impression that Porchia wouldn't know how to ride. Now, with only a quarter moon and a few million stars overhead for lighting, he was glad he hadn't tried this with an inexperienced rider. As it was, he kept an eye on her and Oreo to make sure they were handling the climb okay, but it only took a couple of quick checks to assure him they were having no problems.

He kept them climbing until they reached a level area to leave the horses. He climbed down, tied off Bandit and went to help Porchia. But she was already standing and tying off Oreo when he reached her.

"Are we here?" she asked.

"Almost," he replied with a smile. "A short hike."

"Whew," she said. "Good thing you're cute."

He laughed. "Grab the thermos and let's go."

When the trail opened on the flat rock, Porchia sighed with relief. "This it?"

"Yup." He spread out a blanket. "Sit."

The night sky had begun its transition to morning. The darkness had lightened and shades of pink and purple were just beginning to paint the horizon.

"What colors!" Porchia exclaimed. As she found a seat on the rock, she looked in different directions. "What a view."

"I thought so," he said as he sat. He leaned against the large boulder that acted as a chair back. Porchia's blond hair floated in a wind that'd picked up since they'd left the trail. Up here, without the heat of the sun and with the chilling breeze, she shivered with the change in temperature. "Scoot over here and keep me warm," he joked.

The wry twist of her lips into a smile had his heart racing. He doubted he'd ever tire of looking at her.

She moved closer. "I think I'll use you for warmth instead."

"That works for me."

He pulled her between his thighs, her back leaning against his chest. Bending his knees had her completely engulfed by his body. She snuggled within his embrace.

"How about I crack that thermos?" she asked. "I'll even share with you."

He nuzzled his face into her hair and kissed her neck just behind her ear. "As long as it doesn't require me letting you go."

She held up the silver container of coffee. "Nope." After unscrewing the top, she filled it and took a sip. She let out a long sigh. "That tastes wonderful. Want some?"

She shifted enough that she could lift the coffee to his mouth. He covered her hands holding the cup with his and brought it to his lips for a long sip. Their gazes met over the rim of the thermos cup and held. The heat from the extended stare flowed over him, warmed him to his core. It wasn't the coffee heating him. It was Porchia.

She was the woman he was meant to be with, the only woman he'd want for the rest of his life. There remained no doubt in his mind, but she wasn't ready to hear that. Wasn't ready to hear how deeply he felt about her. How serious he was about making their relationship work. He feared his words would be too blunt, too candid.

No, this was a war of love he was determined to win. To lose was simply unthinkable.

He kissed her fingertips holding the cup. "Thanks. I needed that."

She smiled. "The coffee or the nibble on my fingers?"

"Both." He turned her until her back was once again resting against his chest. "You're too distracting," he complained. "We'll miss the beautiful sunrise if I don't make you face forward."

Looking over her shoulder, she winked at him. "Flatterer."

As the pinks and purples of daybreak streaked across the sky, Darren kept his arms wrapped around the woman of his dreams. If a day could have a more perfect start, he didn't know what it'd be.

She sighed and tilted her head upright. "I love the twinkle of stars. When I was little, I thought those were diamonds winking at me. I was sure that all diamond engagement rings were made from stones plucked from the sky. And the only way a guy could grab a star was if he was really, really in love. One year, Dad had a business meeting in New York and Mom and I went along for fun. We walked all over downtown trying on clothes or shoes. And then we walked into Tiffany's. I remember stopping dead in my tracks. In front of me was display case after display case of shimmering diamonds, just like the ones in the sky. I looked up at Mom and said, 'We must be in heaven.' She laughed and said, 'I think so too.'"

They both chuckled at her story.

"Never been to New York City or Tiffany's" Darren said. "Never felt the desire to be in places jam-packed with people and honking cars." He waved his hand around. "Now this is my kind of place. Just you and me. Perfect, if you ask me."

"Don't forget the coffee."

He snorted. "Right. You, me and coffee. Now the world's perfect."

She sighed again. "Yeah."

They sat watching the pinks and purples turn to orange as the sky lightened just before daybreak.

"You never talk about your parents," Darren said. "I think this might be the first time you've ever mentioned them."

He felt her back get tense at his comment. "We aren't close," she said. "Not anymore."

"What happened?"

She shrugged. "Life. I'd rather not spoil this morning talking about them." Glancing over her shoulder, she added, "Okay?"

"Sure, babe. No problem." He pulled his arms tighter around her.

A small arc of yellow peeked over the edge of the world.

"There she is," Porchia said in a reverent tone.

As the small arc grew, more and more light filled the sky, illuminating the area below.

"We're over the camp," she said in surprise.

"We are. Looks like we aren't the only early risers."

Below, lights came on in the individual cabins as the Montgomery clan woke to a new day.

"You can tell this is a ranching family. Lots of early risers."

Porchia nodded. "Or a bunch of bakers."

He laughed. "Or that."

A truck fired up. Its muffler rumbled as it idled.

"Who's leaving?" she asked.

"That's Singer's truck. Guess he and Lydia are leaving early."

"Speaking of Lydia, isn't that her behind our cabin?" She pointed down. "And she's not alone."

Darren shifted until he had a better view. "I think so. Is that Jason with her?"

"Damn. Where's a pair of binoculars when I need them?"

"Sit up."

Porchia leaned forward, freeing Darren. He leaned over far enough to grab one of the handles on the knapsack and dragged it closer. From the side pocket he pulled a small pair of binoculars.

"I thought we might want them to look at stars," he said as way of explanation. "But looks like they'll have another use."

She put the eyepieces to her face and studied the couple below.

"What are you seeing?"

"They're talking. Ah. He just touched her face. Oh! She just kissed him." She lowered the binoculars. "Think they'll get back together?"

He shrugged. "No idea. They always seemed good together. I don't think anyone but them knows why they split in the first place."

It was light enough now to see more than shapes and figures. They could make out individual people even without the magnifying help. At Marc Singer's truck, Singer and Cash were shaking hands. Lydia had left Jason and was stowing her bag in the back of the truck. The front door of Jason's cabin opened and Katrina walked out carrying her luggage. After Marc helped her get her bags into the truck's bed, she climbed into the backseat and closed the door.

"Looks like Katrina's headed out," Porchia said.

"Yeah. She was only here for the weekend. She said she had to get back. Something about getting the hospital ready for some big inspection. I thought Jason was going to drive her back, but guess she's catching a ride with Marc and Lydia."

"That'll be one uncomfortable ride."

"No kidding."

Porchia settled into Darren's arms and suppressed the contented sigh that wanted to let itself be known. She was happy and relaxed and scared to death. Her relationships with men did not have a nice story. Looking back, most of her boyfriends had been either dull as dirt or some variation of Slade Madden. After her last relationship ended—when the guy forgot his wallet and she had to pay for dinner…for the fifth time—she'd pretty much given up on the whole future-with-a-man scenario. Plus, she'd begun wondering what was amiss with her. There had to be something wrong since she kept making such bad choices in men.

Then along came Darren. Handsome with chiseled cheeks and blue eyes that sparkled like those stars above. Tall. Dark-haired. A smile that could get just about any female between the ages of three and ninety-three to do his bidding. And the muscles. Lord in heaven. Her back was pressed against a granite slab that most people would think was a chest, but she knew better. There wasn't an ounce of fat there, just thick-sinew that made her mouth water whenever she felt him shift behind her.

And while she was on the subject of ridiculous muscles that could make a woman do stupid things, the brawny arms wrapped around her waist could not be overlooked. As she thought about them, she lightly stroked his forearms, running the tips of her fingers along the defined edges of all those rock-hard places he'd built up with grueling ranch work.

One of the many things she liked about Darren was his work ethic. He was so proud of the ranch he and Reno had founded. The brothers weren't afraid of hard work. In fact, she didn't think Darren was afraid of anything. She wished she had some of his fearless nature when she had to face Slade next week.

"Hungry?"

His question pulled her out of her thoughts.

"You have breakfast with you?"

"Well, I did bring something to go with the coffee." When he pulled his hand away from her stomach to dig into the knapsack, she immediately missed the warmth.

"Here." He handed her a sealed package.

She laughed. "Pop-Tarts?"

"It was all we had in the kitchen."

"Mmm. Brown sugar and cinnamon. My favorite. What did you get?"

"S'mores."

"You do realize these are called toaster pastries for a reason. Too bad we don't have a toaster," she said as she pried the envelope apart. "Unless that's a magic bag you're carrying. Can you pull out a toaster?"

"Hmm. Let me look."

The big production he made of digging through the cavernous knapsack had her chuckling.

"Sorry," he said. "No toaster. I did find a wine opener but alas, no wine."

"Wine for breakfast?" she said with an overly dramatic shiver. "I'll stay with my cold Pop-Tart, thank you." She took a bite and chased it with coffee. "Not too bad," she admitted, "but next time, bring a toaster."

Next time? Would this week lead to other weeks? She knew Darren had a crush on her and had had one for a while. However, once the vacation was over and he'd spent a lot of time with her—in bed and out—she fully expected that his fascination with her would be cured. She was the elusive woman who'd not allowed herself to be caught by the ever-so-desirable Darren Montgomery. Once the chase was done and he'd bagged his quarry, he'd be on to the next one. She, on the other hand, would go back to her solitary life style.

Maybe she should get a cat...or six.

"Ready to go?" he asked. "Sun's up."

"Sure. Back to camp?"

"I thought, if you're interested, we could do more riding and exploring. We have a few hundred acres we can investigate."

"I would love it." It'd been a long time since she'd ridden, and she was enjoying the wind in her hair and the magnificent creature beneath her. The major downside was that she'd lose her comfortable back and arm supports.

They gathered up their trash, stowed it in the knapsack with the blanket and started the climb back down to where they'd left their horses.

The jeans, boots and long-sleeve shirt had been barely adequate against the chill of the night air. However, as the sun got higher, the day got brighter and the temperatures rose. So what had been sufficient at five a.m. was getting quite warm by eleven. The outer shirt she'd worn when they'd left was now tied around her waist, leaving her dressed in a tight, skimpy tank. If the looks Darren kept giving her were any indication, he approved.

They rode and talked and explored all morning. By the time they rode back into camp, it was almost noon.

"As soon as we finish getting Oreo and Bandit settled back into the pasture, I want to head for the cabin for some shorts."

Darren nodded. "Sure. You want to have lunch with the crew?"

"Would you mind terribly if we didn't? I adore everybody, but I'm tired and a little brain-fuzzy. You may remember that I didn't get much sleep last night."

He leered. "If you think for one second I'm going to apologize for your, our, lack of sleep, think again."

She grinned. "Nope. No complaints. What do you think about us doing sandwiches by the pool?"

"Babe. That water is going to be way too cold to swim."

"What? Swim? No way. But I could get some sun on my legs and rest."

"Then great idea."

Once they got to the cabin, Darren followed Porchia into the bedroom. She gathered up shorts and a clean tank to put on and headed for the bathroom.

"Where you going?" he asked.

"Um, to change clothes."

"Porchia," he said on a sigh. "I'm pretty sure my tongue has touched every square inch of your body, and you are embarrassed to change clothes in the same room?"

Heat climbed her neck. "I, um, have to do something, um, with my hair."

He grinned. "God, you're cute when you blush."

"I am not blushing." She made the false proclamation and rushed into the bathroom, locking the door behind her. A quick glance in the mirror confirmed her worst fears. Her face was pink and flushed. Her long hair was ratted and tossed in every direction. Dirt from the trail ringed her neck. If Darren thought for one second that she'd be seen by his family looking like this, he needed to rethink.

She rolled the hot and slightly sweaty jeans down her legs, giving a sigh of relief as the cool bathroom air hit her overheated flesh. The rest of her clothes hit the floor with her boots. She flipped on the shower, adjusted the water temp to tepid and climbed in. The coolish water hit her skin and she gave a little shriek. Still, it felt delicious to wash the sweat and trail grime off her.

Once out, she pulled her wet hair into a ponytail and put on fresh clothes. Being clean again improved her disposition immediately. When she reentered the bedroom, Darren was stretched out on top of the bedspread wearing only his boxers. The vision was a smorgasbord for her eyes. Who needed lunch when this meal was laid out in front of her?

"Well, don't you look, uh, comfy," she said.

He grinned, which sent her heart tumbling into her whirling gut. Her mouth actually began to salivate.

"Thought I'd cool off a little while I waited. If you're done in the bathroom, I can be ready jiffy-quick."

Like a model demonstrating the latest in automobiles, she waved her hand toward the door. "All yours."

"Great." He leapt from the bed, stopped long enough to give her one of his patented toe-curling deep kisses.

After he walked away, she continued to stand there as if she'd been turned to stone. The circuits running from her brain to her legs had obviously been fried by that kiss. Licking her lips, she reminded herself this was just a trial-run-relationship. If she tipped her hand and let him know how much a simple kiss affected her, she was sure his interest would wane.

But simple kiss? Who was she kidding? His kisses were blowtorches of heat and power.

She didn't want him to find her standing here in a stupor, even if that's exactly what she was doing. Forcing her legs to move, she went to the front porch swing to wait.

Chapter Fifteen

The lack of sleep, plus the early rising mixed with a postprandial slump and warm sun, tied tiny concrete blocks to Porchia's eyelids. No matter how much she blinked and pulled them wide, they would shutter closed again. Finally, she leaned the poolside lounge chair back and gave in.

Near her, Darren talked with his brother and Magda. Then his parents came by. She knew there was some discussion about the Florida ranch and the selling price, but Porchia had one foot in dreamland, so her brain processed none of the conversations around her.

The bright sunlight on her eyelids dimmed. Cracking her eyes just a tad, she realized Darren had opened an umbrella over her.

"Hey," she said. "Thanks. Am I getting burned?"

When he smiled, it was as if the sun hit her face once again. Good Lord, the man had a powerful presence even when he wasn't trying.

"Not burned, but looked like you were napping. I thought the umbrella would be helpful."

She stretched her arms over her head. "I think I need a nap. Would you all mind if I headed off?"

"Nope. Head on," Magda said.

Standing, Porchia put her hand over her mouth as it stretched wide with a yawn. "I'll catch everyone later."

"I think an afternoon nap sounds ideal," Darren said. He released the catch on the umbrella and let it close. "Ready?"

"More than," she said.

She slipped her hand into the one Darren extended and they started back toward their cabin. She took a quick glance over her shoulder to see if anyone had noticed she'd grabbed his hand. Magda flashed her a thumbs up. Darren's mother gave her two thumbs up. Well, guess their little secret wasn't much of a secret. For a second, a minor panic attack swept through her. What if she and Darren didn't work as a couple? Would she alienate her friends and his family?

Darren squeezed her fingers as though reading her thoughts and assuring her that all would be fine. She glanced up at him and grasped his hand a little tighter, loving the feel of fingers rough with calluses and little scars from his ranching life. A little shiver ran through her as she remembered how those magical fingers had petted and stroked her last night.

"You really sleepy?" Darren looked at her with undisguised interest. "If not…"

Something tugged in her gut. "I think you could keep me awake a while longer."

The responding chuckle made that gut tug even stronger. Shit, she was in deep.

Suddenly, she found herself being hustled across the lawn, not running exactly, but definitely moving her feet like they were walking on hot coals.

When they got to the bottom of their steps, he swept her off her feet into his arms and bounded onto the porch. Her surprised gasp quickly faded to a sigh. Her arms rested on his broad shoulders. She nuzzled her nose into his neck, drawing in his scent.

"Did you just sniff me?" he asked.

"No," she lied, hoping he'd believe her.

He laughed. "Right." She loved that he called her on her little fibs. "Grab the door and I promise to be very, very good to you."

"I was hoping for very, very bad."

"I can do that too." When he chuckled, the sound wound its way around her heart.

She hated moving her arm from around his neck, but she did to open the door. He kicked it shut behind them and strode purposely toward the bedroom. As she nibbled on his neck, she loved how his muscles bunched each time her teeth scraped his skin.

Her gut was now twisting like a tornado, a whirl of energy and excitement that needed to be expressed, preferably with one—or three—orgasms. And she knew just the man for the job.

She kissed him, sliding her tongue easily into his welcoming mouth. The low groan from his chest rattled her insides. The deep masculine sound was like turning a key on an engine. She fired to life, threading her fingers into his short hair, dragging her nails on his scalp.

He sat her on the bed, their mouths still locked in a deep, wet kiss. Breaking the kiss, he rose and looked down. "So I'm thinking, hoping, you've got your second wind?"

"Second and third." She stretched her arms up. "You're too far away."

"And you're wearing way too many clothes."

He dropped to his knees and removed her sandals. When his strong fingers ran up the insides of her calves, lust swirled like smoke low in her gut. With each stroke of his work-hardened hands, her lust grew until its feathery tendrils had infiltrated every cell.

Darren pressed his mouth to her inner knee and left a trail of kisses up her thigh until he reached the hem of her shorts.

"Hmm," he said, his lips vibrating against her flesh. "I seem to have met an obstruction."

"Oh, dear." She furrowed her brow and bit her lip in fierce concentration. "Is it impassable?"

From between her legs he lifted his gaze, which had grown serious. "All kidding aside, I want you, Porchia. Not a minute of today went by that I didn't want to haul you back to our cabin so we could be alone. Tell me I'm not alone in this."

His words sent her nervous system into overload. Electrical sparks and jolts cascaded through her.

Cynthia D'Alba

At the same time, a dark dread filled her soul. Darren was special, too special to hurt.

Still, she laid the palm of her hand on his cheek. "You're not alone," she said. *I'll take this chance with you. Don't break my heart.*

His answering grin sent her heart soaring. He was too sexy, too dangerous to her emotions, but she was here now, and damn if she wasn't as happy as she'd been in a long time.

She put her bare foot on his chest and gently pushed him back. Darren landed on his butt. He arched an eyebrow in question.

The button on her shorts pushed easily through its hole. Standing, she lowered the zipper and let her khaki twill shorts fall to the floor.

"That's one obstruction down."

He saw the change in her immediately. When he got serious, she would turn on the striptease, or try to lighten the mood in some way. This was not just sex for him. He had to make her understand that.

He pushed off the floor and stood.

"Oh," she said with a saucy grin. "You want to play too, huh?"

He caught her hand as she reached for his zipper. Bringing it to his mouth, he kissed her fingers one at a time. Her eyes widened with surprise, but when he brought her palm to his lips and placed a kiss there, the visible pulse in her neck kicked up a notch. Her breath hitched. The cheeky grin slid off her face.

"This isn't play, Porchia. This is real. What I feel is real."

He didn't dare use the word love. She stiffened for a briefest of seconds and he knew his decision to keep the word love out of the room was the right one for now.

Wrapping his fingers around her other wrist, he put his arms around her and tugged both her hands around to her back. The position pushed her breasts out against his chest. He took a step closer so that they were touching chest to chest and thigh to thigh. She rocked her head back and he kissed her and then left kisses along her chin. When he bit the large tendon in her neck, she trembled and sighed. The response sent any spare blood he had, and some he probably couldn't spare, from his brain to below his waist, pumping his cock to a painfully rock-hard state.

He licked her neck and traced the tip of his tongue up to her chin. Her lips were already parted, so he took advantage and slipped his tongue inside to stroke and make love to her with it.

She moaned. The sound was a direct lasso around his heart.

He walked them to the edge of the bed before he released her mouth. Her breaths were ragged and rapid. Her eyes were dilated and a little unfocused. She was as affected by this as he was.

As soon as he released her hands, she slipped them under the hem of his T-shirt and glided them up his chest. Her fingers were like ten individual flames of fire. He burned with need. A shudder he couldn't repress ran through him.

"Raise your arms." She pushed his T-shirt up and off. "I love how you feel." She ran her tongue down the middle of his chest and along the ridges of his abdomen. Reflexively, he sucked in his gut.

"And God, I love how you taste. So hot. So salty. So much man."

He jerked her shirt off and unfastened her bra. She let it slip down her arms and fall to the floor at their feet.

He pulled her roughly against him, harder than he'd meant to, his need for this woman overriding all the control he usually exhibited. But this wasn't just another woman.

Her fingers worked at the button and zipper on his shorts. When she grabbed the waist to pull them down, she caught the elastic of his boxers. She dropped to her knees and tugged both down to his ankles. He stepped from the constricting material, hefting shorts and underwear off with a kick of his foot.

His downward glance rewarded him with the most erotic vision of his life…the woman of his dreams on her knees between his feet. She ran the flat of her tongue up him as though he were a sucker. Damned if his knees didn't quake in response.

She must have noticed, because she glanced up and smiled. And while their gazes held, she ran the tip of her tongue around the head of his cock. Lowering her head, she wrapped her lips around him and slid him inside the wet heat of her mouth.

He groaned and fisted her hair, holding her still—too much movement on her part and this would be over way too soon. Porchia must have sensed his oncoming loss of control, because she secured her hands around the base of his shaft and applied the necessary pressure.

As he began to move in and out of her luscious mouth, she slid her hands up and down his cock. The combination of her hands and the suction from her mouth had him back at the peak too quickly. Holding her head still, he pulled free.

"I can't take more," he said through clenched teeth. He pulled her to her feet and kissed her passionately. His arms under her thighs, he lifted her without breaking the kiss and sat her back on the bed. Once there, he stripped her panties off her.

The musky scent of her arousal hit him like an aphrodisiac. He fell to his knees, hoisted her thighs over his shoulders and drew in a deep breath. Using his thumbs, he separated her folds and licked her. Her hips lifted off the mattress as she groaned her approval. Spicy honey was all he could think of as he continued to lick and suck at her sweetness.

"Enough," she groaned out. "Enough. I want you inside me. Now."

He gave her one last long lap, gently lowered her legs off his shoulders and left them dangling off the side of the bed. "Don't move," he ordered, and she stayed where he put her.

Hurriedly, he ripped open a condom and rolled it on. Then he lifted her legs, held her knees in the crook on his arms and drove into her. Her hips arched off the bed, giving him better access. As he withdrew, she whimpered in protest. When he thrust to the hilt, she moaned with pleasure, which almost sent him spiraling out of control.

But he wanted her to come before he took his pleasure. He pulled out, getting one of her patented whimpers of protest. He flipped her over and lifted her ass high in the air, leaving her standing on tip-toes. He pounded back into her. Her shoulders hit the mattress and she used that surface to brace her hips higher.

Darren wrapped one arm around her waist to steady her for his thrusts, which he could barely control now. With his other hand, he found her clit. He massaged it with his thumb, moving in concert with his thrusts.

Her groans were growing louder. She sounded desperate for release.

He pressed firmly against her nub and drove deep. Rolling her mouth to the mattress, she gave a muffled scream. As she came, her vagina milked him with muscular ripples. Two more thrusts and he was done, grinding into her as he came.

When he returned to the bedroom after disposing of his condom, Porchia had climbed into the bed and pulled the sheet and blanket over her. She met his return with a smile. Flipping back the covers, she nodded to the empty space beside her.

He slipped in and snaked an arm behind her shoulders to pull her over. She rested her head on his chest, releasing a long sigh.

"You okay?" he asked.

"More than."

He felt a little shiver.

"You cold?"

"Nope. Just a little aftershock." She rolled her gaze up to his face. "Best earthquake ever."

He chuckled and kissed the top of her head.

She yawned. "I have to take a nap," she said, and yawned again.

"Sounds like an excellent idea," he said, sliding down the mattress until he was flat on his back. She'd moved with him, her head now back on his chest. Her long flaxen hair spread out behind her and over his arm. He twisted a few of the silk strands around his fingers, noting the extreme contrast between the softness of her hair and the hardness of his hands. As he continued to fondle her hair, Porchia's even breathing told him she'd fallen asleep.

Holding her in his arms felt like coming home. Safe. Secure. Loved. If it were possible, he'd stay in this moment forever.

There were so many ways he could get hurt in life. A bull goring him. A piece of barbed wire springing back to nail a leg or arm. A good, solid slam from a hammer while driving nails into a board. Hell, his leg had been broken when his truck was T-boned.

All those would be minor annoyances to the pain of losing Porchia when this week was done. He had to find a way to make her realize that he was her future, just as she was his.

They slept until almost nine p.m., completely missing dinner with the rest of the campers, not that Porchia minded. She'd looked a little rough for wear when she'd awoken from her nap. The dark circles under her eyes told the world she hadn't gotten much sleep the night before, and the last thing she wanted was speculation, or rather confirmation, of what had kept her awake.

She wasn't complaining. Darren had given her more orgasms in the last twenty-four hours than she'd had in the last twenty-four months, as long as self-induced didn't count, and in her opinion, they didn't.

As they lay in a tangle of arms and legs, Porchia's stomach rumbled loudly. Her silent prayer that he hadn't heard it went unanswered.

He patted her abdomen. "A little hungry, are we?"

She swatted his hand away with a laugh. "You've burned up all my food reserves, what with your insatiable sexual appetite."

His stomach took that moment to give an answering rumble, which made him chuckle. "Ditto, my dear. What do you say we raid the kitchen?"

"A plan I can go for."

It was dark when they stepped off their porch to head to the lodge. Now that all the younger Montgomerys were gone, leaving only the adults at camp, the activity level had subsided to quiet and calm. A thin stream of smoke rose from a fire burning low in the fire pit. Other than the chirps of crickets and tree frogs, the night around them was quiet and peaceful. Some cabins still had on lights, but Porchia didn't see anyone else.

"Let's stay out here," she said. "I can grab the leftover hot dogs from the kitchen for roasting." She sighed loudly. "It's so rare that I get to enjoy a fire. It feels perfect tonight."

Darren pulled a couple chairs closer to the fire. "Works for me. Let's go raid."

They came back loaded down with beer, chips and hot dogs with all the trimmings. Darren stoked the fire. Sparks shot into the sky when he added another log. The wood caught quickly, the flames licking at its dry bark.

He shoved a couple of wieners on a pointed stick and held them in the fire. Porchia cracked open two beers and passed him one.

The cold beer slid down her parched throat and splashed in her stomach. "Yum," she moaned.

They ate and drank and discussed the stars, the moon, the D&R ranch and Darren's family. Porchia kept the topic moving to everywhere but her family and her past. The last thing she wanted was him, or anyone else in Whispering Springs, to know that she'd done something so horrible that her parents had felt they had no recourse but to send her away.

Sadly, even though she'd promised to give a relationship with Darren a chance during the upcoming week, she worried that the next few days were the only ones they'd share. She'd been ignoring Slade's texts, even blocking his phone number the last time, but his threats were getting viler and more descriptive. He'd left her no choice. She'd have to find a way to get away from Darren for a short time tomorrow and telephone her parents. If Slade hadn't contacted them yet, he would. They needed to know that he was back and would make all their lives miserable if they didn't find a way to get him gone.

Chapter Sixteen

It was Tuesday morning before Porchia found herself totally alone and with the privacy to call her father. Darren, Reno, Jason and Cash headed out on the four-wheelers and weren't expected back for at least a couple of hours.

Anxiety flooded Porchia at the thought of talking to her father. She'd seen them last month over the Labor Day holiday. No bad news nor harsh words had been exchanged, but the visit had still been stiff and uncomfortable.

She sequestered herself in the cabin as soon as breakfast was over. Her father would be at work. Her mother was probably dressing for a luncheon at the club. But her father was the one she had to talk to. Her mother always deferred to him.

For a long time, Porchia stared at her phone, trying to get what she wanted to say straight in her head. The conversation could go in a number of directions. Her father could be sympathetic to her concerns about Slade ruining her life in Whispering Springs. He could be angry at Slade, and at her, for making him relive the whole debacle. Or he could react anyway in between.

Her finger shook a little as she hit send on his office number.

"Judge Randolph's office."

"This is his daughter, Katherine. Is he available please?"

There was a noticeable pause before his secretary said, "I'll see if he's available."

The wait for him to pick up seemed to be forever. She was beginning to wonder if he would. Then again, maybe Slade had already made good on his threat and contacted her parents and her father was seriously angry.

"Katherine." Paul Randolph's voice was as formal as a judge, which was appropriate. "What seems to be the problem now?"

Porchia flinched as if each of his words was a direct blow to her gut. "Can't I just call and ask how you're doing?"

"Of course. But since you never have, it would raise suspicions."

"Well, that's true, I guess."

"I hate to hurry you, but I've got a case starting soon. What can I do for you?"

"Slade Madden is out of prison. Did you know?"

"Actually, I did. I was notified when his full sentence was served."

"Has he called you?"

"No. Why would he? We have nothing to discuss."

Porchia chewed on her lip. "He's called me. He wants money."

"Don't we all," her father said. "Of course you didn't give him any."

"No, but…" She took a drink of water to put a little moisture in her mouth. "I know you and Mom didn't approve when I decided to stay in Texas instead of returning to Georgia, but I have a good life here. I want to keep it."

"I see. I'm still not sure what you need from me or your mother this time."

"Slade is threatening to ruin me if I don't give him hush money. And if I don't, he said he'd be contacting you."

"Not that I have any intention of giving that degenerate money, but what did he ask for?"

"A million."

Her father burst out laughing. "Degenerate and deranged. Well, there's nothing he can threaten me with that would make me part with a penny. Frankly, I'm surprised you have given him a minute of your time. Ignore him. He'll go away."

"No, I don't think so. He's pretty determined."

"Has he threatened you physically?"

"Well, no. Not really. Just verbal harassment mostly."

"Then contact your local police or sheriff's department. Let them handle it. That's what we pay taxes for. I'm sorry, but I must go now. The court is waiting on me."

"Sure, Dad. Thanks."

"Anytime. We'll see you at Thanksgiving next month. Your mother misses you."

"I'll try."

She hung up, her breathing constricted by the large boulder setting on her chest. Her *mother* missed her but he didn't? He still hadn't really forgiven her for almost wrecking his appointment to the bench.

She pounded her fist on the sofa cushion. She had screwed up, big time. And, yes, it would have been totally her fault if her father had been passed over for his judgeship. Her and her stupid idea to show her parents they weren't the boss of her. Right. That had worked so well, hadn't it?

The phone buzzed in her hand. She startled and almost dropped her cell. A quick glance at the calling number had her heart crawling up her throat. Mallory James, her nighttime employee, never, ever called her.

"Hello?"

"Porchia? It's Mallory. Mallory James."

"Hi, Mallory. Is everything okay?"

"I'm not sure. I could be overreacting. On second thought, it's probably nothing. I'm sorry I bothered you."

"No! Wait. What's going on? And you don't ever overreact, so talk to me."

"Last Saturday when I came in, there was an old beater truck sitting out front of the bakery."

"Beater truck?"

"Looked worse than my Jeep, and, yes, I know how bad Mabel looks."

Mabel was Mallory's beloved, but old and rusted, Jeep Wrangler.

"Okay. Why did this truck bother you? We live in a small ranching community. All the guys have a crappy truck in the barn. Was it still there when you left?"

"No, but I've seen it near the bakery a number of times. I ran by on Sunday to make a list of supplies I was going to need for a new cake order we got, and the truck was in our parking lot."

The hair on Porchia's neck stood on end. A chill ran down her back.

"Yeah, that's strange. I hope you didn't get out of your car."

"No, I kept going. I can protect myself okay. The military taught me that, but the whole situation felt wrong. When I got here about midnight to start work, it was gone. But when I left Monday morning, it was parked in front of the store again."

"Did you see who was driving it?"

"Not very well. It was a guy. Cropped short blond hair. I think he might have had a tat on his neck. I couldn't be sure. The driver's window was cracked so I got a little view of him."

"Did he say anything to you? Or threaten anyone else?"

"Not that I know of. He looks out of place, if you know what I mean. Like bad news looking for a place to land. I know Tina has seen him too. She mentioned that she had some new boyfriend that'd been meeting her and walking her to the bank for the deposits because she was nervous of the strange guy."

Slade Madden. There was no one else it could be. He wanted her to know that he was watching and waiting. If he was making Mallory and Tina feel spooked, it wouldn't be long before other women were nervous to come in her bakery. This would not do. Not at all.

"Maybe I should cut this trip short and head on back."

"No, no. Don't do that. I'm sure it's nothing, but I thought you'd want to know."

"Have you spoken with anyone from the sheriff's department?"

"No." Her reply was a little too short, too firm. The suggestion seemed to rattle Mallory. "Why would I? What would I say? It's an ugly truck and makes the front of the store look bad? It's a public street. I know he's not doing anything illegal, but it just doesn't pass the smell test."

"Okay, but if this person threatens you or does anything other than park his truck in the area, call Sheriff Singer immediately."

"Will do."

Damn him. Mallory was right. If it was Slade, parking on a public street wasn't illegal or even threatening. And even if she did decide to talk with the sheriff about it, it's not as if Slade's text messages had been more than demands for money. A case might be made for harassment, but she doubted it.

Later that day, she was finally able to get Tina on the phone. Yes, Tina agreed the guy was creepy and that he had black tats on his neck. But she also agreed that he'd done nothing other than park his truck and stare at the store. He'd never spoken a word to her, nor to any of the bakery employees that she knew of. No one was complaining about him, but Porchia's employees had talked among themselves and decided that no one would be in the bakery alone until Porchia got back. There was just something about the guy that seemed sinister.

It was only when she heard the roar of four-wheelers that Porchia realized the entire morning had passed. She hurried to the bathroom to check her hair and brush her teeth before Darren got back. She didn't want to meet him with a face full of worry and concern. Damn man could read her like a book.

"Hey! You here?"

Darren's shout had her doing a quick rinse of the toothpaste from her mouth.

"Bathroom. Be right there," she called back.

Her first sight of him made her groan and laugh simultaneously. He was covered from head to toe in dirt and mud, and the grin on his face reminded her of a kid with a new toy.

"Looks like you had fun," she said, rolling her eyes at the mess.

"Damn Reno. He rooster-tailed me."

"Excuse me?" She covered her mouth to contain her laugh.

"Sprayed me with his back tire," he explained.

"Because?"

He shrugged. "Maybe I might have thrown a little dirt his way."

She shook her head but couldn't contain her laughter. She'd never had a sibling, but if she had, she'd have wanted to be as close to that sister or brother as Darren and Reno were.

"Don't come in," she warned. "You'll have mud everywhere."

"You want me to strip on the porch?" He pumped his eyebrows. "You know all the other women will never be satisfied with their men once they get a look at me."

Her mouth ached from her wide grin. "Yes, I can see how that would be a problem. Leave your boots on the porch and head for the shower. And don't you dare hug me."

After toeing off his mud-caked boots, he walked toward her, the glint in his eyes warning her that he would, without fail, hug her.

"Don't," she warned and danced backward.

"Oh, come on, honey. Give me a kiss." He smacked his lips and moved closer.

"Darren, I swear..."

But that's all she got out before he caught her in a tight bear hug and gave her a kiss that tasted like dirt and sweat and Darren. The kiss should have been offensive, but it was Darren, and to her, nothing he did seemed offensive.

She pushed him away with a chuckle. "You. Shower. Please."

"Going," he said.

"Porchia," he called from the shower. "I can't reach a spot on my back. I could use a hand."

Her momma didn't raise no fool. There was nothing wrong with his back, but what the heck? She'd play along.

She stepped in, shut the door and leaned on the counter. "What's the problem, stud boy?"

"I might need a little help reaching all the muddy areas." The teasing tone totally blew his lie.

"I see," she replied in a serious tone. She quickly stripped off her clothes, which were dirty anyway from his hug. Now that she thought about it, this had probably been his plan all along. "Now, where's the problem?" she asked after opening the shower door.

Darren pulled her under the warm spray and pressed her against his granite chest, slick with water. He kissed her, slipping his tongue into her mouth with practiced ease, touching and tasting her exactly how she loved it.

"Okay, I'm here. Show me the problem."

She slid her hands down his wet, slippery back, appreciating the tone and muscular development formed by daily hard labor. She worked her hands down to his ass until she could grab his cheeks in the palms of her hands. Then she pulled him tight against her.

This was not like her. She wasn't a take-charge woman when it came to sex. But Darren brought out a side of her she hadn't known existed, and it might be hard to get the genie back in the bottle after this week was over.

"You're getting close," he whispered in her ear, making goose bumps pop up on her arms.

She released him and grabbed the bottle of liquid soap. "Turn around," she ordered, and to her surprise, he did. He turned and stretched out his arms, bracing himself on the shower wall. She swallowed…hard. He looked like pure sex standing there.

After lathering up her hands, she worked them down his back, over the rigid muscles and into the valleys between. The dip at his waist and narrow hips sent her heart dropping to her knees. The muscles in his ass tightened as her fingers worked them. Having this powerful man under her control made her head spin and the embers of lust in her gut flare to life.

She squirted more soap, rubbed her hands together and slid them around his hips until she felt the crinkle of his pubic hair. He drew in a breath and held it. When she wrapped her fingers around his granite shaft, he groaned and let his head drop to the wall between his hands.

Slowly, she massaged up and down his cock with a gentle twist of her hands. She dipped down to his sac and rolled the soft flesh between her fingertips. He stiffened at the first brush of her fingers on that delicate area but didn't say anything.

Pulling her hands back around him, she stroked down his legs, enthralled with the strength she found there.

With knees bent, she rested her ass on her heels. "Turn around."

There was a moment of hesitation and then he turned. His face was serious, his eyes dark with passion. His gaze dropped to her sitting at his feet.

She ran her palms over his feet and up his shins, rising up on her knees with the movement.

His velvety cock strained upright on his abdomen and appeared to become even more impossibly hard when she licked her tongue up the inside of his thigh.

He hissed in a breath.

Warm water flowed down his chest, onto his groin and finally onto her as she worked his scrotum with her tongue, lapping at the supple flesh, using the tip of her tongue to roll his testicles between her lips.

Grasping his cock, she pulled it to her mouth and sucked the tip between her lips.

He fisted her hair, tugging it tight. "Fuck," he groaned.

She drew his penis in as far as it would go into her mouth. Then, as she moved off, she scraped her teeth down the sides.

His breathing was erratic and loud in the enclosed space. His gaze never left the space where she tenderly made love to his shaft.

After a few minutes of licking and sucking and even a little nibbling around the rim of the head, he jerked her to a halt.

"I can't take another second of that," he said through clenched teeth. "I'm going to come."

She allowed her eyes to lift until their gazes met, then, while holding his stare, she ran the flat of her tongue down the underside to the base and back up. When she sucked him back into her mouth, he groaned and held her head steady as his hips pistoned his cock in and out of her mouth rapidly.

It didn't take but a few strokes before she felt the hot liquid on the back of her throat. As his cock twitched for the last time, she could have sworn she heard him mutter, "God, I love you."

Chapter Seventeen

The week passed in a blur of contented happiness. Darren poured maple syrup on his pancakes while keeping his eye on Porchia refilling her coffee mug. Even the simple, everyday task of her pouring coffee gave him pleasure. He almost laughed at himself. How he'd made fun of Reno's facial expressions when he looked at Magda. Darren suspected his face bore the same goofy expression Reno's had when his brother had been falling in love with Magda.

Nonetheless, his situation with Porchia was different from any relationship he'd ever had. Since the night in the shower when he'd inadvertently blurted out his feelings, he'd watched for some change in Porchia's behavior. He was sure she'd heard him on Tuesday, but now he wondered. She hadn't reacted then and hadn't said anything about his comment over the following days. She'd neither pushed him away nor drawn him closer. She'd stayed the caring, attentive woman she'd been since she'd kissed him last Saturday.

"I can't believe today's Friday," Porchia said, dropping into the chair beside him. "Where did the time go?"

"You ready to head back on Sunday?"

She shrugged. "Yes and no. I miss the bakery. Getting my hands in the dough. The different aromas in the kitchen. Even miss my night baker, Mallory. But sleeping in every day to almost eight the last two mornings has been a luxury. I'd forgotten what it was like to wake up with the sun rather than before the sun." She sipped her coffee.

"Mom and the rest of the women have enjoyed having you do those baking lessons this week." He put his arm around her and pulled her over for a hug.

"You didn't have to, but I appreciate it."

"Are you kidding? I loved it. Your mom is great. So's the rest of your family. You're very lucky to have them. You know that, right?"

He nodded. "Yup. I do."

And they would love having you as a permanent part of the family, he thought but knew he couldn't say it aloud.

"What's on the agenda today?" She stole a piece of bacon off his plate.

"Reno asked if I'd run to town with him on some errands. Do you mind?"

"Not at all. Magda and I are baking up something special since it's the last weekend, so I'll be tied up most of the day. But we should be done sometime after lunch."

"Great. How about a ride this afternoon?" When she giggled and arched an eyebrow, he chuckled. "I was talking about a horseback ride, but hey, I'm flexible."

"You can say that again."

When she followed the comment with a saucy wink, he laughed, drawing the attention of others at the table.

"What's so funny down there?" KC called from her end of the table.

"Private joke," Darren said.

Porchia squeezed his knee. He laced his fingers through hers and brought their joined hands to his mouth for a kiss.

"Hey, bro," Reno shouted. "If you can tear yourself away, we should get a move on."

"Coming," Darren said, not taking his gaze from Porchia's face. "You and Magda don't get into any trouble while we're gone."

Her answering smile made his heart swell until he could hardly breathe. "Flour, eggs and butter. How can we get into trouble with that?"

"What are you making?"

"I'm not exactly sure yet. I know all the Montgomery kids are coming in this afternoon. Magda said something about Adam loving chocolate chip cookies, so probably cookies for the kids."

"You know I love those too, right? Maybe you could stash a few for our cabin."

She leaned forward and kissed him. "I'll see what I can do."

Darren slammed the door of Reno's truck after he climbed in. "Okay, bro. This had better be some fabulous road trip. You're making me miss time with Porchia."

Reno laughed as the engine roared to life. "How are things with you and Ms. Summers?"

"Okay, I guess. It's like she's got this shell around her that I can't get through."

"So things aren't getting serious?" Reno stopped at the end of the road and waited for the security gate to open.

Darren hesitated. There was no one he was closer to than his brother, but if he actually admitted his feelings out loud, he wouldn't be able to take them back at a later date. And if Porchia finished out the week with a kiss and a brush-off, Reno would never let him forget it.

"Wow," Reno said. "No answer. It's worse than I thought, isn't it?"

"Depends on what you're thinking." Darren decided to not give his brother any ammunition.

Reno glanced over and shook his head. "You've got it bad. Have you told her yet that you're in love with her?"

Hearing the word spoken aloud jarred Darren unexpectedly. He knew his secret but how—

"And now you're wondering how I knew, right?" Reno asked. "It's written all over your face. You look at her and your mouth goes all slack. Your eyes glaze over. And there's this stupid grin that ends up on your face." Reno shook his head. "You're a goner, whether you'll admit it or not."

Darren started to ignore his brother, but at the last second said, "Yeah. Are you the only one who knows?"

Reno laughed. "Are you kidding? Mom has already starting planning a double wedding for me and you."

Darren rubbed his hand down his face. "Shit."

"Yeah, well, I've got that part fixed."

"What part?"

"The double-wedding part."

Darren frowned. "I don't get it."

Reno grinned. "Well, our big trip today is to pick up the marriage license Magda and I filed for this week."

Darren whipped his head toward Reno so fast his neck popped. "Are you shitting me?"

"Nope. Last weekend's surprise wedding was so awesome we decided to steal the idea. We filled out the paperwork for the license earlier this week. The license should be ready today."

Darren slapped his brother's shoulder. "Damn, boy. That is freaking great. I love Magda."

"Me too," Reno said with a laugh.

"What about all the other wedding crap? You know, rings, cake, whatever it is brides have to have to make it work."

"Magda's not like most brides. She doesn't want all the flowers and candles in a church. We picked out rings the same day we filed for the license. Hers had to be sized. It should be ready today too."

"Mom is going to shit a brick," Darren said with a laugh.

"I know, but we really didn't want to do all the parties and big wedding stuff. You know Magda's not that kind of gal. She likes things simple."

"What about her dad?"

"Zeb and Blanche will be in today. They are bringing the older Montgomery kids back to camp for the weekend and staying overnight."

"So this wedding is...?"

"Tonight."

Darren shook his head. "Nuts, man. This is totally wacked."

"But fun, huh?"

"Oh, yeah. It's gonna be fun."

Darren waited in the truck while Reno ran into the courthouse and picked up the marriage license. Then they drove to McRae's Jewelers. This time, Darren got out and went in with his brother.

As Reno made his way to the back of the store, Darren perused the cases of diamond rings. Even if he and Porchia were to that point, which they weren't, he didn't have a clue what her taste in diamonds would be. Round? Marquis? Oval? And then again, he wasn't sure she'd want an engagement ring. And if she did, if she'd want a diamond or sapphire or whatever.

"Can I help you, sir?"

Darren's gaze jerked from the sparkling gems to a trim woman standing behind the counter, a set of keys in her hand.

"Can I show you something?" She indicated the diamond rings in the case.

"Oh. No. Thank you. I was just waiting for my brother. He's picking up a ring for his bride."

"Are you sure? You never know when you might be in the market for a ring."

"No. Not in the market. Thank you."

"You looking at rings already, bro? Damn, man. I knew you were a goner, but this is worse than I thought."

Darren glared at his brother, who'd just walked up carrying a small plastic sack.

"I don't need an engagement ring," he said to Reno through clenched teeth.

"But Mom could have the double wedding of her dreams," Reno chided.

"Thank you," Darren said to the sales clerk. "We're leaving now."

He elbowed Reno hard enough to make him sidestep, but even that didn't ruin Reno's mood.

"Not cool, bro," Darren said when they were back in the truck.

Reno just shook his head. "You do realize that at one time you would have played along, picked out different rings for the three or four fake fiancées you'd make up on the spot to shock the saleslady? Lord, man, you were green just thinking about picking one out. And that's how I know you're in love."

After fastening his seatbelt with a loud click, Darren shook his head. Damn if his brother wasn't right, not that he was going to give Reno the satisfaction of telling him so.

Reno had a few other stops to make, so it was well after lunch when they finally turned back into the Whiskey Creek drive.

"Your future," stated Darren, pointing to the two young boys playing tag in the yard with a black and white dog nipping at their heels.

He'd meant it as a joke, but one look at Reno's contented smile told a different story.

"I know," Reno said. "I can't wait," he added in a quieter voice.

The screen door of the lodge opened and the woman under discussion exited, followed by Porchia.

"You realize we have the two prettiest women here, excluding Mom," Reno said.

"Very true. Listen, there's something you need to know."

Reno looked at him, an eyebrow arched in question. "Yeah? What's that?"

"It's about Magda and when she came to work for us."

A smug smile inched its way onto Reno's face. "You mean the fact that you and Mom cooked up the whole idea of hiring Magda as our housekeeper to get us back together?"

Darren laughed. "Yeah, that one. How did you know?"

"I didn't. Not at first. But it seemed so odd that Mom, so proper about how things are done, would hire someone so close to our age to live in our house. And then when Magda and I came out as a couple, she and Dad were not the least bit surprised. Now that I think about it, she actually had a cocky, self-pleased expression that night. But I'll admit that I appreciate your taking one for the team and breaking your leg."

Darren snorted. "Yeah, well, that wasn't part of the plan. But I'm glad it's worked out for you."

"I think your date has spotted us. She seems to be waving a bag of something."

Darren looked toward Porchia and grinned. "Gotta go. Those are fresh cookies."

He leapt from the truck and hurried over to the cabin. Yes, he knew he wore a shit-eating, in-love grin, but it was impossible for him to suppress it.

"Cookies?" he asked Porchia, knowing full well the answer.

"I'll tell you the same thing I told Adam. Cookies are for good boys. Are you a good boy?" The twinkle in her eye made his heart pound.

Deliberately, he frowned and tried to look sad. "No, ma'am. I can be a very bad boy."

"Oh," she said. "I see. Well, I have something for bad boys too."

He'd noticed the brown paper bag she carried and had assumed it contained more cookies until she pulled a can of whipped cream out.

"Really? In that case, I am a very bad, bad boy."

She laughed and raced up the steps to the cabin with Darren close on her heels.

Later, as they lay in bed a tad sticky but very satisfied, Porchia licked a small glop of whipping cream off Darren's chin.

"I'll never look at a can of whipped cream the same way again."

Porchia laughed. "I know what you mean."

Darren pulled her on top of him. "Let's just stay here the rest of the weekend."

"Okay. Who needs food anyway?"

Lifting his head off the bed, he kissed her. It amazed her that a simple kiss from him could scramble her brain so much.

Darren's large hands warmed her ass. Then he gave her a soft swat on her butt.

"It may be getting close to dinner time. We need to get a move on."

She dropped her forehead on his chest. "Really? I have to move? Sorry. No can do. My bones dissolved about thirty minutes ago."

When he chuckled, his chest vibrated below her.

"Okay," she said. "Just a minute." Propping herself up on her forearms, she raked her fingernails along the side of his head. "I know. I know. I have to get off you."

"Eventually." He adjusted his arms until they were wrapped snugly around her. "In a minute," he said and gave her nose a kiss. "So tell me about your morning."

She wasn't sure what he knew about what was happening tonight. Magda had sworn her to secrecy when they were baking the cake for tonight.

"Oh, you know. The usual. A little baking. Some girl talk. What about you and Reno? Where did you have to go?"

He narrowed his eyes in suspicion. "What do you know?"

"I don't know. What do you know?"

They had a stare down until she giggled, which made him laugh.

"You know, don't you?" he asked.

"Do you know?"

"I know."

"Me too."

"Whew," he said. "I'm glad we got that settled."

She laughed again.

"So that's where you and Reno went this morning? To get the needed supplies for tonight?"

"Would you please stop talking in code? Yes. We picked up the license and Magda's ring. What did you do?"

"We baked a three-tiered wedding cake. Well, actually, Magda made cookies while I made the cake. I told her it wasn't right for a bride to bake her own cake."

"Hope your cake is as good as Magda's cookies were."

She slugged his arm. "You'll pay for that." With a suffering sigh, she rolled off him and stood. "I'm headed for the shower." When she saw him begin to move, she added, "Alone."

"Spoilsport."

The family was gathered at the lodge by the time Darren and Porchia walked over. Well, everyone but Reno and Magda. Sometime while she and Darren had been secluded in their cabin, Marc Singer had arrived, bringing Lydia Henson back with him. However, she was sitting next to Jason, their hands clasped as though one of them would float off if they let go.

One of the things Porchia had come to admire about the Montgomery family was the support they showed their children, even in difficult situations. The family had stood behind Olivia when she was pregnant and unwed. And when Travis and Caroline had the fake wedding. She'd heard all kinds of stories about Cash and what his brothers and parents had done to help him get back on his feet.

Her parents were not like this at all, but maybe it was her fault her family wasn't as close. It had been her foolish decisions that'd almost wrecked her life and her dad's career. Sure they spoke, but they had never discussed that night again.

"Need a drink?" Olivia asked, holding up an opened bottle of wine. Porchia nodded and Olivia passed her a full wine glass. Mitch tossed a bottle of beer to Darren, who immediately popped the top and took a long draw.

"Okay," Darren shouted. "Settle down for a minute. Is everyone here? Who's missing?"

"Reno and Magda are the only ones not here," Clint said. "Have you seen them, Nadine?" he asked.

As his mom shook her head, Darren put two fingers between his lips and an ear-piercing whistle blasted in the air. As soon as he did, the door to Reno and Magda's cabin opened and they walked out.

Reno wore a new, crisp pair of jeans, new white, snap shirt, a black string tie and shiny black boots and a black cowboy hat. Magda wore a white satin dress that was above her knees in the front and dropped to her ankles in the back. Her white cowboy boots sparkled with rhinestones. Her cowboy hat was white and had a small veil that hung off the back to between her shoulder blades.

Darren stepped to the side as Marc Singer made his way down to stand on the concrete walk.

"What's going on?" Nadine said. "Clint? Do you know what's going on?"

Clint shook his head slowly as a smile lifted the corners of his mouth.

"Reno?" his mother asked. "Have something you want to tell us?"

Reno grinned. "I know you've been planning that double wedding for me and Darren, but I can't wait until he finds some woman who'll finally agree to marry him."

"Yeah, love you too, bro," Darren said with a laugh.

Reno looked up at all the Montgomerys crowded onto the porch. "Magda and I thought Cash and Paige had the right idea. You're all here. We're here. And we're getting married."

Nadine's hand flew to her mouth as she cried out. At first, Porchia thought it was in dismay, but she quickly realized how wrong she was. Nadine was thrilled, not upset. There were probably families who would object to their son marrying the daughter of a relative's foreman, but not this one.

"Mom. Dad. Will you come stand over here?"

Nadine and Clint hurried down the stairs and stood by their son.

"Dad? You and Blanche up there?" Magda said.

"Right here, honey," Zeb Hobbs said.

"Will you and Blanche come stand with me?"

"Of course," Blanche said, and they joined Magda.

"Before we start, Magda and Reno wanted to say a few words," Marc Singer said.

Magda turned toward Zeb and Blanche. "Zeb. You may have only come into my life in the last six years, but you've been a wonderful father to me. My life would not be the same without you." She looked at Blanche. "I hope I make Reno as happy as you've made my father."

Blanche dabbed at the tears in her eyes.

Magda turned to Reno's parents. "Nadine. This is all your fault, you know?"

Nadine nodded. "I do good work."

Magda smiled. "That you do. Thank you for making Reno the wonderful man he is."

"Thanks, Mom," Reno said. "I owe all my happiness to your sneaky plan."

Instead of looking embarrassed at being caught at her matchmaking, Nadine blew them a kiss. "A mother knows," she said.

"Dad. I'll try to be as good a husband and father as you are. You're a heck of a role model."

Clint smiled. "Thank you, son. That means the world to me."

Reno looked toward Zeb and Blanche. "I love her, Zeb. I'll take good care of her."

"I know," Zeb said. "That's why I'm gonna let you marry her."

Reno held out his hand and Zeb shook it.

"And last, before we start, Magda and I would like to wish Cash and Paige a happy one-week anniversary."

After the group quieted down from the well-wishes to Cash and Paige, Marc said, "We are gathered here to witness the wedding of Reno Alexander Montgomery and Magda Alicia Hobbs."

The ceremony went off without a hitch, although Porchia's vision was a little blurry from her tears. When Marc pronounced them husband and wife, a loud cheer went up from the crowd. Darren squeezed Porchia's hand and then went to congratulate the newlyweds.

Dinner was loud and festive. Porchia lost track of the number of toasts that required taking a drink of wine. KC helped her set up the wedding cake. If Porchia hadn't let Magda bake her own wedding cake, she sure wasn't going to let her stage it either.

By nine, all the Montgomerys and Landrys under the age of ten were sent to bed with Noah, Caroline Montgomery's brother, as their sitter. Darren joked that must have cost Mitch and Travis a nice sum of money.

It was almost midnight when Magda climbed on top of a table. "Turn the music off. I want to say something." She swayed as she spoke and Porchia was a little concerned, but then she noticed Paige and Cash stepping up to brace Magda. "Okay. Here's what I want to say. I love you all. Love you. Love you. Love you." She pointed around the room with each love you.

Wide grins split the faces in the room. The bride was toasted.

"But I love Reno more than anybody." She staggered, but Reno was there in a flash to steady her. "And now, my husband has to take me home." As she climbed off the table, she said, "Aren't you glad we don't live in the time when people would come to watch us have sex on our wedding night?" She giggled. "I bet they'd be surprised."

Reno kissed her to shut her up as the rest of the remaining campers laughed.

"Need any help getting her home?" Darren asked.

"I'm ready to go," Porchia said. "Why don't we walk with them as far as their cabin? I need some fresh air."

"Good idea," Darren said. "Come on, bro and my new sister-in-law."

"I'll go with you," Marc Singer said. "I have to head back in the morning, so I need to get a little shuteye tonight."

The night air was cool and crisp and exactly what Porchia needed, and she suspected the others did too. The moon was still at about a quarter but the stars were brighter than they'd been last weekend. She took Darren's hand and blew out a sigh of contentment. This was the happiest she'd been in a very long time.

Singer's phone rang. He pulled it from the holder on his belt. "Singer." He listened. "Really. Any idea what time it started?"

He turned his back to Porchia and walked a couple steps away. She tried not to listen, but the night was so quiet the sheriff's voice carried and every word could be clearly heard. All four of them stopped to see what had required a call to the sheriff while he was out of town.

"Everyone out of the building?" Pause. "The fire chief have any idea of where it started?" Pause. "Okay. I'll be on the road within a couple of hours. See you at the station."

"What happened?" Darren asked.

Marc walked over to Porchia and laid his hands on her shoulders. "I am so sorry, Porchia. There was a fire at Heavenly Delights. The entire building was involved."

"But it's out, right? The fire department put it out, right?"

He shook his head slowly. His fingers tightened as he gave her a gentle squeeze. "No. I am truly sorry, Porchia. The fire department did all they could, but it was just too big and spread too quickly."

"It's all gone?" she whispered, not believing what Marc was saying.

Marc nodded. "It's gone."

Chapter Eighteen

Stunned, Porchia stood frozen in place. She tried to force her brain to process what she was being told. Sure, she'd had a number of glasses of wine. And, yes, her brain was a tad fuzzy, but her mind did not want to believe what Marc had told her. Then the words connected and the implications that everything she'd worked for was gone hit her. And not just for her, but for her employees.

Guilt swamped her. This was all her fault. Slade Madden. She knew it. She might not be able to prove it, but in her gut she knew. Her knees began to shake and her legs crumbled beneath her.

Darren caught her before she hit the ground, sweeping her up into his arms. "I'm so sorry, babe. I know this is the worst thing you can hear." He kissed her forehead. "But it'll be okay. I promise."

"It's my fault," she cried out. "My fault."

Marc stepped closer. "What do you mean *your fault?*"

"I should never have come here. Never should have been gone a whole week. If I'd been there, this wouldn't have happened." She struggled in Darren's hold. "Let me down."

"Can you stand?"

"Of course I can," she snapped. "I'm not an invalid. Put me down."

He set her feet back on the grass, but he kept an arm around her waist. She was sure he meant his arm to be supportive, but right now it felt like a vise.

Her breath hitched. "I have to get home. I have to see it for myself." She pulled from Darren's hold and grabbed Marc's arm. "You're going back tonight. I heard you say that. I'm going with you."

Marc's gaze flashed over to Darren. "Of course…if that's what you want."

"Great. I'll get my stuff together."

"Wait a minute, Porchia," Darren said. "I brought you here. I'll take you back home."

She whirled on him. "No. You've been drinking."

"So have you."

"Doesn't matter. I'm not driving. The *sheriff* is." She looked at Marc. "I'll be ready by the time you're ready to leave."

He jerked his head in the affirmative and headed toward his truck and fifth wheel. It would take a few minutes for him to get his camper hooked up, which was enough time for her to throw her crap into her luggage.

She turned and hurried toward the cabin.

"Damn it, Porchia. Wait," Darren called. With his long strides, he caught her before her foot hit the bottom step. "Just wait. There's nothing you can do tonight. We'll head out first thing in the morning."

"I can't. I have to go tonight. I have to make sure no one was hurt." Her vision blurred as tears rose in her eyes. "This is all my fault."

"Hey." He pulled her to him and held her head to his chest. "No. It's not your fault. These things happen."

It was Slade. She had no proof, but in her gut she was sure. Bastard had warned her, hadn't he? He'd said he would ruin her if she didn't pay up. Burning her out might be his first move. Getting others involved would put them within his wrecking-ball reach, and she didn't want anyone else hurt.

When the gunshots had been fired at camp and she'd feared it was Slade, she'd started to tell Darren and the sheriff her suspicions. However, when it had turned out to be kids and she reread Slade's messages, she'd decided he wanted money, not her dead. And really, looking through his texts, he'd put nothing in them that could be construed as threatening. Sure, he talked tough, but a private conversation came down to he said-she said.

Rebuilding her bakery in another location wasn't really an option. Every penny she would get from insurance and the small amount she'd been saving for a horse would go to paying Slade off so he'd just go away.

And maybe after the two romantic weddings the past two weekends, the idea that she could get the money from her trust by marrying Darren had crossed her mind…for about five seconds. She cared about him too much to do something that despicable. Going into a marriage for money was wrong, even one where the couple had deep feelings for each other.

She had a feeling that if she told Darren about Slade's demands, he would insist on giving her the money, but that wasn't the answer. This was her mess to clean up, no one else's. She sighed.

One night. One mistake. Her life forever affected. She pushed away from Darren. "I have to go." She gave him a quick kiss. "Understand, okay? This has nothing to do with you and everything to do with me. I'll never sleep tonight and I'll go nuts until I see all my employees are safe. And I have to see my bakery." Her voice broke during the last statement.

Her bakery.

Something she'd built with her own blood, sweat and tears, and now it was gone. Destroyed by an immoral man with nothing left to lose.

She rushed up the steps and through the cabin to the bedroom. In less than ten minutes, she'd stuffed everything into her luggage and was hauling them to the living room. Darren sat on the sofa looking both forlorn and angry.

"I'm sorry," she said. "You have to understand. If this were your ranch, you'd be headed out too."

"I understand you have to go. I'm not mad at you. I'm mad at myself for drinking too many beers to drive you there myself." He leaned forward, his hands clasped between his knees. "I should be going with you."

"Then come on. Somehow we'll get your truck home. Reno can take the ATVs home."

A knock at the door interrupted her. Expecting it to be Marc, she called, "Come in."

Nadine and Clint hurried through the door.

"Oh, my dear," Nadine said as she hugged Porchia. "We just heard. I am so sorry. What can we do?"

"Nothing, but thank you. I'm leaving tonight. Riding back with Marc."

"Can't you wait until the morning?" Clint asked, concern etched on his face. He looked so much like Darren right now it hurt.

"I can't. I just can't."

Darren stood. "I'm going with them. Mom, will you pack up my clothes and get them to Whispering Springs?" He glanced toward Porchia. "Maybe to Porchia's house?"

Porchia nodded in agreement.

"Sure," his mother said. "What about your truck?"

Darren turned toward his father, who nodded. "I'll get your truck back to town. You go with your lady. She needs you. We'll handle everything here."

Relief flooded through Porchia. Once again, Darren's family had come through when he needed them.

"Let's go," he said, grabbing the two bags she'd set by the door.

Porchia hugged Nadine. "Thank you," she said in a teary voice. She kissed Clint's cheek. "Thank you both."

Porchia scooped up her purse and headed down the stairs behind Darren. The rest of the family was waiting outside to see them off. She wanted to hug each and every one of them for welcoming her and making her feel so at home, and maybe someday she would. But right now, Marc was pulling his truck and fifth wheel out of its parking spot and she'd be damned if he'd leave without them.

Stretched out on the rear seat of Marc's truck, Porchia was asleep within thirty minutes of leaving the campground, more like she'd cried herself to sleep. Darren threw his jacket over her and turned back around.

"Any idea what started the fire?" Darren asked.

Marc nodded toward the back. "She asleep?"

"Yep. Passed out cold."

"Initial report is it looks like arson. We'll know more once we get an arson investigator in."

"We have an arson investigator in Whispering Springs?"

"Naw. Getting someone from the state crime lab to come take a look. You got any idea who'd want to burn her out of business?"

Darren shook his head. "No. None. You?"

"No. I've never heard anything negative about Porchia or her business. This doesn't make a lot of sense."

"Maybe someone wanting her out of business so they can come in?"

"I don't think so. It wouldn't make sense. There can't be enough money in the bakery business to make it worth their while. Now if we were talking oil or cattle, sure. But pastries? Just can't see it."

Darren glanced over his shoulder to make sure Porchia was still asleep. Her breathing was steady. Her eyes were shut and still. Great. She was still out of it.

"You haven't said anything about someone being injured in the fire, but I've got the feeling you were holding something back."

Marc didn't reply for a long time. Finally, he said, "That nighttime baker. James I think her last name is. She was there when the fire started. She has burns, but nothing serious. I think she knows more than she is telling."

"Do you think she might have started it? Some conflict with Porchia that we don't know about?"

Marc shrugged. "I have no idea. Maybe. Or maybe the chick is a psychopath. Nobody knows much about her. She is hardly ever seen around town. Anyway, I thought it would be a good idea to get back before she gets her story set in her mind. Plus, I want to see the bakery the first thing in the morning."

As they parked in the departmental lot of the sheriff's department over an hour later, Darren reached over the seat and touched Porchia's shoulder.

"Hey. Wake up."

A sleepy smile grew on her face. Then her eyes flew open and she jerked upright.

"Where are we?" she asked, shaking her head as if to jiggle the sleep away.

"We're at the sheriff's department."

"Great. Let's go."

"Hold on, Porchia," Marc said. "I need to go in and get a report before we head over. And I need to grab the keys to my car."

"You may need a report and a car, but I don't." She opened the rear door. "I'm walking. I'll meet you there."

Darren saw the determination in her eyes. Even though it was just after four in the morning, she was determined, even if that meant she went by herself. He couldn't let her go charging down to her bakery alone. It wasn't safe. She had no idea that the fire was probably arson. From his way of thinking, that meant someone had a serious grudge against Porchia, or possibly someone else who worked there. The arsonist could still be around just waiting to get another chance to cause trouble. Well, that wasn't happening on his watch.

"Wait a minute," Darren said. "It's too dangerous for you to walk by yourself at this hour. Give Marc a chance to find out what's going on." When he saw that didn't convince her, he added, "We need to check on Mallory before we go too."

That stopped her dead. She whirled around and glared at Marc. "You said no one was there."

"No, I never said that. Your employee, Mallory James, was in the bakery when the fire started."

Porchia closed her eyes. Darren caught her shoulders as she swayed. "Is Mallory dead?" Her shoulders were as rigid as bricks.

"No. She got burned, but the report I got was that it wasn't serious. I need all the information my deputies have before we go down there."

She took a few long, deep breaths as though steeling herself. "Okay." She stared into Marc's face. "I want all the information too."

Turning on her boot heel, she marched through the back door of the sheriff's department with Marc and Darren trailing in her wake. Darren couldn't help but admire her grit and determination. She made love like she lived life... full-out, no holds barred. In the sheriff's office or in the bedroom, she was a force to be reckoned with, and damn if that didn't make him want her all the more.

"Sheriff." The threesome turned toward the male voice.

"Brody," Marc said. "Want to bring me—us—up to date?"

Sam Brody was a new hire to the department. From what Darren had heard, he'd come from the Dallas Police Department looking for a quieter lifestyle. Arson might not be exactly what he was expecting in sleepy Whispering Springs.

"Sure thing, Sheriff." He nodded to Porchia. "Sorry about the bakery, Porchia."

"Thanks, Sam."

Darren was surprised that Porchia knew Sam, but then he realized she probably knew most of the people in town since hers was the only bakery around.

"Well, best we can tell, Porchia, er, Ms. Summers's employee Mallory James walked in on someone burglarizing the place. If the condition of Ms. James's knuckles are any indication, we will be looking for someone who's pretty beat up."

"She served as a Marine," Porchia said in way of explanation.

Brody nodded. "Anyway, the guy hit her with a paperweight on the desk. She went down, and he ran. But he'd already started the fire before their fight. Probably figured the fire would erase any evidence that he was there."

"Do you keep money in your office?" Marc asked.

Porchia shrugged. "I have a floor safe, so sometimes I do, but usually just overnight. Tina Marie has been making my deposits while I've been gone, so I don't have any idea if any money was there last night or not." She looked at Brody. "What about Mallory? How badly hurt is she? Where is she?"

"Ms. James is in Whispering Springs Hospital. She got hit pretty hard on the head."

"And her burns?" Porchia asked.

"Mostly first and second degree. Doctor said she would heal."

At that news, Porchia's shoulders sagged in relief. However, guilt that Mallory had gotten snared and injured during Slade's—and she assumed it was

Slade—vindictive payback ate at her gut. "Thank God." She looked Marc. "Can we go down there now?"

"In a minute. You call in the Texas Fire Marshalls yet?"

"No, sir," Brody said. "I thought you'd want to make that call."

"You did secure the scene?"

"Yes, sir. Deputies Martin and Knue are there."

"Any other stores involved in the fire?"

"The fire department jumped on it pretty quick. Since Heavenly Delights was the end store on that block, the fire was mostly confined there. The jewelry store next door has some smoke and water damage. And the windows of that store were broken out also. The owner is checking inventory now to see if the breakage is from the water hoses or if he was burglarized last night too."

"Go ahead and call the state fire marshal's office."

"Yes, sir."

"Okay, Porchia. Now we can head over," Marc said.

The acrid stench of charred wood burned the inside of Porchia's nose as she stood in her rear parking lot. The asphalt, never in great shape to begin with, was now littered with broken glass, blackened lumber and one burned-out Jeep. Mallory would be crushed about that Jeep. Porchia prayed Mallory had the clunker insured, but she doubted it.

"You okay?" Darren asked.

"No. Of course I'm not okay," she snapped, rubbing the tears off her cheeks. "Sorry. I shouldn't have barked at you like that. This isn't your fault."

He put his arm around her shoulders. "Hey. I can take it." He kissed the top of her head. "This has got to hurt."

"You have no idea."

Marc had loaned them powerful departmental flashlights, which they were beaming around the outside blackened hull that had been Heavenly Delights. Porchia picked her way over to the cinderblock wall that had made up the rear exterior of the kitchen. What had been white was now black from the scorch of the fire. The metal door that led from the parking area into the kitchen was a molten glob.

She took a step over the metal hurdle to enter.

"Stay out here," Marc ordered.

"But I need to see."

"Stay here." Marc's voice left no doubt that he was speaking as the sheriff and not her friend.

She lifted her foot back.

"I want to keep the area as it is for the fire marshal. I'm not an arson expert by a long shot, so we could screw up the investigation by accident. We don't want to do that."

She shook her head. "No. You're right."

The scene and the certainty that everything she'd worked for was gone, was almost impossible for her mind to register. She was right to come. It was hard to ignore reality when it stared you in the face. When she'd first heard, she'd held out hope that some of her store would be salvageable, but it wasn't. She doubted there was a pan in there that would be usable.

"I'm walking around front," she said over her shoulder and started around the end of the building. She didn't have an ounce of proof Slade had anything to do with this. For all she knew, Sarah Jane Mackey had done it to get back at Porchia for being with Darren. Okay, that was grabbing at straws, but still, she didn't have any facts other than it was arson.

There was one person, however, who might know more...Mallory. Porchia needed to talk to her and find out exactly what she'd seen. From the report she'd given the sheriff, Mallory couldn't identify her attacker. Porchia didn't believe it, and if the skepticism on Singer's face was any indication, he didn't either.

Until she talked to Mallory, she'd keep her mouth shut.

Darren followed her, not offering simplistic platitudes or fake optimism, which she really appreciated. It was obvious to anyone with a pair of eyes that the business was a total loss.

The front was no better than the rear. Charred wood. Broken glass. Puddles of water everywhere.

"Sheriff. Can I see you a minute?"

Marc headed toward the deputy who'd called him over.

"Seen enough?" Darren asked.

"I keep hoping to wake up and find this is all a horrible dream." She looked at him. "Not gonna happen, huh?"

He shook his head. "Nope."

"I don't know whether to cry or cuss."

"Maybe a lot of both is in order."

She wrapped her arms around his waist. The position sent a wave of security through her. Still, a sob escaped and her breath hitched.

He held her, rubbing his hands up and down her back. "It'll take a while, but you'll rebuild. And I'll be beside you every step of the way. Whatever you need, just ask."

She realized how easy it would be to give up, just like she'd given up on her parents. Just like they'd given up on her.

She wasn't quitting this time. She asked to go to the hospital right then to see Mallory. However, as Darren pointed out, it was four in the morning, not optimum visiting hours.

The sheriff was still tied up with the investigation at the jewelry store, which had been burglarized. Deputy Brody gave Porchia and Darren a ride to her house. When they walked in, the fresh, clean scent of her house was instantly marred by the reek of smoke from their clothes.

"Lift your arms," Darren said. When she did, he pulled the foul-smelling shirt over her head. "The sight was bad enough for you. You shouldn't have to relive it with this stench. I suggest we set our boots on the porch for tonight and let them air out."

She nodded, but words couldn't punch through the solid lump in her throat.

He set both pairs of boots outside and then turned his attention to her jeans. Once he got them unfastened, he helped her push the heavy material down her legs. She stepped free and stood frozen in place wearing only her bra and panties.

What was she going to do? Her brain was on overload with flashes of ideas and thoughts, and yet nothing was sticking long enough to make an impact. What time was it? Should she make coffee? Offer breakfast? Take a nap? Was the newspaper here yet? Would the fire be in it?

A pair of warm hands on her shoulders turned her. She looked up into Darren's blue eyes.

"Come on," he said. "Let's get you in the shower and get that odor off you."

She started toward her shower as numbness overtook her. He finished removing her underwear and then his own clothes before putting them both under the warm water.

Her salty tears mixed with the warm water. "Thank you," she said, hugging him.

"For?"

"The coffee you're going to make when we get out."

He chuckled. "Whatever you need, I'll be here."

Chapter Nineteen

Porchia woke to an empty bed about noon on Saturday. The sheet beside her was cold, so either Darren had gotten up earlier or he was gone. Staring at the ceiling, she made a mental to-do list. By the time she got to item ten, grief swamped her, overwhelming her emotions.

Throwing off the bedcovers, she stood and stretched. She could accomplish nothing by hiding. But first things first. Some food and then to the hospital to see Mallory. She needed to know what Mallory had told and would tell the sheriff's department about her fight.

In the bathroom, she washed the sleep from her still-puffy, red eyes. Her hair looked pretty much like she'd invited a family of rats to move in. But then she had gone to bed with wet hair, so what could she expect?

The overcast sky set a dreary tone for the day, and that fit her mood perfectly. A bright, sunny day would have been more than her emotions could take.

Dressed in khaki slacks and a sweater set, she headed to the kitchen to find some food, which she knew would be a challenge. Before leaving for Whiskey Creek for her vacation, she'd made sure all the spoilable food was trashed. There was probably at least peanut butter and jelly in the cabinet and bread in the freezer.

Darren entered through the front door at the exact moment she walked into the living room. Startled, she screamed and then laughed at herself.

He slammed his hand over his heart. "Nice way to give me a heart attack."

"Sorry. I didn't think you were here."

"I wasn't. But now I am. Did you know you have absolutely no food in your refrigerator?"

She chuckled. "Yes. I know. Sorry about that. But..." she shrugged, "... better to leave it empty than return to green mold."

"I've lived as a bachelor for years with my brother. We, of course, know nothing about moldy, leftover food."

"I'm sure." She accompanied her remark with an eye roll.

"You better be nice to me." He held up two brown bags. "I brought lunch from the Orchid Deli."

"I'm restraining myself from falling over in starvation." She held out a hand. "Gimme."

He held up identical bags. "Pick one."

"Does either of them have an anchovy sandwich?"

Grimacing, he said, "No."

"Then it doesn't matter. I'll eat whatever is in the sack."

She pointed to the bag in his left hand and he tossed it to her. Inside was a hot meatball hoagie, chips and three peanut butter cookies.

"I love the Orchid's meatball hoagies. How did you know?"

He grinned. "Mental telepathy." Then he pulled out the exact same meal from the second sack. "My favorite sandwich. Good that you love it too."

They sat side-by-side on the couch and arranged their lunches on the coffee table before them. For the next few minutes, there were only groans of gastronomical pleasure.

"Hey. How did you get to the deli? Did you drive my car? How did you know where to find my keys?" Her eyes widened. "Did you go through my purse?"

"Slow down, Columbo. No, I didn't go through your purse or drive your car. My truck was in your drive this morning. I guess my folks packed my stuff last night and drove the truck up sometime early this morning. My bags were in my truck along with this note." He passed her an envelope with her name written on it.

Porchia, we enjoyed spending time with you and hate that it had to end with such a tragedy. You're such a dear. If we can do anything for you, don't hesitate to ask. Love Nadine and Clint and the rest of the Montgomerys

"You have such great parents. Not only were they quick to volunteer to help last night, they did it immediately. That's so nice of them to go to all that trouble for you."

He frowned. "All what trouble? Packing my stuff and bringing my truck home? I'm sure they didn't mind. That's what family is for. It's not like I wouldn't have done it for them or any of my family."

His words stabbed at her gut. What he described wasn't her family, not at all. Her grandmother had been wonderful, taking her in, letting her stay until college, leaving Porchia the house. Her Grandma Summers had been able to show her love for Porchia in ways her parents never had. She'd never doubted that her parents loved her in their own way.

However, now that she'd spent so much time with Darren's parents, she couldn't imagine that Clint and Nadine would have sent any of their children to live with a relative to quiet the rumors.

"What can I do to help you?" he asked. "It's Saturday, so odds are that you can't talk to your insurance agent until Monday. Want me to call Marc and see what's going on with the investigation? We probably won't be able to get into your bakery today to see if anything is salvageable, but I can find out."

"No. Thanks. I think I need a couple of days to get my thoughts together. I thought I'd start making a list of who I need to call and things I need to get done. It's going to be a long list. Why don't you go on to your ranch and check on things there? I'm sure you're dying to get home."

"Come with me?"

"Thanks, but, no. I could use some alone time. It's nothing to do with you or your family," she added. "They were super awesome, but I need some quiet time to think."

"What about your folks? Have you called and told them yet about the fire?"

"No, but I will." Mentally, she flinched at the idea of telling them. They'd never approved of her running her business, much less something as pedestrian as a local bakery. "I'd rather have some firm information and plans before I do."

"I hate to leave you here by yourself. Come home with me. I promise you'll have lots of quiet time at the ranch."

She laid her fingers on his firm thigh. "I'm used to being here alone. I've been alone since my grandmother died twelve years ago. Don't worry about me."

"But you're not alone. You've got your parents."

"Right. I meant on my own in Whispering Springs."

"I just don't feel right going."

"You're not going. I'm sending you away." She gave him a quick kiss. "I really appreciate your concern, but I need to be here. You go on and don't worry about me. I'll be fine."

She could see his mind whirling. He wanted to go home and check on the animals. But, on the other hand, since he was a true Southern gentleman, leaving her probably went against the grain.

"Go," she said more firmly. "Call me tonight. Tell me how much all your cows missed you."

He chuckled and stood. "Okay, I can take a hint." Taking her hands, he pulled her to her feet. "I'll miss you."

"Me too."

"If you need me, or just miss me, call. I'll be on the road back to you before we hang up."

He brought her closer and pressed his mouth to hers. Her heart sighed and Porchia gave up her struggle to remain unaffected by him. Snaking her arms up and around his neck, she held on and enjoyed all the sensations of his tongue delving into her mouth. When he growled and jerked her flat against him, aligning their bodies so they touched chest to chest and groin to groin, the merry-go-round in Porchia's gut lit up and started spinning. Damn, she was going to miss this man.

Their week together had shown her that the age difference she'd thought would be a problem just wasn't. However, it wouldn't be right to drag him and his respectable family into the rabbit hole with her problems. She didn't know what or how Slade would figure in her future. She just knew he brought nothing but bad news whenever he appeared.

When he finally broke from the kiss, he rested his forehead on hers. "I'm going, but only because you're forcing me."

"I'll see you soon. I promise."

After a quick final kiss, she stepped back. "Go."

Once he was gone, the house settled into a quiet so pronounced it almost hurt her ears. The only sounds were her breathing and the hum of the refrigerator. She gave him twenty minutes to get out of town before she grabbed her purse, pulled out her keys and hurried to her car.

The town hospital was small. Most life-threatening cases were sent on into Parkland or Baylor or some other major medical center. However, burns like the ones Mallory had suffered could easily be managed locally, so Porchia was sure her employee was still hospitalized here. She needed to talk to Mallory to find out what she knew about the fire and what she had—and more importantly— had not told the sheriff's department.

An angry voice resonated from Mallory's room, followed by a calming male voice. Porchia pushed open the door. Mallory was sitting in bed, her arms crossed over her chest, her eyes blazing with anger.

"Knock, knock," Porchia said through the open door.

"Porchia." Mallory's voice held a whisper of relief. "Tell this jackass that I can take care of myself."

The jackass under discussion was a man dressed in a pristine white lab coat who looked to be in his thirties with dark hair and a five o'clock shadow. His hazel eyes wore the concerned look of a professional doing his job.

"I'm Porchia Summers," she said, holding out her hand. "Mallory works for me."

"Dr. Salvie. Nate Salvie."

"Nice to meet you." She looked at Mallory. "What's the problem?"

"I need to get out of here. Now! This asswipe says I have to stay another night."

"Some of your burns are quite serious," Dr. Salvie said. "Not to mention the two broken ribs. This asswipe thinks one more night is in order."

"You have broken ribs?" Porchia cried in alarm. "How...never mind. We can talk about it later." She turned to Dr. Salvie. "I'll do what I can to make her stay, even if I have to tie her down."

He gave them both a bright smile. "Great. I'll leave you here to do your magic. And you..." he pointed at Mallory, "...I'll see you in the morning."

"In your dreams," she shouted at his back as he was leaving.

The second the door was shut, Mallory pulled off the hospital gown to reveal a tank top. She pushed her bedcovers to the foot of the bed to reveal jeans and socked feet.

"I'm out of here," Mallory said. "Help me get some shoes on." She stood and gasped.

"Sit," Porchia ordered, pointing to the bed. "And talk."

"I have to get somewhere safer."

"You're worried about the guy who did this."

"Damn straight. He had crazy eyes. I've seen vets like that. People who have totally gone over the edge, and, man, that was him."

"The guy from the beater truck?"

Mallory's gaze flashed to Porchia but she remained silent.

"Was it the man from the truck?"

"You know who that guy is, don't you?" Mallory said.

"Maybe. Probably. Describe him."

"Tall. Blond. Crazy eyes. Prison tat on his neck."

Porchia shut her eyes and drew in a deep breath, trying and failing to calm her racing heart.

"What did you tell the deputy?"

"Nothing about the guy. Only that there was someone and he had your safe open and was shoving money into one of our paper sacks when I walked into your office."

"Why didn't you describe the guy?"

"I don't know. I knew from our phone conversation that you knew this guy, or I figured you did. I owe you, Porchia. You weren't looking for a night baker when I came to you. But you saw what I needed. You adjusted the bakery hours for me. You helped me. I didn't want to put you in a bad spot with the cops if you and this guy were somehow involved."

Porchia staggered and sat heavily in the only chair in the room. "You think I burned down my own bakery?"

Mallory retook a seat on the edge of the bed. "I didn't know. I saw people do stuff in Afghanistan that I would never have thought possible. But until I got a chance to talk to you, I wasn't saying anything to the cops."

"Well, let me assure you that I didn't burn down my own bakery. But you're right that I know who the guy is. And I do think he's dangerous."

Porchia pulled her phone from her pocket and stopped. "Mallory. I am so, so sorry you got hurt. Never in my wildest dreams did I imagine something like this would happen."

"Don't beat yourself up. You couldn't have stopped this if you'd been standing in the office instead of me."

"Thank you. Somehow, I'll make it up to you."

Porchia dialed the sheriff's department.

"Hi, Marc," she said when he picked up. "This is Porchia Summers."

"Porchia. What's going on?"

"I need you to come to the hospital. Room two-thirty-seven. We need to talk."

"Okay. I'm assuming this is about the fire."

"It is. And about the guy who started it. I think I know who it is."

"And you're just now telling me?" His voice was thick with agitation.

"Just come. Oh, bring a deputy to leave on Mallory's room. If the guy is who I think he is, he's dangerous."

"On the way. And Porchia?"

"Yeah?"

"Stay there. You'll be safer. There is already a deputy watching her door."

"So you knew I was here?"

"Yup. See you in a few minutes."

"Why did you call the cops?" Mallory asked, her lips tight across her teeth. "They're useless at best and will probably just make the situation worse."

"Because without them, you and me are in big, big trouble."

Marc was there so quickly Porchia wondered if he'd been in the area, or even in the hospital. But given that a deputy was already stationed on Mallory's room, he might have started to head over when he got the report that Porchia had shown up.

Marc dragged another chair into Mallory's room and took a seat. "Okay, ladies. It's time to come clean." He pointed toward Mallory with a pen. "I don't believe for one minute that you can't describe your attacker. And..." he pointed at Porchia, "...you know more than you've told me. So who's first?"

"Me," Porchia said. "It all starts with me."

Marc poised his pen over a notepad in his lap. "I'm ready."

"I think, from what Mallory has told me, the guy is Slade Madden. He got out of prison in the last couple of weeks."

He wrote down the name. "How do you know him?"

"We went to school together. One night when I was fifteen, I left a party in his car. He was drinking. A lot. I should have known better. I still can't believe I got into his car. But you have to understand. Slade was so popular. He was a senior and captain of the football team. Every girl wanted him. He was so handsome."

"Just keep to the story," Marc said.

"Okay. Anyway, he was drinking beer. I didn't realize how drunk he was until after I got into the car and he drove off. I asked him to take me back to the party. He laughed and grabbed another beer. When I insisted he take me back, he got mad. Called me a baby. He turned around and floored the gas. I think he was just trying to scare me. He took a corner, and I swear, it felt like we were on two wheels. He lost control and jumped the curb and hit an old woman in her yard. He backed up and drove off." She paused, the horror of the night as fresh as if it'd happened only yesterday. "She died. He got a total of eighteen years for negligent homicide and leaving the scene of an injury accident. Plus, a misdemeanor count of driving while intoxicated. Oh, and contributing to the delinquency of a minor. That would be me."

No one spoke as she shut her eyes to regroup her emotions. "I was taken down to the station but released to my parents. No charges were filed against me since I wasn't drinking and had no control over the car. I testified against him. It was horrible. My friends deserted me. No one at school would have anything to do with me."

Porchia clasped her hands together to stop the shaking. It didn't work.

"When the trial was over," she continued, "I moved to Texas to live with my grandmother, my mother's mother. It was supposed to be for a few months, just until all the brouhaha died down, but after a year, I decided to stay."

She looked at Marc. "A lot of the kids and their parents blamed me for Slade going to jail. I didn't have a choice, not really."

When she stopped speaking, Marc cleared his throat. "Why do you think the guy who was in your place was Slade Madden?"

"He contacted me a couple of weeks ago. He's served his entire sentence and is out. He wanted me to give him money, which I don't have. But I promised him I'd give him something in a couple of weeks. I needed to buy some time until I could figure out what to do."

"And you didn't call me because?" Marc asked.

"He didn't do anything wrong. He asked me for money. That's it."

"That's it," Marc said with a lift of an eyebrow. "He thought you'd be such a great sport as to hand over money? No threat?"

She flinched. "Just that he'd tell everyone in Whispering Springs about my history and ruin my name and my business."

"Isn't that blackmail?" Mallory asked.

Marc glanced at Mallory as though he'd forgotten she was in the room. "At this point, it probably doesn't matter. Arson, burglary and attempted murder are enough to send him back. Your turn, Mallory."

Mallory told him about seeing this strange guy hanging around the bakery while Porchia was gone and how she'd called Porchia about it. Then she went over discovering Slade in Porchia's office with the safe open and how they fought.

"How did you get away?" Marc asked.

"I didn't. He pushed me into the side of Porchia's desk and then slammed my head on the top. I think he thought I was dead when I slumped to the floor. The fire was at the door by then, and I guess he decided that if I wasn't dead, the fire would finish the job. As soon as he was gone, I made it to the bathroom and climbed out the window into the back lot. I crawled as far as I could and I guess I passed out. That's where your deputies found me."

Marc glared at both women. "You two ladies are in a peck of trouble."

Chapter Twenty

After reading them the riot act over not coming forward sooner, Marc left a deputy at Mallory's door.

"Sorry, Porchia. I should have known you had nothing to do with that guy."

Porchia hugged Mallory gently so to not hurt her broken ribs and then pushed her shoulders back on the mattress. "You will stay here," she said. "That's an order."

"I will. I promise. I won't even give Dr. Asswipe any problems."

Porchia laughed. "He's kind of cute, you know."

"Not happening."

"Well, you never know. I'm headed out. Grocery shopping and then home. There's nothing in my house to eat."

"Think you ought to have asked the sheriff to put a deputy at your house?"

"No. I know Marc. There'll be a deputy near my house, but I don't think Slade will come there. If he's smart, he's long gone." She scooped up her purse off the window ledge. "I'll check on you later. Since I'm going to the store, you need anything?"

Mallory shook her head. "I'm fine. Thanks."

It was close to dusk by the time Porchia pulled into her drive. Parked down the street was a patrol car. She'd waved as she'd passed. With all the trouble Slade had gotten himself into while in Whispering Springs, she didn't believe he'd dare to approach her. She felt a little guilty about that poor deputy sitting outside for nothing. Maybe she'd bake some cookies to take out to him.

She was later getting home than she'd expected. She'd had to go by the bakery again and just look. Her insurance was good, thanks to her father's advice, but she doubted it would completely cover her losses. The image of her burned-out bakery was branded into her brain, just as the loss had dug a deep hole into her soul.

One of the first items on her to-do list was to help any brides find replacement bakeries, especially those with wedding dates near. It was possible she could make a few of the cakes at home, but she'd have to talk to the other ladies who worked for her to compile a complete list of weddings and dates…if they could remember them all.

All the lights were off at her house, which was comforting since that was how she'd left it. She collected her grocery bags, her purse and the mound of mail that'd been waiting on her at the post office. Balancing it all was quite the juggling act, but she made it to the front door before pieces of mail began sliding off. She left a few envelopes on the porch and let herself into the house. Quiet and still.

After putting away the foodstuffs, she went back to the porch to retrieve the lost mail. A gun greeted her when she opened her door.

"Get back in," Slade said and pushed her backward.

She stumbled, landing across the arm of the couch. She struggled back to her feet. Fear and anger battled to be the emotion in charge. Unfortunately, her fear of Slade was much, much stronger.

"This is a bad idea, Slade. You need to leave before the police get here."

"Nobody's coming, Kat."

"What about the deputy sitting right outside, or did you miss that car with Whispering Springs Sheriff Department on the side? The car with the big blue lights on top?"

He sneered. "I'm not stupid."

She thought he was probably wrong on that account.

"That deputy won't be reporting in anytime soon."

His words made her gasp as her stomach dropped. "What did you do?"

"Doesn't matter. I'm leaving town, and I want that money you promised me."

"I told you it's going to take a while to get it together. I have a little in savings. Maybe a thousand or so. I can get that tomorrow."

He slapped her, sending her face first into the back of the couch. Tears welled in her eyes from the pain. She pushed up, trying to focus on him and what he might do next.

"You have a trust fund. You think I don't know about that?" He jerked her upright by her hair. "You bragged about it enough when we were growing up."

"I…I…I can't get to it yet," she gasped out. "It's restricted until I reach thirty-five or get married. I couldn't get a dime from it if I wanted to."

"Fuck," he shouted and threw her by her long hair onto the floor. "I should kill you for leading me on."

"You took the money from my safe," she said. "That had to be enough to get you away somewhere safe."

He snorted. "That wasn't enough to get me out of the country. I need big money. Enough to set me up in South America. Somewhere with no extradition treaty with the US."

"What about the jewelry store you robbed next to me? Surely he had some good stuff there?"

Slade's face took on a manic expression. He began pacing around the room. "Naw. I haven't found a buyer for that crap. What to do…what to do?" he muttered as he walked.

She found her footing and stood. She had to do something. Slade was just manic enough to kill her since he'd just found out she had no value to him.

He swung the gun toward her. "How much did you say you have in your bank account?"

Looking down the barrel of a gun made her flinch. "Not much. Maybe a thousand." Even as the words left her mouth, she realized she probably should have lied and given him a much higher balance. If he thought he could get more from her when the bank opened, it might have bought her more time tonight.

But damn her mouth and lack of ability to lie when she was scared to death.

"Fuck," he shouted again and dragged his hand through his hair. "Fuck, fuck, fuck." Gesturing with the gun toward her purse, he said, "Give me your purse."

As she picked up the purse, she thought about swinging it at him. Maybe she could dislodge the gun from his hand. Ack. Stupid idea. She'd watched way too much television. She was a baker, not a boxer.

He waved the gun as she took a step toward him. "Slow," he said. "Drop the purse on the table and move back."

She did, but he wouldn't find much in there. There was a secret compartment in her wallet where she hid five-hundred dollars of mad money, but he'd never find that. Should she give that to him and hope that he'd go away?

Was he going to kill her no matter if she gave him money? If he was going to shoot her no matter what, she'd rather go down fighting.

She glanced around the room looking for something, *anything*, that could be used as a weapon. When she got out of this, *if* she got out of this, she was going to get that concealed weapon license she'd been meaning to apply for.

Her eyes alighted on a black and white onyx tray she'd brought home from a vacation in Mexico. The thing was heavier than shit. It would crack him good if she could figure out how to get to it and then get him to stand still so she could brain him with it.

Yeah, she needed a better plan.

Slade dumped out the contents of her purse on the coffee table and tossed aside items of no value, such as tissues, lipsticks and a mirror. Papers from her wallet were tossed onto the table as he searched for any money she might have stashed in the various pockets and slots. His grip on the gun grew lax.

Until she came up with a better plan...she eased toward the tray sitting on the high table under the front window. She'd made three steps when Slade leveled the gun on her.

"Where the fuck are you going?"

She nodded toward the ginger jar on the table. "Checking the ginger jar.

Sometimes I stash some mad money in there."

"I'm watching you. Don't try anything funny."

She reached the table, knowing full well there was no money in the ginger jar. At best, she could hand him a fist of dust from it, but that's about it.

The stomp of boots on the porch reverberated through the door. Slade's head and full attention snapped toward the door. This might be the only chance she had. She wrapped her fingers around one end of the tray and lifted it from the table as her doorbell rang.

"Porchia? You in there?"

Darren. What was he doing back here?

Slade's gaze never moved from the door. He raised his gun and pointed. The doorknob twisted and the door eased open.

"Porchia?"

Darren stepped through the door.

"Don't fucking move," Slade growled.

Porchia hauled back and slammed the thick onyx tray across the back of Slade's head. She heard the crack of bone at the same time as the crack from the gun.

Blood gushed from Slade's head as he slumped to the floor.

She glanced at Darren expecting a broad smile for her actions. Instead, he was looking down at the bright red blossom on his white shirt from the bullet shot by Slade.

Not knowing if Slade was dead or unconscious, she didn't dare let him regain use of his gun. She kicked the gun across the room as her front door slammed open and four deputies followed by Sheriff Marc Singer stormed into the room.

Porchia didn't go to the hospital with Darren for a number of reasons. The main one was that she figured the last person the Montgomerys would want to see was the person who'd gotten their son shot.

Of course, Marc Singer had her sequestered in her kitchen and wouldn't let her leave, but she also didn't put up much of a fight either. The sheriff had a dead man, a shot man, an unconscious deputy and a job to do. Porchia understood that. However, she was going nuts not knowing what was happening with Darren.

The paramedics hadn't told her anything either. As soon as the cops burst through the door, she'd been hustled out of the room to sit at her kitchen table, and that was where she still sat an hour later.

Crime scene investigators were combing through her entire house, not just the living room. From her restricted position, she could see black fingerprint dust on tables in her living room. If she understood correctly, the technicians were also dusting the rest of her house. She suspected, but did not know for a fact, that they were looking for Slade's fingerprints in other rooms of her house. As far as she knew, they wouldn't find them, but what if they did? What if Slade had been in her house without her knowledge? Could they jump to the incorrect conclusion that she and Slade had been in cahoots and that she'd had a part in burning down her bakery?

Marc Singer sat again at her table. "Okay, Porchia, let's go through this again."

She stood. "Enough. We've been through this twenty times. And twenty times, I've told you the same thing. Am I under arrest?"

"No," Singer said. "Sit down"

"Damn it, Marc. You haven't told me anything and it's been hours. Do I need to call a lawyer?"

He hiked an eyebrow. "I don't know. Do you?"

The only lawyers she knew were Darren's sister and Darren's cousin. And she suspected neither of them would want to offer their legal services. Even their new associate might feel like it was a conflict of interest to represent her.

Putting her hands flat on the table, she leaned toward Singer. "Don't you understand? I need to see what's happening with Darren. No one has told me anything." She sighed and dropped back into her chair. "His family is going to hate me."

"Porchia. Don't say anything else until we've had time to talk."

She looked toward the door. Her mouth gaped in amazement as Jason Montgomery walked in.

"Marc. I've been retained to represent Ms. Summers. You are not to question my client any further without my being present."

"Jason? What? Who?" She shook her head. "What are you doing here?"

"Sheriff? I'd like to speak with my client."

Singer stood. "That's fine. I'm done for now anyway."

Jason sat next to Porchia and leaned in close so they could not be overheard. "Darren is going to be fine. The sonofabitch is beyond lucky. The bullet slid between his side and his forearm. He has a nice deep trench on the inside of his arm and the outside of his chest. The docs cleaned out the area and patched him up. He'll be sore and bitch a lot, but he'll be back to normal in no time. They're keeping him overnight but just for observation."

The dam of tears she'd been containing broke. Hot, salty tears streamed down her face.

"I thought he was going to die. I saw the blood and just assumed."

Jason grabbed a roll of paper towels off the counter and handed her one. She wiped her eyes and blew her nose. "Thanks. But I don't understand. What happened? All that blood. What was it?"

"The bullet hit enough vessels to give him a nasty injury. The white shirt made the blood loss look a whole lot worse than it turned out to be." Jason grinned. "Reno told him that he'd been nailed worse by barbed wire than this bullet."

She sagged in relief from the news. "Thank you."

"No, thank you. Darren told us what happened. That without your fast thinking, he would be a dead man. We owe you a debt of gratitude. If you hadn't wacked the other guy on the back of the head, Darren says there was no way the bullet would have just grazed him."

Flinching, she glanced toward the sheriff and leaned in closer. "I couldn't think of anything else to do. I wasn't trying to kill him, only incapacitate him long enough to get away."

"Don't worry, Porchia. It was self-defense and if the sheriff's department sees it any other way, Montgomery and Montgomery will be with you the whole way."

"Thanks, Jason. I really appreciate it."

"Where will you be staying tonight?"

Her eyes opened wide. "Tonight?" She looked around at the deputies and technicians still combing her house for evidence. "I hadn't thought about it. I can call Tina or Tanya or one of my friends. They always have a spare bed."

"KC and Drake have offered you their spare room. KC said that's the least she could do for the woman who saved her brother's life."

Porchia smiled. "Thanks, but I don't want to put them out. I can probably get a room at the Evergreen B&B. Now that I think about it, I think getting a room there would be perfect, unless..." She glanced toward Marc Singer talking with one of his detectives. "Unless they decide to lock me up." She looked at Jason. "Am I going to be arrested?"

Jason took her hand. "No. But I'll go have a little chat with our sheriff and make sure he sees things our way."

In the end, Porchia was released for the night after Jason promised she'd be back at the station in the morning for additional questioning.

Since Porchia had been supplying the B&B with rolls and pastries for the past couple of years, the owners not only found her a room, but gave her the largest and nicest suite in the old house. While she valued their kindness, she was too tired and too drained to fully appreciate the amenities the room had to offer. After a long, hot shower, she hit the mattress face down.

She'd been asleep for only about thirty minutes when a knock at the door rattled her awake. If this was Singer with more questions, she was going to tell him to call her lawyer and slam the door in his face.

Shoving her long hair off her face, she staggered to the door. Bracing herself for Marc in his I-am-the-sheriff persona, she stumbled back a step upon seeing the man standing there. Pale but looking better than a recently shot man had a right to, Darren grunted as Porchia threw her arms around him with a cry of delight.

"Careful," he said. "I'm a little sore."

"Why aren't you in the hospital? Jason said you were staying overnight."

"Stop crying and I'll tell you."

"Can't help it," she said, sobbing into his shirt. "I thought you were dead, and damn Marc wouldn't let me leave to go to the hospital. But I wanted to be there. You have to know that. I thought you were going to die."

"Me too. Probably would have if you hadn't bashed that guy in the head."

She smiled through her tears. "Come in." She pulled him through the door and over to the chaise lounge, making sure to grab the unaffected side. "Sit. Sit. Talk to me."

He sat and made her sit beside him. "I'm fine. A little sore. A lot embarrassed but fine."

"I think you should be in the hospital."

He kissed her. "I needed to see you. I had to thank you for what you did. You were so brave."

"No, I wasn't. I was scared to death." She slugged his good arm. "And what were you doing at my house? Don't you know better than to walk into someone's house when they aren't expecting you?"

"Apparently not." He kissed her again, sending her heart rocketing around in her chest. "I got home. Everything was fine. I missed you. So I came back. And damn good thing I did too."

"What has your family told you?"

"Everything. Jason came back to my hospital room, where I swear every member of my family was, and told us all he could without violating attorney-client privilege. Let me tell you, my family is behind you one-hundred percent. I would be dead without you."

"I am so mad at myself. It's my fault that you and Mallory both got hurt. It's my fault that Slade Madden came to Whispering Springs."

He put his arm around her. "No, it's not your fault. He was a bad seed looking for a place to sprout."

"You know about the woman who was killed while I was in the car?"

He nodded. "Also not your fault. You're the innocent party here. You've done nothing wrong. Not back then and certainly not today."

She kissed him as relief poured through her. "Thanks."

It was nice to hear him say she was the innocent party, even if she didn't believe it. Seventeen years ago, she'd done nothing wrong. But now, she should have never let the situation get so out of control.

She hugged Darren around the waist.

Thank God for onyx trays and bad aims.

Chapter Twenty-One

The state fire marshal confirmed the arson of Heavenly Delights. Neither the money stolen from the bakery nor any of the stolen jewelry was on Slade's body when he died.

It took the sheriff's department a few days, but Deputy Brody found the fleabag hotel where Slade had been holed up when the hotel's owner called to complain about a gas smell. Concerned about the odor, the gas company was notified.

In the area on patrol, Brody met the gas company representative at the Stay-N-Play motel outside of town. The scent was traced to room five, which was in the back and on the end of the hotel. Inside, Slade's limited personal belongings were in the closet, along with two thousand in cash, ten watches, a dozen cocktail rings and a few gold necklaces. In the bathtub were four cans of gasoline.

With Mallory James's testimony and the physical evidence in the room, the sheriff's department and the Texas State Fire Marshal's office closed the case with the finding that Slade Madden had acted alone in the burglary and arson of Heavenly Delights and Randall Jewels and Keepsakes.

Closing the case did not mean slowing the gossip around Whispering Springs. Porchia felt every eye on her no matter where she went. Whispers followed her through stores.

Behind her back, a small group of townspeople who didn't really know her speculated that somehow she must have been in league with Slade Madden. She had even heard that she had probably killed Slade on purpose to keep him quiet about their dealings. She didn't try to defend or explain. That would have been a waste of her breath and her time. People would believe what they wanted to believe.

Close friends and those who knew her understood that all the gossip was just that…untrue rumors spread by nosey folks with too much time on their hands, who believed putting another person down would somehow make them look bigger. That never worked, but mean-spirited gossipers never learned.

For Porchia, the weeks that followed the fire were as if she were reliving her life from all those years ago. It had hurt then to be the subject of rumors and innuendos. It hurt now. Time didn't change that.

Meetings with her insurance adjuster and a couple of contractors confirmed what she had feared since the night of the fire. The bakery was beyond repair. The most cost-efficient option was to demolish the damage and rebuild from the ground up. Porchia just wasn't sure she had the fortitude to go through the months and months required to start again.

Porchia told her employees that they needed to find other jobs. Insurance would pay on her fire claim, but cutting a check of that size took time.

She abandoned the idea of baking from her home and spent days getting all her brides rescheduled with other bakeries, mostly in and around Dallas. Her personal kitchen simply didn't have the equipment required to produce professional cakes. Once that decision was made and all the cakes had been farmed out, she found herself with too much time on her hands and a mind with nothing to concentrate on except how much she had screwed up her life.

Through it all, Darren stood by her. He made her go out to dinner when she might have stayed hidden in her house. He dragged her to Leo's for drinks with the gang and out to his house for horseback rides.

And every time they made love, he made her feel like a princess. The very last thing she wanted to do was hurt him in any way. However, one idea circled through over and over. Maybe her staying in Whispering Springs and trying to rebuild after someone from her past had brought so much trouble to town wasn't the best idea. She had started over in a new, unfamiliar place before. She could do it again, but moving away from a man she loved would be heartbreaking.

As October rolled into November, the days got shorter and the weather got cooler, but she found no answers to all her questions about her future. However, some good did come from those idle weeks. She spoke with her parents more regularly than she had in years.

The initial call to tell them what had happened had been nerve racking. They, of course, had been shocked and scandalized to hear their only child was once again involved in the death of another individual. And while they said all the right words about her losing the bakery, Porchia felt an undercurrent of relief from them, as though they were glad that period of her life was over. When her mother asked her to come home—*home*—for Thanksgiving, Porchia had cried. It'd been the first time in years her parents had indicated they would like to have her back in Atlanta on a more permanent basis. Could she go home again?

Camping with the Montgomery clan had crystalized for her that she wanted a family-centered life. Witnessing the love and interaction among Montgomery family members had brought her an appreciation for family, and in turn, her parents. Sure, they had been hard on her when she'd screwed up, but she had been the one to disappoint them. Could she repair the fence between them?

On days when she and Darren didn't see each other, they spoke by phone, long, drawn-out conversations about anything and everything. Porchia had always known that ranching was a dirty, exhausting job, but seeing it in action when she visited the D&R gave her a greater appreciation for Darren's life. She didn't visit the ranch as much as she could have—after all, time on her hands was ample. But the ranch house was small, and with newlyweds Reno and Magda living there, she felt her presence to be an imposition, regardless of what Darren, Reno and Magda said.

It was about ten days before Thanksgiving when Darren picked her up for dinner. He chose a small, intimate steakhouse in Tyler, a little over an hour away. Bad of her she knew, but she couldn't help but wonder if their numerous dates lately to other towns besides Whispering Springs were because he was tired of all the nasty gossip about her.

The restaurant was located in an old building that had once been a county jail. The cells were still in place, albeit now divided to make single-table, private dining areas.

As they were shown to one of the private dining tables, Porchia said, "I have always wanted to come here. I've heard about it forever."

Darren pulled out her chair and she sat. How chivalrous. Something about a guy holding out a chair for her made all her femaleness stretch and preen.

"I've only been here once," he said. "The steaks were juicy and the beer was cold. I was a happy camper."

She laughed. "A perfect combo."

After they ordered, he brought up Thanksgiving. "The family is getting together at the Bar M ranch. Everyone will be there." He grinned. "It was crowded before all the spouses and children. It'll be positively nuts this year. You're gonna love it. Mom and Dad will be glad to see you."

Her stomach roiled. She had to tell him about Thanksgiving in Atlanta. But every time she looked at him, her heart sighed and rolled over like a puppy demanding a tummy rub. She was head-over-heels in love with this man. She hadn't told him as she hadn't decided exactly what she was going to do about the realization.

"You got quiet," he said, taking her hand. "You know my family loves you. You have to know I love you."

Her lungs seized, making breathing almost impossible. Forcing in a gulp of air, she said, "I…" She hesitated.

He squeezed her hand. "It's okay. You don't have to love me back, but you will. I'll do anything and everything to win your heart."

"Oh, Darren." She touched his cheek. "You are so dear to me. Your family has been beyond wonderful and welcoming. I love them so much."

He winced and then kissed her palm. "Great. Then you'll spend Thanksgiving with us."

Tears formed in her eyes. She hated that crying was her response to every strong emotion, be it anger or happiness. Right now, she was a jumble of conflicting emotions.

"I do love you, Darren. You are the man every little girl dreams of falling in love with."

He grew serious. "I hear a *but* at the end of your sentence."

Darren didn't even comment on her saying she loved him. Damn man knew her simply too well. He heard the hesitation in her voice.

She pulled her hand free from his to use her napkin to dab at her eyes. Damn make-up. "Being with your family has made me realize how much I miss my own. I have been apart from my parents for more than half my lifetime. I want to see if I can have the type of relationship with them that you do with your parents."

He nodded, "I can understand that."

"What I'm trying to say is that I'm going back to Atlanta."

He sat back in his chair, the surprise evident in his expression. "When? And for how long?"

"Soon. My flight leaves on Tuesday."

"When will you be back?"

"I don't know. I honestly don't. I know I'll be there for Thanksgiving. And if we can repair the damage, well, I just don't know. I didn't realize how much I missed having my mom and dad in my life until I met yours."

With the impeccable timing of every waiter in the world, theirs chose that moment to deliver their sizzling steaks. What looked delicious was tasteless for Porchia. She might as well have been chewing rubber.

Darren changed the subject to a new horse he was looking at. Relieved at the reprieve, she grabbed the lifeline he had tossed and they talked horses the rest of the meal. As he paid the check, she dreaded the drive home. His entire demeanor had flipped like a light switch as soon as she'd mentioned going to Atlanta.

"Darren," she said as he pulled from the drive. "Talk to me."

"We've been talking all night."

She sighed. "You're upset with me."

He glanced toward her, his lips forming a tense line across his mouth. "How am I supposed to feel? One minute you tell me that you love me, and with the next sentence, you blast my high like a skeet pigeon."

"I didn't mean… I'm sorry, but I have to try to put my family back together. I busted it apart. It's my job to fix it."

"Bullshit."

The animosity in his voice hit like a tidal wave.

"What did you say?"

"I said bullshit. You were a child. You made a mistake. Hell, all kids do. That's how we learn. You think I didn't fuck up a million times growing up? Reno? KC? You think Clint and Nadine only loved us and kept us safe because we were perfect?" He laughed, but it lacked any humor. "Your parents have done a total mind fuck on you. Every teenager makes horrible decisions. That's what those years are for. Your parents were the adults. If your family disintegrated, it was their fault, not yours."

Hot anger flared inside her. "How dare you talk about my parents like that? You don't know them. You don't understand how much pressure my father is under. You can't understand how important his career is. Paul Randolph is a prominent member of Atlanta society. He makes life and death decisions every day."

Confusion furrowed his brow. "Randolph? You have a different last name from your father?"

"And my mother. I brought so much shame to the Randolph name. Taking my mother's maiden name was the least I could do."

"And they let you?" He scoffed. "Your folks are not only idiots, they're bad parents."

Her back stiffened. "How dare you?"

"How dare *they* let a kid carry such guilt for all these years? How dare they let their only child change her last name because they were embarrassed? Mom and Dad would take turns kicking our asses if any of their kids had tried to dump the Montgomery name."

She turned to stare out the windshield. "I'm done talking about this."

"What if I'm not?"

She shot him her best glare. "Then talk to yourself and leave me the fuck out of it."

When he pulled up to her house after an interminable drive, she opened her door. "Don't get out. I can see myself in." She slid out and slammed the door.

"Porchia. Wait."

She turned. He was standing inside the driver's open door talking over the top of his truck.

"Remember this…I love you. I will always take your side over the world's, even if the world happens to be the two people who gave you life. But that doesn't mean I'll wait for you forever. It's your decision to make."

He got back into the truck and drove away.

Tuesday morning, Porchia boarded her flight, not having heard from Darren since their date. It pained her to leave things so unsettled with him. She had called the house last night but Magda had said the guys were still in the field. There was something in Magda's voice that suggested the story was total BS. She wasn't sure if Magda was protecting her new brother-in-law by her own accord, or if Darren had been standing next to Magda the whole time they'd been on the phone. She'd never know for sure, but what she did know was that he hadn't returned her call.

It was raining cats and dogs when she landed at Atlanta International Airport. When she got to the baggage claim area, a chauffeur was holding up a sign with her name, or rather Katherine P.S. Randolph on it.

"I'm Katherine Randolph." The name sounded foreign on her tongue.

"Yes, ma'am. Your mother had a lunch engagement and could not come. I'm Jimmy North. I work for your parents."

Her first thought was, "Home, James!" but concerned he would think she was making fun of his name, she kept the joke to herself. Embarrassing her parents with stupid comments would not get this visit off on the correct foot.

They pulled through the elaborate iron gates that protected her parents from the hoi polloi, even from those within their own Buckhead neighborhood. Jimmy followed the drive up and around the massive fountain to stop the Mercedes at the front door.

Porchia stepped from the car.

Growing up, she'd thought the large mansion to be magical. Now it looked impressive, as though announcing to the world how much money the occupants must have.

The front door opened and a young, thin, dark-haired woman Porchia didn't know stood there. Dressed in a pencil skirt, matched sweater set and a strand of pearls, she was the quintessential Georgia peach as designed by Porchia's mother.

"Hello," the woman said. "Welcome home. I'm Rudy Wells, your mother's new personal secretary." The woman's Southern accent was so thick Porchia wasn't sure if it was natural or enhanced. There was a tangible lack of warmth exhibited by most Southern-bred ladies.

For some reason, this woman rubbed Porchia the wrong way. Maybe it was her manner of welcoming Porchia into her own family's home. Or maybe it was the way she seemed to be looking down her nose at Porchia, as one did when one encountered a foul odor.

Porchia nodded. "Hello. Is my mother home?"

"I'm sorry. She's been delayed at the club."

The club. Ah. Her mother's home away from home.

"In fact," Rudy added, "Jimmy, as soon as you unload Katherine's luggage, you need to pick up Mrs. Randolph. I'll let her know you're on your way."

Jimmy set the two pieces of luggage on the drive. "Do you need me to take these up for you?" he asked Porchia. "I'll be happy to."

"No, that's fine. I can manage."

Jimmy doffed an imaginary hat and left.

Porchia looked at the snide woman still standing in the doorway. "Well, don't just stand there. Help me with my luggage."

It gave Porchia perverse pleasure to see the stunned face and fish lip reaction on Miss Prissy Pants.

"Oh, and the name is Porchia, not Katherine."

Rudy blew out a breath. "I'll show you to your room," she said, lifting the small carry-on tote bag, leaving the two larger pieces for Porchia.

Porchia stifled a snort of pleasure, grabbed the handles on her bags and rolled them up the stairs and into the grand foyer. Rudy was headed up the curved staircase but stopped long enough to look down at Porchia. Then she tossed her hair over her shoulder and continued climbing.

Did this fool not realize that Porchia had grown up in this house? Did she really think Porchia didn't know about the luggage elevator?

With a roll of her eyes, Porchia wheeled her luggage to the small dumbwaiter, loaded her bags and started the lift rising. Only then did she head up the stairs.

Chapter Twenty-Two

June Randolph arrived ninety minutes after Porchia. From her upstairs bedroom window, Porchia watched her mother gracefully exit the rear seat of the Mercedes sedan. Each fluid movement, high-heeled step and elegant hand gesture announced that June Randolph was a proper Southern lady, which had always amused Porchia since her mother had been born to a lower middle class family in Arkansas. She had moved to Whispering Springs, Texas, when Porchia's grandfather had taken a job in an oil field. All her mother's refinements had come after she'd met law student Paul Randolph.

Porchia's father had been raised in Atlanta by a Supreme Court judge and his stay-at-home wife. He'd been indoctrinated since birth with the charm and grace all Southern gentlemen should exhibit. Not following in his father's judicial footprints had never entered his mind. He searched for, and found, the perfect woman he could mold into a wife to help propel him toward his goals.

He had wanted a male heir to carry on the family name and career, but it was never meant to be. After several miscarriages, he and June had Katherine Porchia Summers Randolph. They had loved Katherine, but she'd fought the constraints of being a Randolph as soon as she could voice her opinion. Nonetheless, they were proud of her academic and athletic achievements. The incident with Slade Madden had destroyed their faith in their daughter.

Porchia wanted to reconnect with her parents. She wanted what Darren shared with his parents…love…trust…respect.

She hurried down the stairs to greet her mother as she entered the mansion. "Mom," Porchia cried.

June raised her gaze to watch her daughter rush down the stairs. "Katherine," she admonished. "Is that how you enter a room?"

Porchia slowed, taking the last four steps with precise, measured movements. "That's much better," June praised. "Now, come give your mother a kiss."

For June, kissing meant air-kisses above each cheek. If her lips were to actually touch another's face, her artfully applied lipstick could smudge, or leave a mark on another's face. Neither outcome was acceptable.

June air-kissed Porchia, a daughter she hadn't seen in months, as though it were a lunch with a friend. Porchia placed her uncolored lips on her mother's cheek, which produced a gasp. But her mother recovered quickly and overlooked the perceived *faux pas*.

Holding her daughter at arm's length, she studied Porchia. "Darling. Your hair." June picked up the strands of long blond hair and tsked. "You know that long hair ages the face of a mature-aged woman."

"I'm only thirty-two," Porchia protested.

"Still," her mother said on an exhaled sigh. "I'll call Mr. Nick and see if we can get you an emergency appointment for this week. It'll be hard because he's the best and everyone in Atlanta wants him to do their hair, but he owes me a favor or two, so I'm sure I can get him to see you."

Her mother sighed a few more times. "And these clothes."

Porchia looked down at her khaki cargo pants and polo shirt. "What? It's all new."

"I'm sure it is," her mother replied, followed by a long-suffering sigh. "But you know how slacks make your hips and thighs look unnaturally large."

Porchia looked down at her size-ten body and couldn't think of anything to say.

"No problem, my dear. This will give us an excellent excuse to do some shopping tomorrow. I do hope you have a skirt for dinner." June checked her watch. "We have time for a quick cocktail. That should give you adequate time to put your face on and change clothes."

Putting her face on meant make-up. Unlike her Whispering Springs life where powder, eyeliner and lipstick would constitute make-up on a good day, her mother felt any woman was underdressed without base, powder, blush, eye shadow, liner and lip color. And Porchia might as well drag out the under-eye concealer or she'd hear about that over dinner.

She allowed herself to be led into a small room off her father's office. Here, her mother had set up her own office. Decorated in soft pastel colors, the room sported a delicate writing desk, lounger, sofa and a couple of wingback, upholstered chairs. In the corner, her mother had a small tea tray with decanters of varying shades of brown down to clear liquid. Her mother was quite the mixologist.

"I'm having a very dry martini," June said. "What would you like?"

Porchia wanted a beer, very cold and preferably in a chilled, icy mug. She knew, however, that request would not be well-received. "What you're having is fine."

The first sip made Porchia's eyes water. She wasn't that much of a hard-liquor gal. The second one went down better, not much better, but at least she felt like she could keep it down.

Her mother stretched out on her fainting couch, as Porchia has always referred to it, and took a long drink from her glass. "Ah," her mother said. "Much better." She caught Porchia's gaze. "The morning was brutal. I am in charge of the Christmas decorations for the flower club and, I'm sad to say, the only taste Mabel Steinbrenner has is in her mouth. The woman thought we should alternate red and white poinsettias in the entry hall. Can you imagine such a tacky display?" She took another gulp of her martini. "Why, we'd be the laughing stock of Atlanta. We've always done solid red. It's so much more dignified and classic."

Porchia doubted they'd be the laughing stock of anywhere, much less Atlanta. No one would even notice the alternating colors. And Porchia could envision a beautiful candy-cane effect with the red and white, but she knew better than to proffer an opinion not sought. So she simply said, "Uh-huh."

"Oh, you remember Sally Pope, don't you? She's married to Dr. Harry

Pope, the cardiac surgeon. I think they had a son about your age. Myron Pope. You remember Myron, don't you, dear?"

Oh, yeah, she remembered Myron Pope. He was a couple of years older than her, had a face so scarred by acne everyone called him pizza face, and—if she remembered correctly—had only a passing acquaintance with soap.

"Uh-huh. I remember him."

"Well," her mother said. "Sally and Harris belong to the same golf club we do, and we saw them just the other night. Myron has moved back to Atlanta to be closer to them. Isn't that great? I told Sally you'd love to see Myron, so we're meeting them at the club for dinner on Wednesday evening. Won't that be fun? You and Myron have so much in common."

"Uh-huh. But that's the night before Thanksgiving. Won't we have a lot to do that evening?"

"I can't think of what. Cook will be preparing the next day's meal. No, I think an evening with the Popes is just the perfect way to start the holiday."

Her mother had called the family's personal chef Cook for as long as Porchia could remember. It didn't matter if the chef was male or female or even if they had a preference of how they'd like to be referred to. It was always Cook.

"Mother, don't you want to talk about what happened in Texas? With Slade and my bakery?"

June stood and walked over to the teacart bar. After refilling her martini glass to the rim, she turned to face Porchia and took a long swallow. "That business in Texas is over. It was unpleasant for me to think about, much less to speak of it. My advice, dear, is to simply put it out of your mind and move on. The past is the past. Now…" She checked the Patek Phillippe on her wrist.

Porchia had never seen that particular diamond watch, so she assumed it was some ridiculously expensive gift from her father.

"Now," her mother continued, "you need to get dressed for dinner. And please put your face on and do something with that stringy hair. I'll telephone Mr. Nick while you dress." She waved her hand. "Go on. I wouldn't want you to have to hurry."

Porchia finished her drink, set the glass on the teacart and headed up to the bedroom assigned her. She didn't really have a designated bedroom here any longer. After she'd opted to not move back home after college, her mother had disposed of all Porchia's clutter and redecorated it as guestroom, not that June and Paul had occasion to entertain overnight that much.

The martini was doing its trick. Porchia felt the intoxicating drink in the swirl of her brain. She had a couple of hours before dinner, more than enough time to lie down and still have plenty of leeway in her schedule. She set her phone alarm for thirty minutes and fell face-first on the mattress.

When she awoke—fuzzy-brained and disoriented—it took a cold shower to clear the cobwebs. After carefully applying her make-up, every layer as expected by her mother, she artfully twisted her hair into an up-do. Dressed in the only skirt she'd brought, a nice blouse and a pair of loafers, she girded herself for her meeting with her father.

She found her parents in the formal living room, each holding a martini glass.

"Katherine," her father said. "How nice to see you."

She'd thought he might come over to her, hug her or at minimum, give her an air-kiss. He did nothing but grant her the smile she'd seen him give large political donors.

"Hello, Father. It's nice to see the house hasn't changed much."

"Oh, well," her mother said. "You know how your father dislikes change."

"It's not that I dislike change," Paul said. "It's that change for change's sake is a waste of good money."

"Yes, dear," her mother said. "Of course."

Porchia wanted to gag, but these were her parents. She'd come here to rebuild those bridges she'd burned so many years ago.

"Well, it's nice to be home," she said.

"What are your plans?" Paul asked.

"I'm not sure. The bakery is a total loss."

"Are you having any trouble with your insurance paying?" Paul asked. "I can certainly give them a call if so."

Porchia was sure a phone call from Judge Randolph would speed the process, but she had never liked to use pull to get something if she could avoid it.

"No, but thank you. My agent has been more than responsive, so I should have my check soon."

"You'll be coming into the trust fund my sister left you soon. Do you have plans for that?"

"Oh, Paul. Let's not talk business. Let's just go in and have a nice dinner." Brackets of disappointment appeared around her mother's lips.

Porchia had no idea how much, or how little, was in the trust fund that Aunt Betty had left her. Her father's sister had died before marrying and without any children. She'd left her estate to her niece when Porchia had been only ten. She did need to learn more about trusts and what would happen when she turned thirty-five, but it seemed more like a story from her childhood than a reality of adulthood.

Dinner was a quiet affair. Mostly the sound of sterling silver flatware clicking on fine china broke the silence. Her father and mother talked about their days, who they'd seen and what difficulties they'd dealt with. A couple of times, Porchia wondered if they remembered she was there. They tried to include her in the conversation but seemed at a loss what to ask her about. However, it became glaringly apparent her mother did not want to talk about the incident with Slade and her father would follow her lead.

The next day, as promised, Mr. Nick met Porchia and June at his shop at eight a.m. Apparently, this was an obscenely early hour for Mr. Nick, who usually didn't take his first client until closer to ten. He immediately declared Porchia's hair a disaster and insisted she needed six to eight inches cut to rid her of such an unsightly mess. Porchia almost left right then. After a long, drawn-out consultation with June and a verbal battle with Porchia, he agreed to cut only two inches.

The sonofabitch, in cahoots with her mother, cut at least five inches off. It still left her with enough length she could pull it back, but the sight of all her hair scattered on the floor made her gasp.

From there, Jimmy drove her mother and her to a small, upscale boutique where the racks were loaded with name-brand items. June pulled a few garments for Porchia to try on.

"Really, Katherine," her mother said. "You just have to have something appropriate to wear for dinner tonight."

Appropriate turned out to be six skirts, eight blouses, five dresses and four pairs of heels. Her mother also tossed onto the growing pile a couple of undergarment foundations to help with that little stomach budge, as June so politely put it.

Dinner at the club with Harry and Sally Pope and their son was as horrible as Porchia had feared. Oh, not that Myron hadn't finally got that acne cleared up and come to love soap. He had. He had a Harvard law degree and an opinion of himself that no one could ever top.

Her mother found him charming and an ideal companion.

Porchia did not.

She made it through Thanksgiving without stabbing herself in the eye, but only because she was worried she'd not die but only be blind. Every time she got the urge to leave, she reminded herself that June and Paul were her parents, the ones who'd given her life. They deserved her love and respect.

After she'd been in Atlanta for a week, she pined for her home in Whispering Springs, but mostly she missed Darren. She picked up the phone to call him so many times his name was the first suggestion under her phone's suggested-call list.

Fifteen days before Christmas, she got Magda on the phone.

"How's married life?" Porchia asked.

"Pretty much the same as unmarried life," Magda said with a laugh. "How are you? We're all wasting away here without all your pastry goodness."

Porchia chuckled. "Thanks, but I'm pretty sure I'm not that missed."

"Depend on who's doing the missing."

Porchia's breath caught. "Someone there missing me?"

"Maybe," Magda said with a laugh. "And if someone was missing you, he'd be a total ass to live with, if you get my drift."

A thrill ran through Porchia. Darren did miss her. For the first time since she'd arrived in Atlanta, she felt like Porchia again, and not like Katherine.

"How are things going with your parents?" Magda asked.

"Oh, they're going."

"What does that mean?"

"It means… Hell, I don't know what it means. It's just so different here. In their own way, I'm sure my parents love me and are glad I'm here. But on the other hand, I think they were used to their lives without an adult offspring living with them."

"So when you coming home?"

Porchia sighed. "I don't know. My business is gone. My family lives in Georgia, not Texas."

"There are different kinds of families. There are the ones you are related to by blood. You have no choice there. But then there are the families you choose to love. Your friends. Your lover. You have to decide which family makes you the happiest."

Magda's words resounded in Porchia. What she said made sense. What was left for Porchia to decide was which family would make her the happiest.

That evening as she dressed for dinner, she reminisced about her years in Texas. How much simpler her life was there. No putting on her face before breakfast, and even when she did apply make-up, it was minimal. Lots of jeans, T-shirts and cowboy boots. Now, it was skirts and more skirts, jewelry and heels. Not that she didn't look great in her new clothes with her new hair style, but was it her? Did she still fit into this world?

Her mother continued to apply what she called motherly concern to Porchia's imperfections. So far, Porchia had undergone a haircut—albeit not as much as her mother would prefer—new clothes, weekly manicures, and now her mother had set her up for tennis lessons at the club.

"I spoke with Tony, and he's penciled you in today for a lesson. I'm sure you don't have an appropriate tennis dress, so we'll need to hurry to get to Tennis and More to get you something to wear."

"Mother. I told you I don't have any interest in tennis lessons."

Her mother frowned, or would have if her botoxed brow would have allowed it. "Golf then?" She clucked her displeasure. "Not really an activity a lady would engage in, but then you have been out of my influence. It's not your fault that my mother didn't teach you all the proper ways of a lady."

Porchia sighed. "Grandma Summers was wonderful to me."

June dabbed her lips with the linen breakfast napkin. "I know she was, Katherine."

Porchia sighed again. "You remember that I told you I go by Porchia now."

Her mother wrinkled her nose. "It sounds like a car. Katherine is so much more dignified."

"Hey. You gave me that name."

"Yes, well, it was a youthful discretion on our part." Her mother's face brightened. "I've been meaning to tell you. Myron Pope is quite taken with you. Sally is over the moon. I was thinking we should have them over for dinner this weekend."

The idea of Myron Pope touching her or kissing her almost had Porchia losing her breakfast. He was a worm.

"Sally told me that Myron said you were an excellent conversationalist."

Porchia laughed. "Mother. All the man talked about was himself."

"Well, that is usually a man's favorite subject, isn't it?" Her mother chuckled. "Now hurry up and change clothes so we can get to Tennis and More when it opens. It is so good of Tony to work you into his packed schedule."

Porchia didn't really want to learn to play tennis, but her brain was slowly but surely shriveling up and dying cell by cell from the boredom. And frankly, tennis was better than another luncheon with her mother. And she needed some exercise.

She missed baking. The one time she'd mentioned baking a cake for dessert, her mother and Cook almost had a case of Southern vapors.

She even missed getting up at five-thirty in the morning. She'd gotten up early a couple of times, headed down for coffee and run into her father, who'd seemed surprised to find her, as though he'd forgotten she was home. About the only time she saw him was at dinner. He left for court before her mother rose for the day. After dinner, he generally retired to his study to read his law journals.

On Friday, the Popes arrived for cocktails at seven, followed by dinner. Porchia dressed in a form-fitting royal-blue dress with a pair of leather kitten heels. After wrapping her hair into a French twist, she put on a pair of chandelier-style sapphire earrings. As she made her way down the staircase, she studied Myron Pope talking with her father. Dressed in a tailored thousand-dollar grey suit, Myron looked like a man who had money, lots and lots of money. He projected an air of entitlement and secure social standing, not that he'd done anything to earn that place in Atlanta society other than be born to wealthy parents.

"There she is," her father said as she entered the formal living room.

"Hello, darling," her mother said, giving Porchia the standard air-kisses.

"She always did love to make an entrance and have the spotlight on her," Myron said with a smile. "You're looking lovely this evening, Katherine." He took her hands and bussed her cheek with his lips. "I'm glad we're together again."

So far, Porchia had bitten her tongue to the point where she wondered if the tip would simply flop to the floor if she opened her mouth. She gritted her teeth and twisted her lips into a smile.

"What are we all drinking?" she asked, pulling her hands free. "Can I get anyone a refill?"

Her mother lifted her martini glass. "Sally and I would love a couple of fresh ones, darling."

At one time, her parents had a butler who would do the bartending duties as well as answer the door. But in an effort to remain in touch with the simpler lifestyle, they'd let the butler go and had only kept a cook, June's social secretary and a maid to help Cook keep the house.

"I've got it, honey," her father said and hurried to the bar. There, he retrieved the icy pitcher of dry martinis. "What would you like, Katherine?"

What Katherine would like was to be called Porchia and for someone to toss her a beer, not that she could verbalize those two opinions. Her mother would need smelling salts to recover.

"A martini is fine," Porchia said. Besides, the alcohol might numb her enough to get through the evening without jerking what she suspected was a toupee off Myron's head.

Cook stepped into the room and spoke quietly with Porchia's father. He glanced over at Porchia and then responded to Cook, who hurried out of the room. Probably some terrible meat emergency that would send her mother into a good old-fashion swoon if she found out. But her father and Cook spoke much too softly for their voices to travel, and Porchia was left out in the cold. However, that little glance from her dad did make her curious. She guzzled the first martini her father handed her and immediately got a refill. The doorbell rang as the rim of the martini glass touched her lips.

"I'll get it," she said, glad to have any reason to leave the room. She hurried to the foyer before an objection could be made.

She threw the door open and her mouth fell agape.

"Porchia?" Darren asked.

Chapter Twenty-Three

It'd taken Darren a couple of days to wheedle Porchia's parents' address out of his sister, KC. He'd finally had to break down and tell her the truth…that he was going after Porchia because he was in love with her. KC had screamed with joy, which had made his ears hurt and got everyone else in the office coming to see what the problem was.

Damn his sister. Now the entire Montgomery & Montgomery office knew how he felt about Porchia. If she kicked him back to Texas, everyone would know that too. Still, he had to try.

Darren was stunned when the airport cab pulled up to the gate of an old, very large, extremely ornate Southern mansion. Porchia had never mentioned coming from money. In fact, he'd even heard her complain about her struggle to make ends meet on more than one occasion.

The cab pulled up to an elaborate iron gate and rolled forward enough to allow Darren to reach the callbox button.

Darren rang and waited for an answer.

"Yes?" a female voice said.

Darren leaned his head out the window and spoke in a loud voice. "I'm a friend of Porchia Summers. I was told she would be here."

"Porchia?"

"That's correct."

"One minute please."

There was a long pause and then the gate swung open slowly.

While waiting through the long pause before the gate opened, Darren wondered if he'd gotten the wrong address. However, this must be the right address since the person at the other end of the security callbox allowed the cab to proceed up a paved curved drive to park in front of a set of double doors.

After paying the driver, Darren set his duffle bag off to the side of the door and rang the bell. While he waited for someone to answer, his heart raced like a thoroughbred coming down the home stretch.

He'd hoped Porchia's reaction to his arrival would be to throw her arms around his neck with a cry of delight. What he got was a somewhat more reserved reaction.

She opened the door, a bright smile on her face that instantly dropped into a stupefied expression.

Darren's hungry gaze ran over her, from her heels, up her legs—was she wearing nylons?—to a dress that accented her luscious curves to her beautiful face—was she wearing eye shadow?—to a hairstyle that made her look elegant and way out of his league.

He looked down at his jeans, cowboy boots and simple snap shirt. She didn't just look out of his league, she was.

He gulped. "Porchia?"

"Darren? What are you doing here?"

"I…" He turned to leave. "I think I've made a mistake."

"Wait." She grabbed his arm. "Don't go."

"Who's there, Katherine?" a male voice asked from the foyer.

Katherine? Did Porchia have a twin sister she'd never mentioned?

"A friend," Porchia answered.

"Well, invite your friend in."

"Um…" A flush climbed up her neck. "Do you want to come in?"

"Katherine? Who's Katherine?" Darren asked.

Porchia shut her eyes for a minute as though gaining strength to continue. "That's me. Katherine is my first name. Porchia is my middle name."

An older man stepped up to the door. The resemblance was uncanny.

"Please come in," he said. "Apparently, Katherine has forgotten every manner we ever taught her."

Darren held out his hand. "I'm Darren Montgomery."

"Paul Randolph." The man's handshake was firm and strong. "Come in."

He stepped back to allow Darren to enter. Porchia moved to the side, her fingers locked in front of her.

By now, Darren was confused. Katherine, not Porchia. Randolph, not Summers. A freaking mansion instead of the simple home he'd expected.

Who was Porchia Summers?

"Can I get you a cocktail?" Paul asked as he led Darren into a plush living room.

"Sure," Darren said. He drew in a breath to ask for a beer but then noticed the other people in the room. He also saw that no one had a beer.

"I'll have whatever you're having," he said to Porchia's father.

"Katherine," her mother said. "Would you like to do the introductions?"

"What?" Porchia's head snapped toward a woman who could only be her mother. "Oh, sure. Darren, this is Dr. Harry Pope, his wife, Sally, and their son, Myron."

Darren shook hands with the Popes and realized he'd walked in on a small dinner party.

"I apologize," he said. "I meant to surprise Porchia, er, Katherine, and I seem to have intruded on your dinner party. I'll finish my drink and be on my way."

"Oh, no, Darren," Porchia said. "You've come all the way from Texas. You really must stay."

"Well, darling," her mother said. "He said he had to be going. We wouldn't want to interfere with his evening plans."

"I think Katherine is right," Paul said. "You should stay for dinner. Katherine, could you let Cook know?"

"Of course." Porchia leaned in to whisper, "Don't leave. I'll be right back."

Paul Randolph handed him a chilled martini glass. "To your health," he said, and lifted the fine crystal to his lips.

Darren took a swallow and almost gasped. Martini, his ass. Why didn't they just call the drink Iced Gin and be done with it?

The fine crystal he held felt fragile in his thick, rough hands. And he knew enough about glassware to realize the thinner the rim, the more expensive the glass. He could only imagine the cost of this single glass.

"So, Mr. Montgomery," Porchia's mother said. "What is it that you do?"

He turned toward Mrs. Randolph. "I'm a rancher, ma'am."

"How nice," she said with a tight smile, and Darren knew he'd been insulted. Oh, not by words, but certainly by tone.

"Well, cowboy," Myron Pope said. "Hope you remembered to knock the cow manure off your boots."

June Randolph chuckled behind her martini stemware. The other woman, Mrs. Pope, openly chuckled.

"You are so clever, honey," she said to her son.

Porchia walked in and looked around at the other adults, then squinted her eyes. "What did I miss?"

"Oh, Myron was making a little joke. He's just so quick witted," her mother said.

A joke at Darren's expense, but to say that would only reflect poorly on him, not on the overgrown momma's boy.

"Dinner's ready," Porchia said.

"I really shouldn't stay," Darren said.

Porchia linked her arm through his. "Oh, but you must." The twinkle in her eye made him a little nervous. "You must get to know my parents and their friends."

He allowed her to escort him into a formal dining room set for seven. Two at each end, three on one side and two on the other. She made straight for the side of the table with two place settings.

"Katherine," her mother said, halting their progress. "Wouldn't you and… your friend like to sit with Myron? I'm sure you'd have much more to talk with him about than I would."

"Oh, no, but thank you, Mother."

She practically dragged him around the table to the side away from Myron. Darren pulled her chair back for her to sit before he took his seat.

Cook entered and served the soup course. It was a watery, beef-based broth. In Darren's opinion, it wasn't much of a soup, but when in Rome… He lifted his spoon and sipped.

As soon as possible, he was sending a large bouquet of flowers to his mother. Growing up, his family never ate with formal restrictions. However, she'd made sure every one of them knew what spoon, fork or knife to use. That information had come in handy only once in his life…when he'd been an escort for a debutante. Who would have thought he would need the information again?

"Tell us more about yourself, Mr. Montgomery," Porchia's mother said. "Growing up in the wilds of Texas must have been interesting."

"Yes, ma'am," he said. "I'm sure it would be. However, I wouldn't know. My family ran a cattle ranch in Florida. My brother and I moved to Texas after college to start our own ranch."

He started to tell her to call him Darren, but at the last minute thought, screw her.

"How industrious of you. Would we know the owners of the ranch your parents worked on?"

Porchia opened her mouth, but he put his hand on her knee and squeezed.

"I doubt it, Mrs. Randolph. The ranch was the Double Down. Are you familiar with it?"

She looked at her husband, who shook his head. "I'm not." She turned to her friend. "Sally. You and Harry go to Florida often. You ever heard of the Double Down?"

Sally dabbed her lips with the crisp, white linen napkin. "I'm sorry, June, but Harry and I just don't have anything to do with Florida industry."

"Unless you're talking your personal support of the clothing stores there," her husband said.

That brought chuckles around the table. Darren smiled, but he doubted he'd ever dined with more self-important prigs in his whole life. And what was blowing his mind was how easily Porchia fit into this circle of snobs.

"Mr. Montgomery."

Darren looked across the table at the only other unattached man in the room. Oh, he saw clearly that the two mothers were scheming, and neither they nor the son seemed happy that Darren had shown up to throw a monkey wrench into their match-making plans.

"Yes? It's Myron, right?"

"That's right. I was just wondering how long you were planning on being in town."

Darren sat back in his chair and draped his arm ever so casually on the back of Porchia's chair. "Well," he said with a drawl. "I guess that's up to Po— Katherine. I might be a day. I might be here a week."

The scowl on the other man's face conveyed his displeasure.

"Katherine has quite a heavy holiday party schedule, don't you, dear?" her mother said. "I believe our first engagement is tomorrow evening. That reminds me, Katherine. Did you remember to send Jimmy to pick up your evening gown for tomorrow night's ball?"

Jimmy? Darren looked at Porchia with an arched eyebrow. "Jimmy?" he mouthed.

She shook her head. "Yes, Mother. Jimmy picked it up at the same time he got yours. Remember? You were unhappy with the color of my gown."

"That's right." June looked at Sally. "The young people these days. Katherine's gown is yellow. I tried to tell her it will never work with her skin tone and white hair, but would she listen to me? Of course not." She drained the remainder of the martini she'd brought to the table.

"I think you'll look lovely tomorrow night," Myron said. "A little extra blush and I bet you will not look washed out at all. Isn't that right, Mother?"

Sally Pope nodded. "I think Myron's correct," she said to June. "He has an eye for things like that."

The salad course came and went. If his life depended on it, Darren was fairly certain he could not list one vegetable in it other than lettuce, and even that had been purple.

He turned to Porchia's father. "Por—Katherine tells me you're a judge."

"That's correct."

"You must have had some interesting cases come before you over the years."

"A few," Paul conceded.

"Tell him about the case of the woman who stole hams by putting them up her skirt."

Paul chuckled. "That was a good one."

"And definitely not dinner material," Porchia's mother said, her brackets of disapproval reappearing around her mouth. "Myron, tell us about the law practice you've joined here in Atlanta. I'm assuming you're in line for a partnership."

Myron began telling his life history, or maybe it was the history of cheese. Darren didn't know and didn't care. He wasn't listening. His mind was churning at a million miles an hour. He sat back and observed the table interactions. He was not sure if he should be amused at how ridiculous these people were or disconcerted that they didn't realize it.

Out of the corner of his eye, he watched Porchia's exchange with her parents and their guests. Her table manners were impeccable. She knew when to smile, when to encourage the speaker to continue, when to ask questions. Her social grooming was evident in every action and word. She was the perfect society hostess. Now he understood how she could so easily fit in with his family. She was a chameleon.

"Hey, Cowboy."

Darren looked across the table at Myron.

"I was asking where you left your luggage? Or do you have a bedroll tied to the back of your saddle?"

Darren wasn't positive, but he was fairly certain he could knock a few of this guy's caps off with one solid punch.

"Myron," Porchia scolded. "That wasn't nice."

"Oh, Katherine. Lighten up. Cowboy here knows I was joshing with him, right, Cowboy?"

Darren hiked an eyebrow and channeled his father. "Were you? I apologize. I stopped listening to you some time back. My grandmother—" He looked at Porchia. "I'm sorry you never got to meet my Grandma Helen." Looking back at Myron, he continued. "My Grandma Helen taught me never to engage bullies or fools."

Red tinged Myron's cheeks. Probably anger that Darren hadn't reacted to the intended insult.

"How dare you impinge my reputation among these excellent people!"

Darren wiped his mouth on his napkin and set it at the side of his plate. "I'm not sure you know what impinge means. You might want to look it up when you get home." He stood. "Mr. Randolph. Mrs. Randolph. Thank you for an enlightening evening. I believe I'll take my leave now."

Porchia grabbed his arm. "Don't go, Darren. Mother, tell him you'd like him to stay."

Her mother shrugged. "Mr. Montgomery, you're welcome to stay for dessert."

If Darren had ever heard a less sincere invitation, he couldn't remember it. "Thank you, Mrs. Randolph, but I believe it's time for me to leave."

Paul Randolph stood. "It was nice to meet you. Let me walk you out."

Porchia stood. "I'll walk him to the door."

Her father turned his gaze on her and she sat.

"This way, Mr. Montgomery."

Darren followed Paul Randolph, expecting him to head straight for the door. When Paul instead headed for his office, Darren let him take the lead. Apparently, Porchia's father had something he wanted to say.

Once they were inside, Paul shut the door. "Would you like a drink?"

Darren shook his head. "No, thank you. I'm assuming there's something you'd like to say to me." He gestured to the closed door.

Paul poured himself a drink, a scotch if Darren had to guess. Using the hand that held his glass, Paul pointed to a chair. "Have a seat for a minute."

Darren sat. Paul took the chair directly across from Darren.

"I'm not sure what you know about Katherine's history."

"I know it all, sir."

Paul arched his eyebrows in surprise. "Ah, well, then you know why she was living with my wife's mother."

Darren crossed his legs and settled in the chair. "I understand that she believes you sent her there because she was an embarrassment to you and your wife. And that you left her living there because it was better for your career." He shook his head in disgust. "What you did was nothing short of mental child abuse." He allowed his anger and abhorrence of their handling of the situation to color his voice and his face.

Paul sipped his drink. "We'll just have to disagree on that. However, Katherine is back home now. My wife is happy, which makes me happy."

"And what about your daughter? Is she happy here, or does that even matter?"

Darren knew his best course of action would be to stand and walk out before his mouth got him knee-deep in manure.

"Regardless of what you think of me or my wife, we've always wanted what was best for our daughter."

"And you think that stuffed shirt at the table is best for your daughter?"

Paul gave a slight shrug. "You may not like Myron Pope, but he's an intelligent, up-and-coming attorney. He can provide her the quality of life we want for our daughter."

"You think I'm some dirt-poor cowboy from Texas trying to get your daughter's money." Darren gave a hoarse chuckle and stood. "Thank you for your hospitality, such that it was. I'll call a cab from the drive."

"Don't bother. Our driver can take you to your hotel. It'll save you cab fare."

Darren almost blurted out that not only could he afford cab fare, he could probably buy the entire cab company with the financial gift his parents had given him and his siblings from the sale of the Florida ranch. In the end, he decided it simply wasn't worth the effort and hitched a ride with the Randolph's driver.

He checked into the airport Hilton more than a little disappointed. He'd had higher hopes for this trip. He hadn't expected to find Porchia living in a mansion. Nor had he expected to crash her family's dinner party.

Once he'd changed his return flight to tomorrow, he stripped to his boxers and ordered a bucket of beer from room service. The knock on his door came sooner than he'd expected. Throwing on a robe, he opened the door to let the hotel staff in with his beer.

But it wasn't the hotel staff.

Porchia stood in the hallway, her hair hanging limply around her face. "Can I come in?"

He hesitated and then stepped back. She entered and shut the door.

Darren turned and walked back to where he'd been stretched out on the bed. "What can I do for you, Princess?"

"I'm so sorry for how you were treated. It was unforgivable."

He gestured to the only chair in the room. "Sit."

She did.

"I came to Atlanta to find Porchia Summers. I needed to see her. I needed to tell her that I love her."

"Oh, Darren—"

He held up his hand. "I didn't find her. I found Katherine Randolph. I don't know Katherine. I don't think I want to know Katherine. What I know for sure is that I'm not in love with Katherine. Porchia, yes. Katherine, no."

"I'm still the same person."

"No, you're not. Porchia Summers would have never let a man speak to her like you did that jackass Myron. She would never have let dinner guests behave so rudely to another guest without comment. Porchia has a spine. She has respect for herself and others. I respect Porchia. Katherine is a boorish woman who lets others walk on her. I do not like or respect her."

"But what can I do?" she cried. "I came home to make amends with my parents. This is the only family I have. Without them, I'm alone in the world."

"You have me. You have my family. We all love Porchia. You would never have been alone. Come home."

"I don't know." She stood and paced. "You're asking me to give up my parents, to walk away and never see them again."

"No, I'm not. I would never ask you to do anything like that. But I can't love Katherine. You are the only one who can decide if you're Katherine or Porchia. And until you know who you are and what you want, I think it'd be better if we went our separate ways."

Chapter Twenty-Four

Porchia left the hotel with Darren's words ringing in her head. Who was she? Was she Porchia Summers, the Texas baker who struggled some months to pay all her bills? Her parents didn't seem to like that woman very much.

Or was she Katherine Randolph? Daughter of Judge Paul Randolph and his wife? Heiress to the Randolph fortune? Society snob in the making?

She went home and slept on it. In the morning, when she woke, she knew beyond a doubt who she was and what her future held.

Dressing quickly, she raced out early to reach Darren. She had to explain her epiphany. But he was already gone when she arrived. He'd taken the first flight out of Atlanta.

That evening, she had a long talk with her parents. She explained how much she'd missed them over the years. How much she loved them and needed them in her life. Their lifestyle in Atlanta was perfect...for them, but not for her. She hoped with all her heart that they would forgive her, but she had to go back to Texas.

"I'm more Porchia Summers than I am Katherine Randolph," she explained. "I love my life in Texas. I'm happy there. I have friends. I have to go home."

Her mother cried.

Her father actually smiled and kissed her cheek. "I suspected as much," he said. "The young man. He's your future?"

"I certainly hope so."

"Then I wish you happiness and love," he said, shocking her. "Be sure we get invited to the wedding."

At the mention of wedding, her mother wailed louder. It was all Porchia could do not to roll her eyes.

"Invited? Heck, Father. You'll be paying for it."

His laugh was rusty, as though he didn't use it enough. She hoped he practiced it more.

"I'm going upstairs to pack." She hugged both of them, her mother clinging on to Porchia for a long time. "I'll be back," she told her parents. "Not to stay," she clarified. "But for visits. And I'll call. And you'll call. And you'll come to visit." She smiled. "It's not like here at all."

In the end, she didn't fly to Whispering Springs. Instead, as an early Christmas present, her parents bought her a new, and completely too expensive, sport utility vehicle to take back. She thought about saying no, but they sincerely seemed to enjoy giving it to her. Since she'd given her sedan to Mallory after hers had been destroyed in the fire, the gift was received with pleasure.

It took a couple of long days on the road before she pulled into the drive at her home.

Around her, houses blinked with multi-colored Christmas lights, large Christmas decorations and one Santa that opened and closed an empty trailer. It was almost Christmas. She didn't have time to get all her boxes of decorations out to get her house into the Christmas spirit tonight. But tomorrow? Her house was getting a makeover.

Her house. Man, she liked those words.

Now to go get her man.

She liked those words even better.

Scratch that. She wanted more privacy than they could get at his place with Reno and Magda listening in, so she needed him to come here. She called his cell.

"Hello?" He sounded calm and totally unaffected by her call. And he had to know it was her by the caller ID.

"Hey. It's me."

There was a pause before he said, "Is this Porchia or Katherine?"

"Porchia."

He said nothing.

"I wondered, if you're not too busy or anything, if you could come over to my house this evening."

"You're home?"

"I am." She started to say she was home to stay, but at the last second she decided she'd wait and see what kind of reaction she got from him. If he totally hated her and wanted nothing to do with her, she'd...well, she didn't know exactly what she'd do. She crossed her fingers. "Can you come?"

"What time?"

She smiled. "I'll cook dinner, so whenever you get done." She glanced at her watch. That'd give her time to get to the store and grab some food, since she was sure there was nothing edible in her kitchen.

"I can be there about seven. That work?"

"Perfect. See you then."

A trip to the grocery store that should have been twenty minutes tops turned into an hour as people greeted her or hugged her or just stopped her to tell her how much they'd missed her. Most asked if she was going to rebuild the bakery, moaning about how much they longed for her pastries. All the kind words and hugs caught her off-guard. She hadn't expected this kind of response from the townspeople. She found herself tearing up more than once.

One more stop and she was back home.

She made a roast with potatoes, carrots, green beans and creamed corn. She even had enough time to make fresh yeast rolls.

By six-thirty, she'd showered, dressed in jeans, a soft sweater and a thick pair of socks. She was done, done, done with nylons and high-heel shoes. Her toes thanked her.

When she heard the rumble of his truck in her drive, Porchia's heart charged up her throat. Whatever happened, she was laying it all on the line.

He knocked at the door, and for the briefest of seconds, she remembered opening the door to Slade and all that had transpired afterward. But that was the past. Darren had been right. She had done nothing wrong, not seventeen years ago and not a month ago.

She opened the door, her gut tugging nervously. He'd never looked better than he did tonight. Dressed in fresh jeans—thanks, Magda—a snap shirt, boots and a leather jacket, he stood with his hat held at waist height. Her eyes ate up the vision.

"Come on in."

He walked, studying her as though she might turn into a butterfly at any minute. She smiled.

"It's me. Porchia. Katherine was laid to rest in Atlanta."

But he still held back affections except to say, "Good. I didn't like Katherine anyway."

"Me neither, to tell you the truth. Take off your coat. Dinner is ready. I know you come home ravenous."

He smiled. "That I do." He draped his coat over the sofa. "Smells good."

She deliberately arched an eyebrow. "And it'll be good too. Can I get you a beer?"

"I'd love one."

"Great. Grab a chair. I'll be right back."

She brought a couple of beers to the table. Not because she wanted a beer with dinner, but more of an overt sign that she'd made her decision.

While they ate, she apologized again for the dinner at her parents' house. And she told him about her conversation with them, about coming home to Whispering Springs, about wanting to rebuild her life.

He let her talk, nodding in appropriate places, but not asking many questions.

"So," she finished up. "Once my parents understood my need to come home, they bought me a new SUV as a Christmas present and sent me on my way. I was surprised they took it so well." She chuckled. "Sort of well. Mother cried and then insisted on buying me the most expensive SUV she could, which was fine with me. I felt so bad about Mallory losing her car because of me, that

I gave her mine. And before you tell me the fire wasn't my fault, I know. But giving her the car made me happy."

He nodded and smiled. "That was a nice thing to do."

"Which brings me to why I asked you here."

Setting his fork and knife across his plate, he studied her. "Okay."

"I'm here because being in Whispering Springs makes me happy. I want a happy future, and I only know of one way I'll be happy."

"And what's that?"

"To be with you."

"Are you sure, Porchia? Really sure?"

She stood and walked to where he sat. Then, dropping to one knee, she said, "Will you marry me?"

The stunned expression on his face scared her more than actually saying the words. But then a broad smile crawled onto his lips.

"Do you love me?" he asked.

"With all my heart."

"And I love you." He pushed back his chair and pulled her into his lap. "I have missed you so much," he said and kissed her.

When his lips touched hers, a rain of sparks went off inside her. She loved how he smelled, how he tasted, hell, how he breathed. This was her man.

"Hey," he said. "Where's my engagement ring? When a guy asks a girl to marry him, he always presents a ring."

She laughed. "I got you something better. Hold on."

She hurried to her bedroom, grabbed the two boxes she'd picked up this afternoon and raced back. She found Darren in the living room sitting on the sofa. She skidded to a stop and sat on the couch beside him.

"Wait. Before you get these, you didn't answer my question. These are *engagement* presents. I have to have an answer *before* you get them."

"Well," he said, "I'll give you a provisional yes. Now let me see what you got me." The twinkle in his eye made her smile. Man, she'd missed that twinkle.

She laughed and put the boxes behind her. "A provisional yes?" She forced her mouth into a pout. "Not good enough."

"Fine. I'll marry you. Now let me see what you bought."

She handed over the presents. He ripped the paper off, his eyes growing wide at the Resistol box. "You bought me a Resistol?" He jerked the lid off and lifted a silver-toned, felt cowboy hat from the box. "It's gorgeous." He set it on his head. "And a perfect fit. Thank you," he said. "I love it."

"One more box." She set the large, square box on the floor.

He looked at her, took off the hat and set it behind him. "Porchia. You don't have to buy me anything. I love you. Don't you know that? I want to marry you. I'd marry you tomorrow if you'd agree. I've wanted to marry you since day one of the camping trip. But I knew if I told you that back then, you'd have run for the hills."

Nodding, she chuckled. "Yeah. I probably would have."

"Do you believe that I love you?"

She held his face in the palms of her hands. "I know you love me. You faced my family for me. There's no doubt in my mind I belong here with you."

Their lips met in a hot kiss full of pent-up desire and years of love.

"Well," he drawled when he broke the kiss. "Funny you should want to ask me to marry you." He put his arm around her and pulled her snug against him.

"Yeah? Why's that?"

He reached into his front pocket and pulled out a black velvet box. "Great minds and all that." He popped it open and an embarrassingly large diamond winked at her. "I told myself that if you came back, I was never, ever letting you go again. I've been miserable without you."

She looked into his eyes, although hers were a little watery.

"I love you, Porchia. I want to be your husband. I want to be the father of your children. I want to spend the rest of my life loving you."

"Yes! Yes. Yes. Yes," she said, adjusting her position on the couch until she could throw her arms around his neck. She kissed his mouth, his cheeks, his chin. "I love you, Darren Montgomery."

He slipped the ring on her finger. "I love you, Porchia Summers, soon-to-be Porchia Montgomery."

She kissed him again. "Wait. I got you another engagement present."

Grinning, he said, "Since we *are* engaged, I think I should open it, don't you?"

He hefted the box off the floor and into his lap. Once he got the lid off, a pair of black leather, ornately decorated cowboy boots rested inside.

"These are incredible, honey."

"I thought they'd look good on our wedding day."

He smiled. "But nothing will be more beautiful than my bride."

Porchia would always love her parents, even if she didn't understand or agree with them all of the time.

In Texas, she'd found unconditional love and acceptance.

With Darren, she'd found family.

They turned off the lights and their phones and went to the bedroom to plan their future. A future that held their shared dreams built on a foundation of love and trust.

A future that was family.

About the Author

New York Times and *USA TODAY* Bestselling Author Cynthia D'Alba started writing on a challenge from her husband in 2006 and discovered having imaginary sex with lots of hunky men was fun. She was born and raised in a small Arkansas town. After being gone for a number of years, she's thrilled to be making her home back in Arkansas, living in a vine-covered cottage on the banks of an eight-thousand acre lake. When she's not reading or writing or plotting, she's doorman for her two dogs, cook, housekeeper and chief bottle washer for her husband and slave to a noisy, messy parrot. She loves to chat online with friends and fans.

You can find her most days at one of the following online homes:

Website: www.cynthiadalba.com

Facebook: www.Facebook.com/cynthiadalba

Twitter: @cynthiadalba

Pinterest: www.Pinterest.com/CynthiaDAlba

Newsletter: http://cynthiadalba.us2.list-manage.com/subscribe?u=13edc42ab44c965943cbcccea&id=fd9f2bcd88

Or drop her a line at cynthia@cynthiadalba.com

Or send snail mail to: Cynthia D'Alba PO Box 2116 Hot Springs, AR 71914

He plans to take the wander right out of her wanderlust.

Texas Bossa Nova
© *2015 Cynthia D'Alba*

Texas Montgomery Mavericks, Book 5

Magda Hobbs's job as ranch housekeeper—and its daily dose of cowboys—wreaked havoc on her libido. Especially one certain cowboy she couldn't resist. Scared of going down the same path as her mother, Magda jumped on her motorcycle and hit the road.

Five months later, her father's mild heart attack has forced her back to Whispering Springs. While she's grateful for the cleaning job at one of the Montgomery ranch houses, she's not so thrilled one of the cowboys she's looking after is the one she fell for last spring.

Reno Montgomery's parents hiring a housekeeper for him and his brother is a nice surprise, but he's shocked to discover it's Magda, the woman who up and left just when things were getting serious between them.

When a freak snowstorm cuts off the outside world, the isolation rekindles their desire. But when the weather and the roads clear, Reno has to work hard and fast to keep the woman of his dreams from accelerating right out of his life again.

Warning: Contains a woman born with a bad case of wanderlust, and a cowboy determined to show her that life's a dance that doesn't have to two-step her out of his life.

Real bad boys can grow up to be real good men.

Texas Twist
© 2014 Cynthia D'Alba

Texas Montgomery Mavericks, Book 4

Hit hard by the death of her parents, Paige Ryan needs to figure out what to do with her life. She moves to Whispering Springs, Texas, to be near her stepbrother. But just as she starts to get her life on track, the last man she ever wanted to see again sends it right back off the rails.

Cash Montgomery was on the cusp of having it all. Three bull riding titles, fame, fortune and respect from his family. Until a bad bull leaves him injured, angry and searching for comfort at the bottom of a bottle. With nowhere to go, he moves into his sister-in-law's old ranch house in Whispering Springs—which he's surprised to find already occupied.

As Cash rebuilds the dilapidated home and Paige starts out on her medical career, their old friendship begins to reemerge and sparks are ignited. Paige knows that Cash is nothing but a heartache waiting to happen. But maybe this bad boy has grown up to be a real good man?

Warning: Watch out for falling lumber, falling in holes, and falling for the wrong guy…again. You can leave your hard hat on.

Two weeks on a beach can deepen more than just their tans.

Texas Fandango
© 2014 Cynthia D'Alba

Texas Montgomery Mavericks, Book 3

KC Montgomery was eleven when she met the love of her life. Of course, seventeen-year-old Drake Gentry didn't know she existed, but that didn't stop her girlish fantasies from growing and changing over the years.

Now, after enjoying a front-row seat to his breakup with his latest girlfriend, she's been handed an all-grown-up fantasy come true—two weeks at the Sand Castle Resort. With him.

Drake most definitely noticed KC a long time ago, but the timing's never been right. Now that he's facing a lonely vacation that was supposed to be for two, it seems only natural to accept KC's offer to fill in. And as far as her terms go… No strings. No expectations. No holds barred. Drake is no fool—he's all over it.

But once they're back in Texas there are invisible strings still hanging between them. Strings labeled attraction, affection…even love. And the more they try to untangle the knots, the tighter they're bound together.

Warning: Beware of sunburns, whirlpool sex and sand in delicate places.

SAMHAIN

PUBLISHING

It's all about the story...

Romance

HORROR

www.samhainpublishing.com

Bruce County Public Library
1243 Mackenzie Rd.
Port Elgin ON N0H 2C6

CPSIA information can be obtained at www.ICGtesting.com
Printed in the USA
LVOW11s0455150116

470661LV00009B/1029/P

9 781619 232389